**WHAT**

*Turn Around…* seems to be a very fitting title for a book that so draws the reader in so well that you feel like "you just *turn around* and you have come to the end of the book – and left wanting more."

Though *Turn Around* certainly conveys the centrality of the message that Jesus preached, it is not "preachy" or "churchy" at all. Jesus told His followers that they lived in a kingdom. "The kingdom is here. The kingdom is now. You just need to *turn around* (repent) to see it."

Bob's grand novel with its picturesque scenery will appeal to followers of Jesus who are no longer satisfied with "church as usual", and who will no longer settle for some impotent variety of religion that poses as Christianity. *Turn Around* will also appeal to spiritual seekers who may have never seriously considered following Jesus. *Turn Around* aptly conveys the message that there is more – much, much more – involved in being a follower of the One who changed the world. He has invited us into His kingdom and He wants to give us a full life. The reader of *Turn Around* begins to experience in novel form what Erwin McManus, Brian McLaren, Myles Munroe and Rick McKinley have been theologizing about for years.

Hooray for Bob Ledbetter and *Turn Around*! May our culture and world *Turn Around* and see Jesus.

—Pastor Mike Lawrence
North Eugene Faith Center (Foursquare Church)

I read this book in two sittings because I didn't want to put it down. Through his knowledge of many vocations and his intimate knowledge of Colorado and Alaska, Bob Ledbetter brings the story to life. Drama, adventure, travel, and spiritual warfare are four of the action settings that captured my attention. But it was the concept of prayer that kept me glued to the pages. Having read copiously from teacher/authors such as E. M. Bounds, Frank Peretti, and Jack Taylor, I am aware of the dynamics involved in prayer. But in *Turn Around*, Bob Ledbetter described spiritual warfare and the necessity of prayer in ways that left an indelible impression on me.

—GENE LINZEY
Teacher, Author, Former Pastor
Siloam Springs, Arkansas

I was impressed from the beginning of the book. Bob's forthright ability to capture spiritual activity in the lives of ordinary men and women is refreshing. Bob colors his characters with a perception beyond coincidence and leads the readers to explore the reality of a spiritual dimension too often dismissed in religious circles. I enjoyed the interplay and is an easy-read with ordinary folks. I have encouraged hundreds to purchase this book and have suggested it to script writers as movie material. Bob has captured Randy Alcorn's flavor in common dialect with ordinary mannerisms.

—William M. Conklin
Pastor
International Speaker: Spiritual Roots of Disease

*Turn Around* by Bob Ledbetter. I enjoyed the ride very much, especially the second time around.

—Jerry Chapman,
Drumspeaker to the nations
Sto:Lo First Nation

Bob Ledbetter has managed to capture the essence of the power of prayer and its relationship to unleashing God's awesome saving grace into the lives of people upon the earth. To read TURN AROUND is to take a walk through that place that allows us to look at the spirit world as well as the earthly realm and to note that one does not operate independently of the other. In fact, we find them to be one and the same.

This is the story of struggle, hardship, turmoil, death, life and victory. The author weaves a tale of intrigue which includes trains, trappers, police officers, old ways, modern life, angels and God Himself.

When I finished reading the last page, I was struck with the realization that our Lord will bend Heaven and earth in order to save the souls of men. His greatest desire is that none would be lost; but all would come to Him through the Cross of Christ.

—Dan Lundy
Founder, Messenger Ministries

# TURN
# AЯOUND

# TURN
# AROUND

BOB LEDBETTER

TATE PUBLISHING
AND ENTERPRISES, LLC

Published by Tate Publishing & Enterprises, LLC
127 E. Trade Center Terrace | Mustang, Oklahoma 73064 USA
1.888.361.9473 | www.tatepublishing.com

Tate Publishing is committed to excellence in the publishing industry. The company reflects the philosophy established by the founders, based on Psalm 68:11,
*"The Lord gave the word and great was the company of those who published it."*

Book design copyright © 2013 by Tate Publishing, LLC. All rights reserved.
*Cover design by Leah LeFlore*
*Cover photograph by Bob Ledbetter*
*Interior design by Lindsay B. Behrens*

Published in the United States of America

ISBN: 978-1-62902-726-5
1. Fiction / General / Christian
2. Fiction / Relgious / General
13.08.16

# DEDICATION

FIRST and foremost this work is dedicated to Father God, Jesus, and Holy Spirit, whose ideas, inspiration, gentle prodding, love, sacrifice, and protection made everything possible for this project.

Then to Jeff, Julie, and Jon. I am so privileged to be their Dad.

To Meg, my partner, and love of my life who encouraged and supported me in finishing this project.

Bill Conklin has been invaluable in his encouragement and support. Thanks, Bill

Finally, to you my readers of this Real Fiction. My prayer is that you will "Say a quiet yes to God and He'll be there. Quit dabbling in sin. Purify your inner life. Quit playing the field," as it says in James 4:8 in *The Message.*

God Bless you all

# ACKNOWLEDGMENTS

I WOULD like to thank the following people for their assistance and/or tolerance while writing this book.

Smokey Joe, Union Pacific Conductor/Brakeman
Meg MacGregor,
Bill Conklin,
Peter Marshall, M.D.
Scott Deal, North Pole Police Department
Eric Nichols - KL7AJ
Mike Sambuco - AL7KC
Pete Vinton - Captain, United Airlines

# FOREWORD

M AN's Basic Struggle is of Good over Evil.

The following, almost true story, is established on the premise that each of us at birth was assigned not only a Guardian Angel, which represents the Good, but also a representative of the Evil side, whom the Bible calls "Familiar Spirits".

In this story the Angels are members of the Hemispheric Angelic Forces (the HAFs), while the evil ones belong to the Network of Atmospheric Agents of Sub-Terrestrial Impieties, the naastis, a.k.a. The Hafnots.

Take note that the name satan and related names are not capitalized. I have chosen to not acknowledge him or them, even to the point of violating grammatical rules.

The names of the principals have not been changed to protect the innocent because there are no innocents, and any resemblance to persons living or dead is purely coincidental.

Although the events are based upon true happenings, they have been re-arranged to make a better story.

**The End, however, is as it will be.**

# CONTENTS

# AW, BILGE

A N icy breeze wafted across the sleeping man. Awaking to the brisk feeling on his face, Frenchy rubbed the sleep from his eyes and gave an involuntary shiver as he glanced at the thermometer hanging outside the window. "A tad chilly this morning," he said to himself, swinging his feet to the floor. "Twenty-three below. Not bad for the beginning of March."

He looked at his watch. "Eight o'clock," he said to himself, "won't be really light for another hour, but I might as well git up and head for home," and with a stretch and a groan Frenchy began his day.

To separate his feet from the cold wood floor, he put on the moose hide moccasins he'd made three seasons ago, then his wool pants went over his long johns as he dragged himself to the wood stove. Before going to bed last night he had prepared his coffee for morning. After stirring up the fire he slid the coffee pot over the fire on the stove and held his hands over the stove to warm them a bit. His suspenders went over his shoulders as he stuck his head out the door and hollered.

"Hey, Smo-ki, Griz', Jake, Suzie, Sly, Max, Hidey, Radar, Sophie, Chena, Watts, Volts. Wake up, you bunch of fish burnin' sled draggers, we're burnin' moonlight. If ya 'spect to git home before sundown, ya better git up. We only got ten miles t'go, so up an' at'em an' let's git t'gittin'."

The response from his team was a display of toothy yawns. Each dog had its own wooden house, but none of them had felt the need for the extra warmth and had slept curled up, noses tucked warmly under their tails, on beds of straw in front of their houses.

thordan, a Lieutenant in the network of atmospheric agents for sub-terrestrial impieties (naastis), was watching his Project from his perch on the cabin wall, and thought Frenchy looked much too comfortable in his goose down sleeping bag and had blown a slight breeze of icy air across the sleeping man's face.

thordan had been given the assignment to control John Patrick 'Frenchy' LeBlanc when Frenchy was born, but, much to his chagrin, it did not include killing him. He was only to cause him as much pain and trouble as possible, reinforce the image of self-sufficiency, and above all keep his Project from going Vertical. He accomplished that by constantly reminding him of the man John Patrick had killed, and if that required a use of force, or the bitter memory what "the church and Christians" had done to him after the killing, so much the better.

The day was dawning as clear and cold as glacier ice, with a cloudless sky, and the full moon in the northwestern sky casting it's light on the snow. It was bright enough to see everything in detail. Even though the air had a frigid tooth to it, it was quite comfortable inside the cabin.

While Frenchy went about preparing a breakfast of oatmeal for himself, and a blend of fish and dried food for his twelve Alaskan sled dogs, thordan moved silently—like a rustling in the trees. He had learned a long time ago that the twelve dogs were not only Frenchy's mode of transportation, they were also Frenchy's 'alarm' system. More than once the dogs had alerted Frenchy to a 'circumstance' he had devised against his Project.

Smo-ki and team were part Siberian Husky and part Malamute, and weighed from 80 to 110 pounds each. By sled dog standards, they were big, almost huge, but Frenchy had no need for a team of Iditarod runners. He did, however, need a strong team and for that reason he had built his team for strength and endurance. Smo-ki, his silver-grey leader, got her size from her dad, a big-boned, barrel-chested, 117 pound teddy bear of a work hound, and her smarts and pale blue, almost white, eyes from her mother.

Griz and Smo-ki had been the beginning of Frenchy's team, and except for his yellow eyes, Griz could have been Smo-ki's identical twin. However, there was no blood relation, and the pair had produced a quality team of working pets. Dogs that not only answered quickly to commands, proving their intelligence, but ones that could endure the hard paces Frenchy and the trap line required of them. Most trappers thought Frenchy a fool to maintain a pack of such large dogs, but Frenchy was no normal trapper, and, ignoring the men who mushed teams of six or eight smaller animals, he kept his reliable team of twelve lovable giants.

As Frenchy was taking food to the dogs, thordan pulled back the top of a large spruce tree. The tree groaned in protest, and Frenchy looked up at the sound.

"Hey Smo-ki," Frenchy said to his buddy and lead dog, "Whadya think that was?" Smo-ki vocalized her response with a yip, but with nothing of a warning in her tone Frenchy gave it little thought as he made the rounds to the rest of his hungry mouths. As Frenchy dished out the food, thordan yanked the tree again, and cursed the dogs when they sensed, more than heard, the tree groaning in protest. Stopping their eating they began sniffing the air worriedly. Looking around, Frenchy saw Smo-ki was upset, but couldn't tell why. The only thing he saw was a slight breeze stirring the tops of the trees.

"NICE time for a battle," Nadia pointed out. "Now always is," Obed agreed.

Nadia and Obed were attending a meeting of the high echelon commanders of the Hemispheric Angelic Forces held in the Operations Center of World Space Defense Command, WORSPADCO. The topic of discussion was, as always, the upcoming conflict. The final conflict. In attendance was Lt. Colonel Nadia Ben-David, Commanding Officer of the Northern Hemisphere Angelic Forces, COMNORHAF, Lt. Colonel Obed Shalom, his Southern counterpart, COMSOUHAF, and The Angelic Agents.

"I'm glad it's beginning to end," Nadia continued. "It's only been a couple thousand of their years, but it must seem like ages to them."

"True," Obed said with a slight nod. "But only a few have actually understood what Advocate meant when he said 'It is finished.' Most have been able to grasp the idea—some better than others—but since UNICINC directed SID to inform them, they're beginning to get the big picture."

Specialized Instruction Division (SID), under the direct command of the Universal Commander In Chief (UNICINC), was responsible for instructing the Verticals who showed a certain propensity for the things of the future and how those things concern everyday life. Many Verticals, those fragile earthbound vessels who had accepted what Advocate had done for them, were gaining a true understanding of things to come.

"Yes, especially since UNICINC gave the directive. Have you noticed how much SID's activity has picked up?"

"It really has. Now, as long as they remain Vertical and firmly committed to the cause..." Nadia continued.

"... Yes," Obed picked up. "Then we will be able to carry out what must be done to rid creation of this pervading evil once and for all."

A LARGE portion of the Operations Center of WORSPADCO was set aside for en masse meetings and resembled a large auditorium with deeply padded seats. In the backs of the seats was a drop-down desk and on each desk was a device, which in appearance looked like a laptop computer. However, any similarity was only in appearance as the capabilities far surpassed any and all hand-held computing devices available to earthlings, both Vertical and non-verticals. The input devices were not limited to the mouse and the keyboard. Each angel could access their device with the touchscreen as well as their thoughts.

"Gentlemen," UNICINC spoke, giving pause to the small pockets of conversation throughout the room. "Now is the time to consider fully what the next action will be. I have noticed the earthlings have somehow gotten the impression that there is going to be some kind of celebration, However," he paused and directed His attention to Advocate, "Advocate, have you seen any signs of your bride being ready?"

"No, sir," Advocate responded, "not yet. She is making progress, but as for being ready for the wedding, no sir."

"Ah, well then," UNICINC continued, "we can continue helping the Verticals demonstrate our Kingdom to the other earthlings.

"OKAY Smok," he said, "whadya think?" By far, Smo-ki had the most trail smarts of his entire team and Frenchy had learned long ago to pay attention to her reaction. However, this time her response was more of a question than a reply, as her warm breath curled in the cold air with her whine.

"A freeze break? It just ain't cold enough for a tree ta freeze break, gal. Whatever it is, though," he said as he turned the conversation to another of his friends, giving Watts a scratch between the ears, "the sooner we skeedaddle outa here, boys 'n' girls, the sooner we git home." Watts, however, wanted more than a little scratch between the ears, and just when Frenchy was slightly off balance she playfully grabbed Frenchy by the sleeve. Frenchy went down on one knee as Watts nuzzled her nose in Frenchy's long, black beard. They snuggled a bit before Frenchy continued his rounds and the dogs went back to their food.

This particular camp, the closest to his main cabin, boasted most of the comforts of home. A twelve-by-sixteen foot log cabin with a wood stove, a "bunk" of spruce boughs, and outside, in four of the trees about ten feet above the ground, a log cache to protect his supplies from varmints. The previous owner had built the cabin out of spruce trees at the edge of the forest, about 50 feet from a creek. During the spring and summer, the creek was a source of relaxation as well as water. But during the winter, it became Frenchy's frozen highway between his main cabin and the clover leaf-shaped trap line trail that branched out from his home three miles south of Wiseman, Alaska.

As Frenchy stowed the dried dog food in the cache, and placed the ladder next to his cabin, thordan saw his chance to strike.

Grabbing the top of the tree, he lunged backward until the tree was snapped off about twenty feet from the top. Then, he threw it at Frenchy.

The ominous cracking noise recoiled like the shot of a rifle, shattering the morning quietness. Smo-ki and crew barked their warning in unison, and as Frenchy looked around toward his dogs he caught a glimpse of something moving. A huge white spruce tree falling his way. Reflexively, he raised his arm for protection, but it was too late. All 347 pounds of his six foot seven inch frame were slammed mercilessly onto the frozen ground.

thordan laughed a hideous cackle and sneered unheard, "There you go, you stinkin', low life human. Get out of that one. I can't kill you, yet, but I can make you wish you were dead."

A few times Frenchy had almost succumbed to the urgings of the Verticals, but thordan had always managed to worm his way back into Frenchy's thoughts, convincing him he could take care of himself. That he needed no one else. Certainly not God!

skulban, another naasti, had been in charge of Jean Pierre, Frenchy's father, and when he'd received his orders from naasti Headquarters to do away with him, the two demons decided to give thordan a little more control over his Project. The unbearable pressure skulban put on Jean Pierre was too much for the man to cope with, and he began arguing with his son. skulban saw to it the argument got out of hand, and pointed to the rifle over the door. Jean Pierre grabbed the rifle and pointed it toward his son. As Frenchy was trying to wrestle the gun out of his father's hands it went off before he realized his finger was on the trigger. Actually, Frenchy had never touched the trigger, but thordan wasn't about to let him know that.

The court ruled it accidental, but the wound was made, and his father was dead. From then on Frenchy had been very easy to control. A little flash memory of his father's life draining onto the floor of the cabin was enough to bring Frenchy back under control.

However, all that had changed when Frenchy met a fellow trapper. A Vertical. One of the Verticals able to speak The Code—that dreaded language which none of thordan's kind could understand. The Code had been designed and written by Creator as a means of permitting the Verticals to communicate with Himself, and The Angelic Forces, without the naastis being able to listen in. The Verticals called it 'praying in the spirit', and because of it, thordan had not been aware of a planned encounter. The message in Code had brought the assistance of the Vertical's Force Leader, a counterpart that even now caused thordan to tremble.

The Vertical's Force Leader had a name, but thordan hated to even think about it. Somehow the mere thought of the name seemed to give him even more credibility. Shaking the worrisome image from his mind, thordan gloated over his latest feat of dastardly do. This ought to get him some hearty praise from...

thordan stopped in mid-thought. Someone was watching. The only name that came to mind was Jireh. Frenchy's HAF. He must be close. Too close. Even as the thought flashed through his mind, Jireh struck, and thordan had no more time to think. He had to counterattack. He couldn't let all of his hard work be for naught!

Coming to his senses, Frenchy found himself in the embrace of the massive weight. He tried lifting himself with his arms, but a stabbing pain lanced through his side, and when he tried moving his legs they felt like lead weights and would not budge. He could move his head from side to side, but he couldn't get a decent breath of air. Frenchy figured he must have some broken ribs, or worse. Scowling beneath the burden, he knew panicking would be a useless waste of energy, and no one would hear him even if he did call out. Besides, it would only use up precious energy that he needed to stay alive.

"Aw, bilge," he thought loudly, "hadn't counted on this today."

2

# CODE

T HE great philosopher A. Nony Mouse once articulated "There is no known cure for an obsession with trains," and Lew Andrews was certainly proof of that. His father had worked for the railroad, as had his father before him, so it was natural that Lew thought he had more cinders in his blood than corpuscles, and all he had ever wanted to do was "run trains". As a child he had watched them with longing, yearning to be on any that was leaving from, or arriving in, Seattle. He remembered more than once watching Great Northern's Empire Builder pull out of Seattle and thought, *'Tonight, he'll be going through Spokane. Then tomorrow morning, through Glacier Park, and tomorrow night, through Minot, and get to Chicago the next afternoon. Wish I was going along.'*

Years later, those far away places with cool sounding names had become reality when Lew went to work for the Burlington Northern Railroad in Seattle. He never ran as far as Chicago, since the Brotherhood of Locomotive Engineers, the union, restricted him to a hundred mile run, and neither did he get to run the Empire Builder as Amtrak had taken over all passenger operations and he didn't have enough whiskers—a railroaders term for seniority. However, he was running trains.

A major upheaval in his life caused a need for a change of scenery, and one day he woke up. He decided to move to Colorado. Since the first time he'd been there on vacation with his family, he'd thought it would be a nice place to live.

He'd driven from Seattle to Denver, and upon his arrival, his first stop was the headquarters of the Denver, Salt Lake & Pacific Railroad. That was when he learned they needed an engineer for helper service in Minturn. That sounded good to him, so heading west out of Denver on I-70, he went past a herd of buffalo just west of Denver, through Dillon, over Vail Pass, and found the Minturn turn-off. Driving through town that first time Lew knew he had found the right place.

The first Saturday after moving to Minturn he was at the only grocery store in town and some folks were giving away St. Bernard puppies. That's when he found his friend. An extra large, roly-poly pup of white, with brown ears and large brown spots on his back, huge paws, and eyes that grabbed Lew by the heart and would not let go. Lew looked at the pup's 150 pound mom and 185 pound dad and calculated, hoped really, that the pup would be at least as big as the mother. Looking at the pup, Lew knew he'd been adopted. He called his new friend Cupcake.

That same day, he and Cupcake had also found the perfect spot for relaxation and contemplation. The north side of Tennessee Pass, a few miles south of Minturn. Camp Hale. Not a camp anymore, only the ghosts of buildings, people and goings on from a long time ago.

Minturn, a small burg nestled in the mountains a few miles west of Vail, was put on the map, and kept on the map, by the railroad's need for helper engines to get trains over Tennessee

Pass. Lew knew he was going to be back on the Extra Board when he hired on, but it didn't matter. The pay was the same, and he could still run trains. The only difference was never being sure when he would be called to work, but the intriguing thing had been getting away from the crowds of Seattle, and he had not been disappointed.

That first weekend in Minturn had been one Lew would never forget. Not only had he found a faithful friend and a place to re-group, but also a gathering of people who welcomed him as one of their own. It wasn't long until he had become very involved with the local church and discovered an insatiable appetite for being with Father God. Although the pastor had been out of town that first weekend, over the years they had developed a firm friendship.

Lew had been raised in a railroader's home by parents who knew absolutely nothing about God and Jesus. It had been some friends in high school who had invited him to a Youth For Christ meeting one Saturday night, and it was on that night he'd met Jesus, as personal Savior. He had gone on to receive his degree from a Christian college, but soon determined that was not enough. Through a process of growth, he was finding there was more to life. More to Christianity. Much more.

Lew smiled at the memory and then at the glorious scene which surrounded him. He'd been off work for two days and had been camping in his "study". It was a lazy, leisurely kind of rest that prompted him to think deep thoughts on important matters.

"Hey, Cupcake," he called to his furry friend, "let's take a hike." Lew's suggestion was met with enthusiasm, and with a woof and a bound the 172 pounder joined his master on a romp through God's Country.

Since Lew had started understanding and accepting the Kingdom of God and worship in a whole new way, his life had been completely turned around. He'd been praying less and worshiping more in the last few months, and knowing the difference. He also knew that God Almighty wanted him, Lew Andrews, to let Him, Father God, be a part of his life all the time. He had a somewhat difficult time with this line of thinking until he discovered his pastor had also been doing the same spiritual thinking. He was, in fact, studying and teaching along those same lines and the more they discussed their understanding, the tighter their friendship became. His pastor, David MacIntyre, a one-armed, former railroader, began teaching more and more on the Kingdom of God, worship, intercession, and spiritual warfare, as well as the importance of those things in the everyday lives of Believers. He pointed out the difference between a "Christian" and a "Believer."

"For instance," Pastor Mac had said, "Believers do what the Word of God says, whereas Christians don't necessarily do much of anything."

Lew smiled at the memory. While climbing the hill just above their camp he was thinking about this and wondered aloud if there was more to it. Cupcake was just looking at him with his head cocked to one side, as if to say, "Um, could be."

FRENCHY had an incredible headache, no feeling in his legs, and it was beginning to snow again. That was both a good thing and a bad thing. Good because it meant it was getting warmer. Bad because if it snowed a lot, which it could very easily do, it could bury him. However, having been raised to be totally independent and self-sufficient, he was unprepared to ask help of anyone, anytime for any reason. The fact that there was no one around for miles did not enter his mind. He just knew he needed to get out from under the massive tree. He was not frightened, but things were starting to wear on him. There was the awful pain, the limited hours of daylight, and the cold, and it was snowing. Hearing the agitated voices of Smo-ki and the other dogs he strained to listen, but he could only hear the wind in the trees above him.

As he tried raising the tree an inch or so, a sharp pain knifed through him, and he felt the sticky wetness of his own blood under his arm. He concluded a branch must have pierced his many layers of clothing, and after considering all the options, he figured the tree must have been unusually weak and the heavy burden of snow had caused it to break.

Thinking back to the decision to move out of town and into the bush to live full-time on his trap line he figured he'd had enough hurt for one man and decided Number One was the only person to be concerned about. In the intervening years, his independence had been tempered to an unbreakable degree. Although he would admit it to no one else, he did have to level with himself about his inner-most feelings.

Prompted by the reaction of the church folks after he'd accidentally killed his father he moved to the bush. He remembered it had felt like someone had reached into his chest and pulled out his heart by the roots as he saw his father's life draining into a growing, gooey red puddle on the floor. But the biggest scar was the one that remained after his 'friends' at church had totally, and completely, let him know, in no uncertain terms, that he was no longer needed or even wanted in their presence. At a point when Frenchy needed them most, he decided 'church folks' were very definitely the people to be on guard against. They had the ability, and inclination, to give a person a hug and stand on their toes at the same time. They would smile and say, "I love you, Brother", then turn right around and spread gossip about them.

"Sure you love me," he thought out loud, anger welling up like a blizzard. "NOT! You love me like wolves love moose. If folks don't happen to measure up to your standards," he went on berating the air, "then you say 'you were never really saved in the first place' and then go on about your own self-righteous business."

Frenchy didn't realize what was happening, and certainly could not see thordan, who was sitting on his head inserting those ideas into his brain, and preparing to inflict further injury.

Although invisible to the human eye, thordan was about three feet tall and looked like a monkey with bat wings, owl eyes, and a long, pointed tail. His dirt brown, leathery skin was stretched tightly over his scrawny body, with two short arms protruding from under his wings. Those arms ended in two, long, finger-like claws, which he used to jab and poke at his Project and fill Frenchy's mind with memories. Memories of the wrongs and hurts from people he'd once cared for. Memories thordan must now use to convince Frenchy that Christians were folks to stay away from. At all costs, thordan had to prevent his Project from going Vertical.

Shuddering, thordan twisted his face into a monstrous scowl. If Frenchy did go Vertical, he would be in for more horrible beatings. He knew he was under constant surveillance, and that lucifer, the Supreme Commander of the naastis, knew everything when it came to the Projects and their status as Horizontals.

thordan could still feel the scars of the beating he had received when Frenchy had just spent the better part of a day with an earthling named William, but called Word. kije, a fellow naasti, was responsible for Word and had also been there. He remembered kije telling him of the wicked torture he'd endured when Word had gone Vertical. Since then kije moved with a noticeable limp and one side of his body was caved in from a blow that would have killed a mere mortal. But, since their kind could not die, he was forced to maintain as best he could.

As if that weren't enough, not only had kije's responsibility for Word been increased, it seemed that Word's resistance had also increased. Especially since he had mastered The Code. The Code the Holy One had given him.

thordan and kije discussed their Projects regularly. Indeed, at each meeting of the naastis, all Projects were thoroughly discussed, and there were millions to consider. Punishments were meted out to the unlucky agents who "earned" them when their Projects had gone Vertical, and dreaded glory stripes were applied.

lucifer called the scars from beatings "glory stripes" and thordan thought they were too frequently handed out and punishments too eagerly given. However, he knew better than to voice those opinions, as lucifer and his henchmen seemed to know every word the agents spoke and every thought the agents thought.

More than anything thordan wanted out. They all wanted out. But of course, that was out of the question. thordan and his kind had made their decision to follow lucifer, and with that decision, had sealed their own doom to an existence of being constantly driven to do the bidding of a demented mind. A mind that took out its anger on whomever, or whatever, was closest at the moment. To make matters worse, when they were carrying out missions against their Projects, especially against the Verticals, the light they had to endure was just as excruciating as the beatings they received later.

thordan was instantly shaken out of this thought pattern by a plea for help, but he could not believe his pointy ears. John Patrick "Frenchy" LeBlanc was asking, calling, painfully seeking help. The spear he had so cleverly designed had somehow been blocked.

"WE'VE received a message, sir." The Watch Commander was speaking. "It's a request for help from a Horizontal."

At the word 'Horizontal', Lieutenant Colonel Nadia Ben-David became attached. "In one of our sectors?"

"Yes sir," the WatCom replied. "Interior Alaska."

"Could be important. Especially now." Nadia had just returned to his Headquarters from the series of meetings at WORSPADCO. "Any Intel from DSI?"

"Yes sir, but it's Eyes Only for COMNORHAF, Encrypted For Transmission Only," the Chief responded, passing the hand-held terminal to Lt. Col. Ben-David.

Nadia read the communique:

E Y E S O N L Y

COMNORHAF

E F T O

| 2125Z | DSI INTSIG BULLETIN |
|---|---|
| ~ ~ ~ | RE/naasti OPS |
| 469991 | MESSAGE FOLLOWS |

AT 2114Z DSI MONITOR STATIONS FAIRBANKS MANLEY AND COLDFOOT RECORDED AN EHF TRANSMISSION FROM NASQUAD EHF FACILITY SEMIVISAK XX

MESSAGE DURATION 1 MINUTE 23 SECONDS XX

EHF SIGNAL EVALUATED AS "ATTACK" TRANSMISSION TO NASQUAD AIR AGENTS IN SEMIVISAK XX

AT 2112Z AN "ALL AGENTS" TRANSMISSION WAS MADE BY NAASTI HEADQUARTERS INTERNAL TRANS STATION FAIRBANKS VIA SATELLITE SIX-SIX-SIX XX

BANDS USED: ELF VLF VHF UHF EHF XX

MESSAGE DURATION 27 SECONDS WITH 2 REPEATS IDENTICAL CONTENT MADE AT 2113Z AND 2114Z XX

SIGNAL COVERAGE AS FOLLOWS: NORTHERN SQUADRON AREA INTERIOR ALASKA SQUADRON AND COLDFOOT WING XX

NOTE SOUTHERN SQUADRONS NOT REPEAT NOT AFFECTED BY THIS BROADCAST XX

NUMEROUS ACKNOWLEDGMENT SIGNALS EMANATED
FROM ADDRESSES IN AREAS CITED ABOVE XX

BEGINNING AT 2120Z DSI MONITOR STATIONS FAIRBANKS
MANLEY AND COLDFOOT RECORDED INCREASED
UHF AND EHF TRAFFIC AT NASQUAD BASES NORTH
POLE AND MANLEY XX

ORDERED WITH ASSETS REPORTING AVAILABILITY AND
STATUS XX

| | |
|---|---|
| 2125Z | END BULLETIN |
| ~ ~ ~ | DSI SENDS |
| 469991 | BREAKBREAK |
| | * * * * * |

In English the message read:

EYESONLY
COMMANDER NORTHERN
HEMISPHERIC ANGELIC FORCE
ENCRYPTED FOR TRANSMISSION ONLY

Time stamp: 9:25 p.m. Greenwich Mean Time
Department of Strategic Intelligence
Intelligence Signal Bulletin regarding naasti Operations
Message Number 469991
Message Follows:

AT 9:14 p.m. Greenwich Mean Time, Department of
Strategic Intelligence Monitoring Stations at Fairbanks,
Alaska; Manley, Alaska; and Coldfoot, Alaska; recorded
an Extremely High Frequency transmission from naasti

Squadron Extremely High Frequency facility called Semi-visible in Alaska XX

Message Duration 1 Minute 23 Seconds XX

Extremely High Frequency signal evaluated as an Attack Transmission sent to naasti squadron air agents in semi-visible in Alaska XX

AT 9:12 p.m. Greenwich Mean Time an "all agents" transmission was made by naasti Headquarters Internal Alaska Transmission Station at Fairbanks, Alaska via satellite six-six-six XX

Transmission bands used: Extremely Low Frequency; Very Low Frequency; Very High Frequency; Ultra High Frequency; Extremely High Frequency XX

Message duration 27 seconds with 2 Repeated transmissions of identical content made at 9:13 p.m. and 9:14 p.m. Greenwich Mean Time XX

Signal coverage as follows: Northern Squadron area—Interior Alaska Squadron—Coldfoot Wing XX

NOTE: Southern Squadrons Are NOT, Repeat NOT Affected by this Broadcast XX

Numerous Acknowledgment Signals Emanated from Addresses in Areas Cited above XX

Beginning at 9:20 p.m. Greenwich Mean Time Department of Strategic Intelligence Monitor Stations at Fairbanks, Manley, and Coldfoot, Alaska recorded increased Ultra High Frequency and Extremely High Frequency Traffic at naasti squadron bases in North Pole, Alaska and Manley, Alaska XX

This is Ordered with assets reporting availability and status XX

Time Stamp: 9:25 p.m. Greenwich Mean Time
End of Bulletin
Department of Strategic Intelligence sends

~ ~ ~

Message Number 469991
End of Transmission


Nadia reacted before the messenger realized what was happening. "A Horizontal is being attacked. Alert the 981st Intercept Wing to prepare to provide whatever support is necessary."

"Yes, sir," the Watch Commander replied. Nadia had seen many such communiques from the Department of Strategic Intelligence and it was common knowledge that DSI knew everything there was to know about the Humans.

"Rapha, what is the status of your Vertical?" Nadia "spoke" through his Direct Thought Link with Lew Andrews' angel, preparing to send back-up if necessary.

"Sir, this will be his first trip, but he is in the proper frame of spirit for the transertion process." Rapha replied, while flying over a man and his dog. Descending to a lower altitude brought the scene in clearer as Lew and Cupcake hiked to their choice spot in the woods near their camp.

"Excellent. Jireh," Nadia was now communicating with Frenchy's angel in Alaska. "How is your Horizontal?"

"Frenchy was attacked by thordan again," replied Jireh, "and he lost a lot of blood. I slowed his metabolism a bit and patched him up."

"Very good," Nadia said. "Keep us informed."

Jireh and Rapha, Guardian Angels, ten and half feet tall, had been assigned to their humans, Frenchy and Lew, at birth. Several years ago their colleague, Nissi, had succeeded in convincing William Orville Randolf Davis, Word to his friends and Frenchy's closest neighbor, to join the family. Now, it appeared Jireh might have similar success with "Frenchy" LeBlanc. And, because Rapha's human, Lew Andrews, had shown such a deep desire to be with UNICINC, he was being prepared for an IntraPlanetary Transertion to provide more than a little help.

L EW was thinking about the kingdom, intercession, worship, and strangely, Alaska. He shook his head at the thought. Up to that point, Alaska had been the furthest thing from his mind. Sitting down on an outcropping of granite he looked at the intensely blue Colorado sky.

"Cupcake, m'man, I do believe Colorado has the most amazing weather in the world. Think about it, yesterday we got 6 inches of snow, and today it's 45 degrees and not a cloud in the sky. Bet it's not like that in Alaska, y'know what I mean? I've even heard it gets so cold up there that things actually break. Can you imagine it being 50 or 55 degrees below zero?" Cupcake ducked his head beneath both front paws, as if he fully understood his master's words. Lew just laughed and patted the mammoth head.

Time was passing pleasurably while Lew sat watching and listening to nature, when suddenly, he was conscious of barking and a groaning sound. Almost human in nature. Looking around he noticed the scenery had changed, and he was in a dense forest of birch and spruce. Snow was piled deeply on the spruce boughs and the birch were standing in their midst like white sentinels. He saw several dogs, began counting them and realized Cupcake was not with him. Then he heard the groan again and for the first time he felt the cold. Glancing down, Lew realized he was standing in several inches of snow, wearing only a T-shirt, his heavy, flannel shirt-jacket, blue jeans and sneakers.

"Brrr, probably get cold tonight," he thought. As he stretched and changed position, he saw familiar territory and realized he was in Colorado.

"Boy, Cake, ole buddy, the brain box is a funny thing. I was just thinking about Alaska, and it was so real, I thought I was there. Hmm, go figure." Looking around he continued, "Y'know, this is really a great spot. Nowhere on God's green earth is there a better study. Right big guy?" he said, grabbing his bear-sized buddy and giving him a good hug.

The small hill Lew and Cupcake had climbed was above the highway and overlooked the train tracks. From there, he could look uphill to the south and see the headlight of any train that was approaching. To the north, the expanse of the valley spread before him like a diorama with the Rocky Mountains rising from either side. These same mountains defined the term "mountain railroad", with their twisted curves and torturous grades. The eastbound trains traveled in a southerly direction through here, straining hard uphill, and the west-bounders, with dynamic brakes screaming and mechanical brakes smoking, struggled valiantly to hold their own against gravity's relentless pull. Even though running trains over these rails was a daily way of life for Lew, he still got a kick out of watching them inch their way through the reverse curves to conquer the steep four percent grade. It was a kind of defiance to nature—a mastering of impossibilities—and Lew couldn't help but thank God for giving man the ability to tame the resources He'd so generously provided.

Lew enjoyed his private praise session, soaking up the beauty around him and training his mind to a state of worship. A few weeks had passed since he and his pastor had enjoyed a lengthy talk about worship and The Kingdom, and his thoughts turned to the people in the church. Some of them were taking to it like trains to tracks, but others were not so sure, especially after Pastor Mac had introduced flags and banners into praise and worship. Some folks uncomfortably thought they were taking things a little too far. But one brother mentioned that a banner in church was like a pin on a lapel, or a sticker on a bumper.

Just then, a loud groan again caught his attention. "Trees don't groan," Lew said aloud, as he got to his feet. "They crack and creak when the wind blows, but that was definitely a groan! A human sound!" Lew studied the area for the origin of the sound. The only sign of a human were the dogs, and they were all tied together somehow. They reminded him of something he'd read about dog sleds and dog teams. That must be it.

Cocking his head to one side, Lew strained against the silence. Then without warning he heard it. It was faint but nevertheless clear. Someone was calling out. Lew listened. "God, send me some help," Lew heard.

"**S**IR, Lew has made the trip successfully." Rapha was giving Nadia an update on the condition of his human. "I had a bit of trouble with the transertion process because of the temperature difference, but I warmed his air a bit to make him more comfortable and everything is going as planned."

"Excellent, Rapha," replied Nadia, "help him all you can without being conspicuous."

"Yes sir."

Nadia then contacted Nissi, Word's angel, and told him to put Word in touch with Frenchy. He knew Frenchy could use a friend with a Handbook.

**F**RENCHY could not believe his eyes. 23 degrees below zero, at least four feet of snow on the level, and yet, before him stood a guy in a flannel shirt-jacket and jeans. Where had he come from?

"Don't you have a coat?" Frenchy questioned, momentarily forgetting about his situation.

"What?" Lew asked hesitantly. There was no one else to be seen.

"A coat. Where's your coat?" the voice asked again.

"Oh, uh, guess I left it home. Where are you?" Lew asked still looking around, trying to find the source of the voice.

"Under this dad-gummed tree! Where do you think I am?"

"Where?" Lew responded, searching for the man. "I can't see you. Wave your arm."

"Wave my arm!" Frenchy gasped. "You gotta be kiddin'! If I could wave my arm I woulda been outa here an hour ago."

"You're mighty snippy for someone who's stuck."

"Hey look, cut the comedy crap and get me outa here. I'm off to your right, wearing a size triple large spruce tree. Forest Green's the color."

Smiling, Lew worked his way over to the fallen giant. "I think I've found you. That is, I found your tree." He strained to find some sign of the buried man.

"Here, let me get this thing outa the way," Lew said, battling the branches of the twenty-foot treetop. "How'd you get under there, anyway?" It looked to Lew like the tree had been snapped off about twenty-five feet above the ground and fallen right on top of Frenchy.

"How'd I get under this thing? How d'ya think I got under it? It fell on me! Now, if you'll quit flappin' yer yap and lift up the end," Frenchy was saying as Lew worked his way through the branches, "I'll try and wiggle out."

Lew had a better idea, and without thought to the weight, he simply picked up the tree and threw it to one side.

After the snow had settled, Frenchy shook his head. "I can't believe you just did that. It must a weighed a ton."

"Uh, yeah. Prob'ly did." Lew replied. "Nothin' to it when you have a little help from a friend. Now, God said you needed some help. What can I do for ya?"

As Lew was speaking Jireh landed a solid blow to the side of thordan's head, sending him spinning head over end into the space just above the trees. Earlier when thordan had heard Frenchy ask God for help, he'd gotten a little closer to his Project, and through the trees he saw a cloud of powdered snow where the twenty foot projectile had landed. He heard Lew and didn't want to believe his ears. He had heard about this Vertical who was so intent on getting close to "Him", but had never anticipated a face-to-face meeting. He'd always thought, 'It'll never happen to me'. Worse yet, thordan knew that if this Vertical was here, his Force Leader, Rapha, would be somewhere close by.

All agents knew, and feared, Lew and his kind. All they ever did was, well..., thordan had always found it difficult to even think "worship" or "intercede" much less actually say the words. However, that is exactly what they did. Always! ALWAYS!

thordan and his kind had hoped to gain more control over Lew when sapphira had convinced his true love to leave him. Instead, he'd turned to this. lucifer had said it would drive him their way, but, as usual, he had been wrong.

"Stay where you are, thordan!"

He recognized Rapha's booming voice immediately and knew he was beaten before he started. However, ignoring the obvious he moved with blinding speed and reached an ugly claw through the hole in Frenchy's coat.

"Who did you... AARGGH!!!" Frenchy howled.

Upon hearing Frenchy's scream, Lew reflexively rebuked the pain. "satan, you foul spirit of infirmity, you no good, stinkin', lyin' creep, in the name of Jesus, get your hands off this man," Lew commanded.

At the word "Jesus" coming with such tremendous authority, thordan winced in excruciating pain, and was momentarily blinded by an extremely bright light.

Jireh sprang into action, and thordan was caught off guard.

At that precise instant Rapha's blow between the wings slammed the demon's claw out of Frenchy, and Jireh landed a widow maker on thordan's pointy little chin.

"Do you have a Bible?" Lew asked.

Frenchy stared blankly at Lew for a moment before realizing what he was up against. "Oh, for cryin' out loud," he groaned. "You're all I need. Another lily-livered, two-faced wus of a Christian. Get outa my face! I don't need no back-stabbin, son of..." Frenchy's words faded as he struggled to move. "I got in here on my own and," groan, "I'll get out the same way."

thordan felt the searing pain as he went flying through the air. But when he heard Frenchy say 'two-faced' Christian', his hopes rose and he headed straight for Frenchy again.

"Listen here, satan," Lew began, "you have no authority coming in here like this. In the Name of Jesus Christ of Nazareth, I command you to get your hands off this man." Frenchy was mesmerized as the stranger spoke, and thordan again winced painfully at the name 'Jesus.'

The reaction was not lost on the Angels. Maneuvering so as to put thordan between them, they attacked together.

For an instant, as his thoughts were interrupted by simultaneous blows, thordan wondered if he had indeed heard Frenchy correctly. The combination knocked him momentarily senseless and that was all the Angels needed. Rapha grabbed thordan by the tail and sent him streaking toward his place of torment. They knew they were not finished with him yet, but at least he was out of their way for the time being.

"Hi feller," Frenchy heard through the trees. Looking around, he could not understand, let alone figure out, what had happened. At least he thought it had happened. He was no longer bleeding and he didn't seem to be hurting, and the broken tree was lying about twenty feet from it's stump. Tourist, however, was no where to be found. He could see the footprints and the blood stain in the snow, but no "Tourist". Turning around, Frenchy saw the trapper he had met back in October. "Hi your ownself. What're you doin' here?"

"Thought you could use a Bible," Word said. "looks like there's been quite a ruckus 'round here. What happened?"

"Yeah, s'pose it does," Frenchy responded, looking around, "but I sure ain't needin' no Bible, or a stinkin' Bible thumper, for that matter. Not sure what happened, but I was mindin' m'own bu'ness and packin' up ta get back home when that tree over there fell on me."

"What do ya mean that tree fell on ya? If it fell on ya here, how'd it get over there, where it is?"

"Just what I said, it fell on me. Then Tourist picked it up and threw it over there."

"Tourist!", Word exclaimed. "What tourist!?"

"There was this tourist-type who dropped in and picked up that tree and threw it over there."

"Wait a minute," Word said, while walking around the area. "Slow down will ya. You mean to tell me that here we are, ten miles from Nowhere, a spruce falls on ya, some tourist-type waltzes in here, picks up the tree, by himself no less, and throws it over there, then splits?"

"Yeah, well, that pretty much sums it up."

"Right." Word was unconvinced.

"Well..." Frenchy began, "...he was here..."

"That's a fine how do you do," Word said, and then thought, *'Father, you work in mysterious ways, but this one's a real doozy. You mind splainin' what's goin' on?'*

As if on cue, Frenchy answered, "Listen, I can't explain it, but it's like I told ya. Tourist-type shows up, picks up the tree, throws it over there, and asks me if I have a Bible. I tell him, in no uncertain terms, that I don't have a Bible, and furthermore I don't need no stinkin' Bible, and now I don't know where he's at." Frenchy was truly confused, but equally convinced of what happened. "Anyway," he calmed down a little and continued, "why are you here?"

"Well, um... I really don't know. I just had to find ya, I guess."

Nissi and Jireh were hovering over the trees and rather enjoying this exchange, but decided it would probably be a good idea to help them sort it out. Nissi gave Word an idea. "Wait a minute," Word said, "I just had a thought. Maybe we can piece this thing together. Tell me, slowly please, step by step, exactly what happened."

"Well, let's see," Frenchy said while Jireh, his angel, refreshed his memory, "I was packin' the sled and the dogs were actin' like they heard somethin', 'specially Smo-ki, then the cold snapped off that tree. Over there's where I was under the thing until Tourist-type showed up."

"Hey wait a minute," Word began. "It ain't cold enough for the cold to snap the tree. You sure that's what happened?"

"Yeah, I know it's not cold enough, but, it's the only thing I can figure. It sure sounded like it split 'cause of the cold, but like you said, ain't cold enough."

"Oh well, forget it. Go on. Then what happened?"

"Okay," Frenchy went on. "Well, I tried to get out and couldn't. I couldn't even move 'cause some of the branches had trapped my coat. As I as tryin' to wiggle or squirm, do anything to get out, I felt a stabbing pain under my arm. That's when I could tell I was bleedin'."

"You're hurt?!"

"I was," Frenchy answered, "but I'm okay now."

Then Word remembered the blood in the snow and saw Frenchy's coat. "You've lost a lot of blood. We better take a look at it."

"Well, I s'pose you're right, but let's not take all day," Frenchy said while heading toward the cabin. "The sun'll be gone in a couple hours and we're still 10 miles from my place."

Frenchy's coat, both shirts, thermal underwear and cotton T-shirt were all stained with blood, but when he saw there were no marks on his skin, Frenchy was as speechless as the Northern Lights. He saw the thermometer and wondered about Tourist-type. He had only been wearing sneakers, jeans and a flannel shirt!! *A lot of things need explaining,* he thought as he re-dressed putting his shirts on backwards so the holes would be away from the one in his coat.

"Okay, then what?" Word said putting his parka back on.

"Well," Frenchy continued, "it seemed like I'd been in there forever, hurtin' like crazy and beginnin' to wonder if I'as ever gonna get out. That's when I saw Tourist. He was right over there. See?" he said pointing through the window. "There's his tracks."

They went out to the tracks, and what they saw shocked both of them. They were expecting sno-pac tracks, but what was in the snow was a very clear foot print with k-o-b-e-e-r pressed into it. "What's k-o-b-e-e-r spell?" asked Frenchy.

"Hmm, k-o-b-e-e-r. Let's see," pondered Word. "Think about this. What'd we get if we spelled that backwards?"

Frenchy's mind did a glitch, "If we spelled that backwards we'd get t-a-h-t."

"No, no," Word flabber-gasped. "Spell k-o-b-e-e-r backwards!"

"Oh," Frenchy grinned. "You said spell that backwards, so I did. Anyway, k-o-b-e-e-r backwards would be r-e-e-b-o-k. That's it! Tourist was wearing Reeboks. He looked like he'd just stepped off the plane from Outside. Why he wasn't even wearin' a coat! I asked him if he had one, and he said, he'd left it home. Man, you'd think a guy comin' to Alaska in the middle of winter would have sense enough to bring decent clothes. Outsiders. Man I tell ya, ya just can't fix stupid."

"Mebbe he didn't know he was comin'," Word offered, then went on, "then what?"

"Then he told me to wave my arm so's he could find me. I told him I couldn't and that's when he picked up the tree and tossed it over there."

"Let's go see the tree," Word suggested. By the marks in the snow, it was plain to see that someone, or some thing, had thrown it like a javelin. The top ten or so feet had bro-ken away, leaving a deep gouge in the earth and snow. Word observed, "Don't look to me like this tree was freeze-broke.

That splits'em, and this looks like it's been snapped, kinda like a pencil."

"Yeah, you're right," Frenchy agreed.

"Okay, go on," Word said.

"Then, he said, 'God sent me'."

"Oh yeah?" Word was genuinely interested in that remark, but decided to leave it 'til later. "Then what?"

"Then he said somethin' really strange. Don't remember exactly," Frenchy said, scratching his beard, "but somethin' about a ghost or spirit or somethin', and infirmary, and Jesus name, and asked me if I had a Bible."

"Really?" *'This,'* thought Word, *'is gettin' good.'* "What'd you say?"

"I said I didn't and that I don't want one. I still don't," Frenchy added emphatically.

"Go on," Word urged.

"That's it."

"What do ya mean that's it?" questioned Word.

"That's it. Finished. Over. Done. Fini," Frenchy concluded.

"Then what happened to this guy?"

"Dunno." Frenchy answered. "He was gone. Like he just up a disappeared or somethin' and you showed up. Say, what were you doing all this time?"

"I was on my way to your place. You know, come to think of it, I made incredible time gettin' here. That's kinda strange, too, 'cause I wasn't trav'lin' any faster than normal, but when I'd check, I'd find myself a lot further than I thought I should have been. F'rinstance, from the Glacier River through Bear Flats to Whiskey Creek normally takes a good two hours. But, by my watch today, it took 43 minutes! And I had to dodge a pack of wolves, too."

"You expect me to believe that?" asked a puzzled Frenchy. "What's wrong with your watch?"

"Nothin'. Don't think so anyway... what time you got?"

"Quarter after Ten," Frenchy said.

"Me, too," Word said, looking at his watch. "That means I made it from my place to your place in an hour and ten minutes!"

"You tellin' me that you left your place shortly after nine?"

"Yeah. Why?"

"That's when the tree fell!" Frenchy exclaimed. "I heard it break, turned, saw it fallin', put up my arm and saw my watch. 9:05. Then wham! That musta been when I hurt my side."

"Very interesting", Word remarked while he was praying on the inside *'Father, you brought me here for a purpose. Show me what to do.'* "What're ya doing today?", he asked as the idea popped into his head.

"What?" The question came right out of the blue and caught Frenchy off guard.

"What are you doing today?" Word repeated.

"Oh," Frenchy thought out loud, "just gonna work on these furs, I guess. Why?"

"Well," began Word, "what do ya say we head back to your place and I'll help ya with'em?"

"Sounds fine to me," said Frenchy, "but why do you want to help me? Don't you have your own furs to get ready?"

"Oh, I've already done mine."

"Well, awright," Frenchy continued, "but we'd better hurry. By the time we get back, it'll be time to eat. Y'know? I just happen to have a Caribou stew that's just itchin' to git et."

# 3

# JUNE'S

THE blast of a locomotive horn broke rudely into Lew's thoughts, and he unexpectedly found himself back in Colorado. Smitty, a good friend and the engineer on the west-bounder, gave him a friendly wave. It was time to drag the eastbound perishable to Salida.

"Okay, Cupster," he said, shaking his head to think clearly, "time to head for home so's I can go play trains." It took about fifteen minutes to get back to the Jeep, and since he had already taken down his tent and put the Coleman stove away, the only thing left was to drive down the mountain. "Hop in," Lew said when they got to the Jeep, "let's head for home."

There had been a passenger seat when Cupcake first saw the Jeep, but after a while, Lew had taken out the seat and replaced it with a piece of plywood covered with carpet. When his master did that, Cupcake couldn't even see out the front window and had wondered why his best friend had done that to him. It wasn't too long, however, before he discovered Lew's Jeep had changed, and he was able to see out. Then his master had made something else for him that was even better. His own seat, and it was right behind his master so he could get a head scratch any time he wanted.

Lew arrived in Minturn about forty five minutes ahead of the train he was scheduled to take over the hill and figured a cup of coffee and a full tank of gas was in order. Pulling into the QuickStop across the tracks from the yard office, he noticed a fellow pumping gas into a pick-up/fifth wheeler combination with Alaska license plates. Lew couldn't decide if the fellow was smaller than average, or if it was a big truck, but as he approached it became apparent the man was shorter than average. Of course, at six foot four inches, Lew generally looked down on people. "I noticed your plates," he said, trying to strike up a conversation, "you from Anchorage?"

"Nope," the guy replied. "Fairbanks. Only good thing about Anchorage is it's so close to Alaska. Ever been to Alaska?"

"Nope. Don't think so." '*Now why did I say that,*' Lew asked himself. He wondered if the guy even heard him. If he did, he kept quiet.

"Well, it's a great place to visit and I really like livin' there. It's my first trip to Colorado though, and you can color me impressed. Name's Davis," the guy said, extending his hand to Lew, "Bud Davis. I'm a train nut and I've been chasin' an eastbound freight. You know anything about trains and/or where to take some pictures?"

"Strange you should ask," Lew answered, accepting Bud's hand in a firm grip. "You see that rascal with 3099 on the point?" Lew asked, gesturing to the lead engine on the train just across the road from the filling station. "I'm gettin' ready to take'im over to Salida. By the way, I'm Lew. Lew Andrews."

"Nice to meet ya, Lew. You kiddin' me?" Bud exclaimed. "You're an engineer on the Denver Salt Lake and Pacific?"

"Sure am."

"Those locomotives are SD40 dash 2's, aren't they?"

"Yup, sure are. You really know your locos. Now I'm the one who's impressed," Lew exclaimed.

"Just nuts about trains. I ran in to that guy just the other side of Grand Junction, and been chasin' him ever since. He's got six o' those monsters," he said referring to the engines. "Those SD forty's are 'bout three thousand ponies each, aren't they?"

"Yup. Dyed in the wool train nut, aren't ya?"

"Yeah, I guess I am," Bud agreed. "But my brother, Word, he lives in Alaska, says I'm just a trained nut. Tell you what, though, I'm sure nuts about Colorado. This is one neat place. You know that canyon just this side of Glenwood Springs?"

Lew nodded and said, "Oh, yeah," thinking about Glenwood Canyon.

"Well, I paced him right through there. Now, that's some country! Very similar to a place on the Alaska Railroad. You oughta come up and see it sometime. Matter of fact," Bud continued, "when you do, let me know and we'll get together and chase some trains." Returning to the present, he pointed south. "I understand from here to Leadville is the steepest part of the D-S-L-n-P."

"Sure is," Lew responded, thinking this guy was either lonesome for somebody to talk to or simply a 'motor mouth.' "We pull 4 percent just before we crest Tennessee Pass. That's why they're gonna give me a shove with four more of those rascals."

"You don't say!" Bud exclaimed. "Eighteen thousand horsepower on the point with twelve thousand more giving you a kick in the rear. Must be some kinda power trip having all those horses under your hand."

"I s'pose," Lew answered nonchalantly while all the aspects of his job were rolling through his mind, "it's just a job. Tell you what, though. It sure beats working."

"Yeah," chuckled Bud. "Guess it does at that. Changin' the subject. Is there a good place to get some pictures when you're pulling that 4 percent? I've been gittin' a lota stuff with my digital, but I really wanna drag out the four by five."

"What's a four by five?" Lew asked.

"It's a camera," Bud said. "Makes a negative that's 4 inches by 5 inches. It's pretty good sized, so I need room to set up a tripod."

"Oh, okay." Lew decided this guy must really be into photography. It also registered that the fellow hadn't used any off-color language, which was a big change from hearing the guys at work. He continued, "Tell you what ya do. Head south out of town a few miles until you see the old Camp Hale site. It'll be on your left. You can't miss it."

"Famous last words," Bud interrupted, a gleam in his eye.

"Right, I hear ya," Lew chuckled and continued, "but, seriously, if you're lookin' for it you can't. It's an old abandoned Army Post, and there's a huge clearing. Anyway, you go about a mile past the site, up the hill, and you'll see the reverse curves on your right. It's a great place, and plenty of room for you and your rig."

"Sounds good to me," Bud responded.

"Say," Lew shifted gears, "while we're waitin' on the westbound perishable, let's go grab a cup of coffee. I'm buyin'."

"Fine by me," Bud began, "but I thought you were headin' out right away?"

"I am, but it'll be awhile before that west bounder gets here and since there's only one siding between here and the top o' the pass, and he's already passed it, I can't leave 'til he clears the main here in town. I'll just check in with the dispatcher and let him know I'll be over at June's," Lew explained, thumbing over his shoulder toward June's Café.

"Well, okay, then. Let's get that coffee." Walking beside Lew, Bud revealed an aspect of his life that topped both trains and photography. "Don't suppose there's a Bible study anywhere in town tonight, is there?"

"Oh?" Lew asked. "You one of those Jesus Freaks?"

"Uh, well, yeah," Bud started to get a little defensive, "I guess you could say I'm a freak for Jesus." He then saw the twinkle in Lew's eye.

"Me too," Lew exclaimed. "I go to Minturn Community Outreach and we have a get-together on Thursday nights."

"Good, I'll be there. What time's it start?" Bud asked.

"Well, folks start showin' up around 6:30 or so, but actually doesn't start 'til seven o'clock. It's on Main Street, down a block from June's."

"Great," Bud said. By this time the two had ambled over to the dispatcher's office where Lew checked in. They then went to Minturn's 'meeting hall', June's Café. Minturn was a typical small town, everybody knew everybody else, and Lew saw many friends as they walked in.

"Hey, Lew," someone on the far side of the room shouted, "how ya been?"

"Just dandy. How 'bout yourself?" Lew called back, making his way to Will's table. A cattleman, Will owned a ranch a few miles out of town, and didn't get to town all that often.

"Well, if I'as any better, you couldn't stand me. Who's that ya got with ya?" Will asked.

"This is Bud, my new friend from Alaska," Lew spoke, approaching Will's table.

"Alaska, huh?" Will said, making room for the three of them in the booth. "Join me. What part of Alaska?"

"Fairbanks," Bud answered. "Ever been up there?"

"Yup," Will confirmed, "matter of fact I have. Not in Fairbanks, though. I'as out in the Aleutians durin' the Cold War. Too much isolation for this guy, so's I bought me a ranch when Uncle Sam got tired o' feedin' me. Whatcha do up there?"

"Oh, I fix computers," Bud responded, "take a few pictures on the side and just generally try to stay outa trouble."

"Um," Will retorted, "sounds boring."

"What?" Bud asked, "Fixin' 'puters or takin' pictures?"

"No. Stayin' outa trouble," Will said with a mile wide grin.

"I heard that," Bud replied.

As they were having coffee, a strange series of thoughts kept intruding into the back of Lew's mind. He sensed flashes of a forest, a fellow caught in a tree, knowing it was cold but not feeling it, and dogs barking. Just bits and pieces came and went all during the time he and this guy from Alaska were talking. He learned Bud's brother lived alone and ran a dog team. He trapped in the winter, hunted for gold in the summer, moose and bear in autumn, and read his Bible every spare minute. Bud told Lew about Word's most recent thoughts on worship and the Kingdom of God and how he sees it as an all day, every day, relationship with Father God. He sees that God, Father God, wants us to treat Him as the real, caring, loving Father He really is.

Lew was astonished beyond words, as that was exactly what he saw. He mentioned his only want was to be with Father God, and Bud said that was the way his brother was, and that he was also beginning to see it. They both agreed that when they made a conscious effort to be with God all the time, the things of life that needed attention were taken care of, and better than before.

Tsidkenu, Bud's angel, and Rapha, Lew's angel, were sitting on the roof directly over the heads of the two men. Tsidkenu had grabbed sacre, Bud's naasti, and Rapha had grabbed zoltan, Lew's naasti, and had tied the two demons with their long tails and were bouncing them like basketballs. Neither angel could help but chuckle. If Bud and Lew REALLY knew what was going on, their minds would short circuit.

"Just think, Tsid," Rapha said, "after all this time they're finally beginning to see."

"You are so right, Raph." Tsidkenu replied. "When people like Lew and Bud and Word..."

"...don't forget Frenchy," Rapha interjected.

"...and Frenchy," Tsidkenu complied, "as well as the host of others who see the truth of what the Kingdom really is. Then we can go knock heads."

"Yeah. You should've see the look on thordan's face as he went flying by," Rapha said, smiling. "He reminded me of the human song, 'Oh, he flies through the air with the greatest of ease, old nasty thordan will soon bow his knees'."

# 4

# PRAISALUJAH!

T HE red "on air" light over the door of the main control room of KMGC radio went on as the morning
man opened his microphone. "We found that one by the
Fifth Dimension in the files of seventy-one. Good morning, I'm Scott Dennis on Magic 99. It's six twenty-nine this
Wednesday morning with 28 sunny degrees, and our eye in
the sky tells us the mouse-trap caught a semi this morning.
Here's our Sky-Pilot, Rodger Lee."

"Thanks, Scott. Good morning, all bodies. Boy oh boy,
it's gonna be a long year this morning. About fifteen minutes
ago, a semi going from I-25 southbound to I-70 eastbound,
jack-knifed and rolled onto it's side. Police on the scene say
there are no injuries, but traffic will be tied up for the rest
of the morning. The truck was carrying a load of hay and
several bails went over the rail and onto I-25 southbound.
Fortunately, no cars were directly under the falling bails at
the time.

"We are over the scene and see southbound traffic already
backed up to 58th avenue. Eastbound I-70 traffic is slowing
from Federal. Northbound I-25 has not been affected yet, but
westbound I-70 is beginning to show some problems due to

the number of folks going to southbound I-25. Folks, if you can, take another route this morning.

"Elsewhere, the system seems to be running smoothly with only minor slowing out on the south end with 225 westbound merging with I-25 north. Keep the shiny side up, everyone."

"Rodger Lee, Magic 99 Sky-Pilot. Back to you, Scott."

"Thanks, Rodger. It's six thirty and here's Xan Franklin with the morning's news."

"Thanks Scott, good morning everyone. LARS, the Local Area Rail System, has claimed another life. About 3:30 this morning a car traveling south on Colorado Boulevard was struck by a light rail train. Police say the only occupant was the driver of the car who was pronounced dead at the scene.

"Another shooting overnight. Lakewood Police report a minister of the Lakewood Christian Fellowship Church was attacked in his office about one thirty this morning. Details are sketchy, but a spokesperson for Lutheran Medical Center says 'early this morning, Rev. Dan Andrews underwent an emergency procedure for a gun-shot wound'.

"In other news, the implementation of the cashless society is one step closer. The President's Chief Economic adviser says the entering of the names of every person in the world into the data base has just been completed. President Marshall says the next step in the switch-over will be the issuing of an RFID, a Radio Frequency Identification Device, in driver's licenses and credit and debit cards. This will be handled by local banks and the DMV, and, according to Marshall, will begin next week.

"On a related note, despite protests from Coloradans everywhere, today is the first day new driver's licenses will have RFIDs implanted in them.

"We'll have details on these and other stories we're follow-ing on The News In Depth at Eight.

"Weather-wise, it's going to be clear and chilly today with a high of about 34. That's all the news that is the news on Magic 99, I'm Xan Franklin."

"Thanks, Xan," Scott said while pushing the PLAY button on the CD Sequencer. "At six thirty-two we're back into the music you want to hear with Chicago on Magic 99, KMGC, Denver."

As Xan closed her mic, she wondered about the man named Andrews.

L EW was walking through the door as the phone was ringing. Due to the hour, 6:30 AM, and the fact that he'd just gotten off work, he had a gut feeling that all was not well. "Hello," he said apprehensively.

"Lew?"

"Yes."

"Lew, this is Pastor Mac. I have some bad news for you. Maybe I should come over." About a year and a half ago, Lew had successfully 'bumped' into a 'hotshot' run, a regular, fast freight. He had been fortunate to keep that run and he could schedule his time much easier. He was still 'married' to his phone, but, basically, he knew when he was going to be called, now that he was no longer on the "helpers roster". He had just walked in from bringing a hot shot from Salida.

"No, Pastor, that's not necessary. We can talk on the phone."

"Sit down, Lew," Rapha, Lew's angel, advised, "this isn't going to be easy."

"Lew," Pastor Mac began as Lew braced himself.

"Dan's been shot."

"What! No! When?! Who?!"

"His wife called and said he was at Lutheran Medical Center. That's all I know."

"Okay, Pastor," Lew said while sinking into his chair, "I guess we'd better pray." Lew was too shaken to pray. Dan was not just his brother, he was his best friend, and since he had moved from Seattle they had become even closer.

"Let Mac pray," Rapha said.

"You took the call," Lew said, "so you pray and I'll agree."

"Our Heavenly Father," Pastor Mac began, "we bring to You Lew's brother, Dan. satan's hand in this is too clear to ignore, and Father we thank you for the authority you've given us to set the captives free. Now, satan, in the name of Jesus, get your crippled hands off Dan. He is God's property, and you have no business messing around with him. Father God, I ask for divine health for Dan even as we speak. We know there is no distance in the spirit world, and we bind any hindering spirits that would minister to Dan, and we loose Your peace on him. We thank You for this Father, in Jesus Name."

"I agree with that," Lew said through his tears. "Thanks Mac, and thank You, Father."

"Tell him," Adon said, "to go to Lakewood", Adon, Pastor Mac's angel, was giving the direction, "Dan will be glad to see him."

"You've probably got some time-off coming, why don't you go on over to Lakewood? Cupcake's more than welcome over here."

"Thanks. I was thinkin' the same thing. See ya in a bit."

With the few necessities out of the way, he was soon heading over the mountain to Denver. Anywhere in that huge metropolis was Denver to him, and he could never comprehend why anyone would want to live in a place like that. Just look what happened. He started thinking and blaming it on the "big city", but he could not shake the impression that this was a direct satanic attack, so he began praying.

As he was going over Vail Pass he was praying for his brother, and somehow his thoughts turned to the first time he had seen his pastor. He had been bringing a westbound perishable train into Minturn and as he was rounding the curve at the south end of the yards he had seen a one armed man walking across the tracks, and knew that the man was, or at least had been, a railroader. He had the unmistakable "railroader's ramble". The almost comical, almost bow-legged, gait that comes only from having spent many hours walking on a moving train. At the time Lew had wondered about the man, but little did he know he would see him at church the next Sunday, much less as the Pastor.

About a year later, Lew and Mac, had been talking about nothing in particular and everything in general, and the subject of railroading came up. It was at that point Mac told Lew how he had lost his arm. It seems he had been an "old teenager", as Mac put it, and was working for the Santa Fe in Salida as a summer job during his college days. Somehow, Mac was not quite sure what happened because it all happened so fast, he found himself on the ground with a boxcar running over his left arm. Mac said there was no pain, and very little bleeding, and that after the boxcar had passed he'd gotten to his feet, picked up his arm and walked to the dispatcher's office. When he got there, Mac said the dispatcher passed out in a dead faint, so he had gone to the Yardmaster's office, who called the hospital. Several years had passed and Mac's hair was gray and thinning, but he had not lost his love for trains, and often went down to the Yard Office to have coffee with whoever was on duty at the time. All the guys knew him and welcomed his visits.

Lew was driving up the west approach to the Eisenhower Tunnel when his thoughts then turned to his brother. He knew Dan had been working with some ex-members of the local witchcraft group, and he had mentioned several times their discovered plots against him, his church body, and individuals who had been set free. If this was related, it was the most serious and most blatant since Dan had moved from Seattle, Washington and started the church four years ago.

"CAN I get a little help over here?" Jeff Wolfe, Dan's Music Director, was speaking. He had been working in the sound room when he heard the shot. As a Navy corpsman in Viet Nam he knew what to do, so instead of wasting time waiting for an ambulance, he had put a pressure bandage on the wound, called the police and the Emergency Room, and had taken Dan to Lutheran himself. "Here's the man with a gun shot in the abdomen," Jeff said as he opened the Emergency Room door. Immediately the Emergency Room Personnel were there with a gurney.

"I need vitals, stat!" It was the Emergency Room doctor speaking while they were putting Dan on the gurney. "Start an I.V. Using 16 gauge in both arms, left and right wide open." The police were also there, and Jeff spoke with the officer as the ER Personnel took over.

"BP 80 over 40 with heavy bleeding," responded the ER Medic.

"That's worrisome," said the ER Doctor. "Minimum code. Palpate the pulse. Type and cross match, prepare 4 units, stat. Nurse, call OR Surgeon, stat. Medic, I want a CBC, stat."

The medic spoke, "He's pretty clammy, Doctor, BP 70 over 30."

"Prepare to transport to OR, stat. Begin fluids. Let's roll, people. We're burning the clock."

"We've got a Life-pac 8 with us, Doctor," the nurse informed as she helped guide the gurney toward the elevator.

The Operating Room charge nurse called on the two-way, "OR's prepped and ready."

"Good. Have 'em meet us at the door," the ER Doctor said into the intercom on the elevator.

"We think we've got him stable. His heart's assuming on it's own," the ER Doctor said as they rolled the gurney out of the elevator.

As soon as the door was open far enough to squeeze through, the OR team took the gurney and wheeled it into surgery, and the Medic volunteered, "BP's 60 over 20."

"Okay, thanks," responded the OR Doctor, "we'll take him from here. We're prepped and ready."

Their part over, the ER team of Doctor, Medic, and Nurse stayed on the elevator and went back to their domain. "You think he has any chance at all?" asked the Nurse.

"He has two," replied the Doctor, "slim and none."

"BUT sir," kije pleaded, "I've laid many traps for him. I even sent a wolf pack after him, but..." He was caught short by another blow to the face. He was being held by four demons, each of whom had a grip like an iron claw, while stench was administering the "correction".

stench's ugly, gnarled, crippled claw was gripping kije's throat, stretching his neck beyond endurance, but death could not come. stench and his kind, the upper echelon of the naasti hierarchy, were humanoid in appearance in that they moved on two legs in an upright position. Grotesque, malformed, foul-smelling and obnoxious, stench and company were the epitome of ugliness. The interrogation was taking place deep in the bowels of a massive, dark, stone structure. lucifer was asking the questions and ordering stench to do whatever his demented mind could dream up. "But..." gag, gurgle... "sir... Nissi... was... there..."

When lucifer heard 'Nissi' he tore kije from stench's grip and slammed him into the ground. "What!?!" he screamed.

"Nissi... sir," kije cowered.

"Nissi? Are you sure!?" lucifer blasted out.

"Yes... sir." kije gasped, "and... Jireh too."

"And Jireh!?!?"

"Yes... sir."

"Where was thordan!?" lucifer yelled.

"They... sent him... to you just... as I arrived."

"Oh, yes," lucifer sneered. "stench!" he demanded, "see that these two bumbling idiots are properly reprimanded. Eight or ten glory stripes should knock'em back in line."

"Yessir!" stench responded, the very picture of fear. He knew lucifer was on the verge of losing his temper.

"Do whatever is necessary," lucifer went on, "then send them back to their Earthlings." While he was speaking, lucifer had grabbed stench by the throat and held him out at arms length. "And you go with them. Show them how to properly carry out an assignment. Don't fail me, stench!" lucifer yelled while throwing him into the massive stone wall for emphasis. The grip on stench's throat had broken his neck and his head rolled crazily from side to side. He'd hit the wall head first, deeply gouging his cheek and eye.

"You did not do what you were told," stench shrieked at thordan and kije as his head flopped backwards, "and your failure has caused me to endure lucifer's anger again. This re-education is going to make all the others seem like a stroll in the park." stench had never felt anger like this and he was going to pass it on by re-arranging a few of their parts. thordan and kije were not going to be the only ones to feel his fury.

"Boy, that bullet really hammered him. It flew around in here like a space ship out of control. What a mess! I haven't seen anything like this since Nam." The Chief Surgeon had been assigned to the 3rd Medical Battalion in Nam and had seen everything anyone would never want to see, and was talking while removing the pressure bandage

Jeff had applied. "Did the guys in ER put this bandage on?" he asked.

"I don't think so," responded Ranaye, "why?"

"Something else I haven't seen since Nam."

As the bandage was removed, damien, Dan's naasti, reached his dirty, ugly, claw into the jagged hole in Dan's side and grabbed the spleen.

"Doctor," said the assisting Surgeon, "his spleen's hemorrhaging."

"We are losin' him," confirmed the anesthetist.

Silently, but fervently, Ranaye, the nurse, was praying for the man on the table as damien tightened his grip.

"BP 50," said the anesthetist.

"Prepare for splenectomy," ordered the surgeon.

At that order, the nurse got down to some serious praying and began rebuking satan and any harm he would throw their way. She had worked in this room for years, had seen satan steal life from folks too many times, and decided it was time to put a stop to this bunch of death. "*No way, satan,*" she began praying silently, "*you cannot take him. I don't know if this guy's a Christian or not, but I have the authority around here and you cannot have him. Now, in Jesus' Name, get your filthy, lousy hands out of him and let God and the doctors do their work.*"

On hearing the nurse's prayer, Roi, Dan's angel, swooped in from the ceiling and grabbed damien by the back of his bony neck, kicked him like a football out of the hospital, and began repairing Dan's spleen.

"Doctor," said the assistant, "take a look at this. His spleen has stopped hemorrhaging. The wound seems to closing on it's own."

"That can't be," retorted the Chief Surgeon.

"That's what the books say, but take a look for yourself."

"I don't believe what I am seeing," the Chief Surgeon said without believing.

"Praisalujah," the nurse said out loud.

"What did you say?" asked the chief.

"Praisalujah. It's a combination of Praise the Lord and Hallelujah."

"Oh that's right," began the chief, "you're one of those Christians, aren't you?"

"Don't stop her," picked up the assistant, "whatever she's doing, it seems to be working."

"BP 60 over 30," the anesthetist interjected.

"Is it fixing itself?" the chief asked incredulously.

"Seems to be," replied the assistant.

"BP 90 over 60," said the anesthetist.

"Amazing," both Doctors said in unison.

"Thanks, Dad," said the nurse.

"BP 110 over 80," said a joyful anesthetist.

"Thanks who?" the assistant asked.

"Father," the nurse replied. "You know, Who art in Heaven."

"And here, too," said the anesthetist.

"BP 130 over 90."

"He's stable," said the chief. "Prepare to close. Call ICU, and tell'em we have a customer for them. I really don't believe what just happened here."

"I don't either," the assistant continued, "but we don't have much choice. All four of us saw it."

"I know," said the chief while suturing the wound, "but it was absolutely amazing. One minute his spleen was bursting open like an overripe melon, and the next it's returning to normal."

"So, Tom. What are you going to put in your report?" asked the anesthetist.

"Haven't decided yet. What do you think, nurse?," the chief asked Ranaye.

"Search your heart," she answered. "God knows what happened, and He will enlighten you."

"I suppose you're right," the chief said, "but I still don't believe it."

"You don't have to believe it now, it's over." the nurse said. "Just thank Him.

# BATTLE

VERNA Phillips was flying faster than she had ever moved before. Even when she had been in 'that big thing' going to Dayton, Ohio to see her Air Force son, she had not moved so fast. Ahead of her she could see what looked like a huge cloud of dust, and every now and again she could see flashes of lightning and thought it strange she never heard the thunder that always accompanied lightning.

As she got closer she could hear men's voices. Some irate, others blissful, and still others were in absolute torment. The entire area spanned from one horizon to the other and the dust was so thick in some places she could not see through it, while in other places it was like a mist. The wind was tugging at her hair as she flew, and as she approached a particular area she observed a battle in progress. Above it, yet on the same level at the same time, she saw little, monkey-like critters; larger creatures that moved on two legs; and very tall beings with large white wings dressed in white with gold sashes around their waists. From time to time she would see a monkey-thing go whizzing past. They were either going up or down, and, judging by their hideous screams, something had hit them. If they were going up, the expression on their faces was of sheer terror, and they were shielding their eyes from a shaft of brilliant light that was shining on their faces. If they were going down, they moved with utmost urgency and had a very determined, yet very painful appearance.

Simultaneously the two-legged creatures were wreaking havoc on the monkey-things and battling the whitewings. They would grab a monkey-thing and twist and stretch and punch it while yelling unspeakable things at it. They would then grab it by the tail and throw it down and it would either go through the mist-like cloud at her feet and disappear, or hit with a sickening thud and lay there writhing in pain until another two-legged picked it up to continue the misery. The whitewings used very large, very heavy swords to slice the two-leggeds in two. The parts, writhing in pain would then move toward each other, and when they got close enough they would reunite into a semblance of the two-legged they had been, but the parts would not always return to the correct places. She saw a two-legged with it's head attached to it's leg and some kind of dark, black ooze coming from where the head had once been. Another had an arm attached to a foot. Wherever the two parts touched they would attach themselves, until that part was severed again. After the parts had re-united they would then attack the whitewing that had done the awesome deed, only to be run-through, decapitated, or otherwise mutilated. The two-leggeds could never touch a whitewing.

Using their heavy swords like extensions of their arms, the whitewings simply moved them where they wanted them to be, as though the sword was as weightless as a snowflake. Whenever a whitewing swung his sword, whatever was in its' pathway was cut in two, and when the sword struck a two-legged, a brilliant flash of light would momentarily light up the entire area.

Verna felt herself being drawn toward a particularly large battle. There were monkey-things with whitewings standing on their necks. Two-leggeds engaged in fights-for-life with whitewings and their swords, and other monkey-things were coming up from below and the two-leggeds would grab them and begin torturing them. The whitewings would rush in and attack both kinds of demons with their swords, and the two-leggeds would throw the monkey-thing down.

At one point she was following a monkey-thing that was on the way down. It went screaming past her, through the "ground" and headed toward earth. Following it she saw it was headed for a small fire directly below her. Getting closer she saw it was a building on fire, but not being consumed by the flame. When she was on the same level as the building she was amazed to see it was a church building. Her church building.

She looked up through the clouds at the battle raging over her head. She looked down at her church and recognized different people. There was Lew Andrews and the guy he had told her about. She saw Lew's brother, Dan, and the beings behind his shooting. There was Mac and Sharon, his wife. She also saw a young girl she did not know but felt an immediate kinship with and whom she knew she would meet soon. There were several people she did not know by name, but knew they were in Dan's church body.

Then the scene changed and she was hovering over another building in another place. She moved closer to the building in order to read the sign, but the only thing she could read was 'Dan Andrews, Pastor'. It, too had fire on its' roof.

The third time the scene changed, she found herself in her own room, in bed, early in the morning. Her Big Ben alarm clock indicated 4:35, and she knew what must be done. Reaching for her phone, she dialed a familiar number.

"Pastor," she said when the receiver at the other end was lifted and she heard his voice, "this is Verna."

"Yes, Verna," Pastor Mac answered. "You sound concerned. How can I help?"

"We need to call the prayer chain. They need to pray for the people who were involved in Dan's shooting, as well as Dan's church body."

"I was just praying about that. You call your people and I'll call mine. Tell them we don't know anything more than we did."

"Another thing Pastor," Verna continued.

"Yes?"

"I think you should go over to Lakewood and teach them how to intercede, how to worship, and how to make spiritual war. They are going to be attacked in a major way. I don't know the details precisely, but it's going to be bigger than anything any of us have ever experienced."

"You're right," Mac agreed, "I've been praying about doing that very thing, and had asked for confirmation. Thanks."

After Verna and Mac had completed the task of calling every person on their prayer-chains, each of them began their own prayer vigil. They hoped the others would be praying.

6

# GUARDIANS

"HEY, Bro," Lew said, walking into his brother's room.

"What are you doin' here?" Dan replied, completely surprised to see Lew.

"Hi, guy. Good to see ya. Donna called Pastor Mac and he got hold of me as soon as I got to town. Understand you stopped some lead."

"I guess so," Dan replied, not at all groggy, and glad to see his brother. They did not get together as much as they used to since he was busy at the church and Lew, it seemed, was always playing with his trains. It was nice for them to be living just a little over a hundred miles apart rather than the thousand or so it had been for several years.

"Any idea who it was?" Lew inquired.

"No," Dan answered, "but a Detective Cruz just left, and he said they'd found somethin' to go on."

It was the second time the detective had been by to ask questions. Especially about Larry. Dan had given them a description of his attacker, and told them all he knew about Larry and his friends, but was not sure if they still considered any of them suspects. He could not see any of them being involved in this at all.

"What kind of something?" Lew's mind was in a whirl with a mixture of thoughts and emotions. He was furious at whoever had done this to his brother, and, at the same time, also knew it had not been the person, but the spirit working through the person. That knowledge made him even more angry.

"He asked if I knew a Nick Craddock," responded Dan.

"Well, do you?"

"Never heard of him. Have you?"

"No. Can't say that I have. You know it's possible that satan could be behind this." Lew knew Dan didn't need to get upset and tried to not to show the emotions which were raging and churning inside when he answered his brother

"Yeah, I know it is, Lew."

"You said that you've been workin' with a guy who was delivered from the satan-worship life style. Could he have had anything to do with this?"

"You mean Larry? No, nothin'. I know he did not have a thing to do with this." Dan had complete faith in Larry, and knew deep down he could not be involved. True, Larry had been deeply linked with the satan-worshipers in the past, but he had broken off from them a couple of years ago, and even though there had been some opposition from them at first, it had stopped. There had not been an incident for about two months, until this shooting. Was there a connection? Dan's mind would not let him drop it. It kept hanging on. Like a leach. "Larry just told me that something was going to happen."

"Did he indicate what kind of 'something'?" Lew asked while making 'quotation marks' in the air with his fingers.

"No, he didn't. I really didn't think much about it at the time, but I did tell Donna and she called the intercessors. They seemed to think there was quite a bit to it, especially with all that stuff going on in Colorado Springs." Dan was referring to the problems a church in Colorado Springs had been having with the local witch's covens. He went on, "I am beginning to see how right they were. Man, all my married life, Donna's been sayin' "trust your wife" and I thought I had been, but I guess I didn't this time. Say, how'd you know where I was? You said Donna called Mac, but how did she know?"

"I don't know," Lew answered. "I 'magine Jeff called her after bringing you in."

"Oh," Dan said, satisfied with that answer. "So," he continued, changing the subject, "enough about me. I understand you had quite an experience recently? Tell me about it?"

For quite some time Lew had been doing a lot of studying about intercession, worship, and prayer, and how they influence the daily lives of 'ordinary' people. He had been told all his life about the 'guardian angels' and believed that folks do have them and had read several books on angels and about the various ways they show themselves to the human world. One particular account stuck with him.

Somebody had left their car unlocked with a lot of very valuable equipment in it, but did not realize they had not locked it. When this person did remember not locking the car he asked God to protect it and its contents, and went on about his business.

Then, some time later while on vacation in Dallas, Lew had been watching a Christian TV program, and a guest on the show was telling about how he had found Christ. The guest was an ex-con, and before he became a Christian he had seen a car with a lot of electronic gear in it. When the name of the city was mentioned, Lew perked up his ears, because it was the same city in which the account he had read had taken place. The guest told about wanting to steal all the stuff, and had even figured out how to fence it. However, when he was starting to go over to the car, he saw two men, dressed in white suits, standing right next to the car. They were not in any threatening position. They were just standing there. So this guy waited. He waited and waited. For about an hour he waited. Then another fellow came out of the building, got into the car and drove off. The guest watched the car go down the street and then looked back to see what the guys in white were up to, but they were gone.

Then, as strange as it sounds, a few years later the two fellows met. The ex-con turned Christian and the one with the unlocked car. By the time they met, God had developed a ministry in both of them and when they began comparing notes, the events coincided and they were shown that the men in white were actually angels on assignment. That TV program had really been the first in a series of steps he had taken in his search for the real meaning of worship. When Dan asked the question, all these thoughts flashed through his mind. *"Where to begin,"* he thought.

"I really don't know where to start," Lew said.

Rapha, Lew's angel, gave him an idea. "Start with Mac's comment about worship," he prompted.

"I guess," Lew began, "it began when Mac made a comment about worship bein' a heart condition, rather than a doing of somethin'. I always thought worship was what we did in church on Sundays, and somewhere got the idea that those who like to make music had an 'in' when it came to worship. I was prayin' 'bout that after Pastor Mac said what he did, and I felt the guiding of the Holy Spirit to do a word study on 'worship', both in the Old and New Testaments. My ideas were pretty close in the Old Testament, but way off base in the New."

"How so?" Dan questioned. He had been thinking and studying quite a bit about the end times and thinking about worship was not at the top of his list of things to study.

"Well, in the Old Testament 'worship' means 'to bow down, fall down flat, do reverence', but the New Testament word comes from the word which means 'to kiss, like a dog lickin' his masters' hand', and that word is from the word which means 'by the side of'. It was at that point I got serious about finding out what New Testament worship is all about. Father God then told me to pay close attention to Cupcake whenever I came home."

"Cupcake?" Dan asked. "You mean your St. Bernard?" When their father died, it had affected Lew the most. That was shortly after his wife had left him, and the combination had almost broken his spirit. Dan knew he had to do something for his brother, so he had asked God to fill the void with something tangible. Cupcake was pretty tangible. Since then, Lew and Cupcake were almost inseparable.

"The very same, Bro, but I didn't question that too much because I remembered how God spoke through a donkey once."

"You got a point there. So what happened?"

"Well, for the next few days," Lew went on, "God was quiet, and I just watched Cupcake, lookin' for somethin' strange or different to happen, and when nothin' outa the ordinary took place, I asked Father God what I was supposed to see, and his response was "Open your eyes and see the gift I have placed before you."

I told Him I'd been doin' that, and He replied, "I know. It's hard to see the dog for the fur. What does he do when you get home?"

"He jumps up and down," I said, "and generally makes it known that he's glad I'm back."

"Does he lick you?"

"Father," I said, "why d'you think I call him a St. Barnyard? You ever been licked by a St. Bernard?"

"I get your point," God said, with a chuckle, "but do you get mine?

"You're not letting me off the hook, are you," I asked.

"You said you wanted to know about worship, right?"

"Right," I said.

"Okay," He said, "watch Cupcake."

"Lew," Dan interrupted, "this sounds like a replay of a conversation."

"Dan, that's exactly what it is. Father God and I were talkin' just like you and I are right now. That's part of worship."

"Right," Dan stated incredulously. "Where'd that bullet get me?"

"In the gut. Why?"

"That's what I thought they said, but I was beginnin' to wonder if it hit me in the head, 'cause, my dear brother, I don't understand a thing you're saying."

"That, my dear brother, was also my reaction at first. But after a few days of watchin' Cupcake, my lightning fast mind began to catch on. Cupcake reacts to my comin' home in the only way he can. You see, I've also learned to understand fluent St. Barnyard, and Cupcake is showin' me that he absolutely worships the ground I walk on, and out of that adoration he bounces and twists and tries to smile and say so, but his talkin' comes out as grunts and growls. However, if I watch him as though I were a St. Bernard, I see what he's sayin'."

"The form is not the worship," prompted Rohi, Dan's angel.

"I think I am startin' to see it," Dan said, "Cupcake's form, quote unquote, of worship is jumpin' up and down, etc., but that's not the worship that's in his heart. It's just the only way he has of showin' you how he feels."

"Yeah." Lew said, "You remember what 'worship' means?"

"By the side of."

"That's right. What's it come from?"

"To kiss," Dan replied, "like a dog licking his master's hand. And a dog licks his master's hand because that's the only way he has to express how he feels toward his master. Lickin' is not worship, merely an expression."

"Now you're gettin' it, but there's more," Lew went on. "How do you suppose it makes me feel when I see Cupcake so, um... enamored with me?"

"Well," a thoughtful Dan replied, "I imagine you like it."

"Like it? Like it? No, I love it! In fact, it makes me want to do whatever I can for him. I mean, he's only a dog, but he loves me no matter what. He doesn't care what I've been doing, where I've been, who I've seen, or anything else. Cupcake is so glad to see me he just can't stand still. When I realized that is how Father God reacts to our worship I saw why He said through His Son, our Brother, 'seek the Kingdom first and My righteousness, and these things will be added to you.' When I see how much, really how much Cupcake loves me, I mean, uh... well I wouldn't let anything happen to him any more than he'd let anything happen to me. That's the way God reacts to our worship."

"Aha... So, are you saying God battles our problems when we worship him?"

"Yes! That's exactly what I'm saying. But that's not all. There's more."

"More?"

"Yea, more. Cupcake not only likes it when I come home, he also likes to go with me."

"Yeah, so?"

"God does, too."

"What d'you mean 'God does, too'?"

"Likes to go with me."

"What d'you mean He likes to go with you?" Dan asked with a puzzle in his voice. "He's with you all the time. He is omnipresent."

"That's true," Lew conceded. "However, imagine yourself in a lecture hall with a speaker that is anything but interesting. You're with him, and everybody else in the room, but you're not really with him. See what I mean?"

"You mean you're not with him mentally, right?"

"Right. We hafta change our minds about God, like the Apostle Paul said. You see, Dan, God wants us to let Him be with us all the time, and we must make a conscious effort to invite Him along wherever, and whenever. But, this is a very difficult thing to do. Any idea why?"

"Prob'ly," Dan thought out loud, "because we know He knows everything about us, and we don't wanna remind ourselves of that fact by inviting Him along."

"Exactly. We've believed the lie that God'll let us have it for every little thing we've done wrong, when the fact of the matter is, if we've accepted Him as our personal Savior, He has chosen to not even remember if we ever did anything wrong."

"That's absolutely right." Dan was seeing how Mac and Lew had both been completely turned around by this way of seeing the gospel. "You s'pose," Dan went on, "that's what Paul the Apostle was talkin' about? He cautioned the Galatians to not mix anything with the cross because that would dilute the power of the cross. When he said all things were lawful, but not expedient, was he saying performance was no longer the issue with God?"

"Exactly, Dan. What was the curse of the law that we're redeemed from?"

"Fear. Fear of what would happen to us if we did, or didn't, do a certain thing."

"Right, but isn't even more basic than that? Isn't the curse of the law performance?"

"Of course!" Dan almost shouted. "I see it now. We've been saying that the blessings of Abraham are ours, which is true, but we've been teaching the blessings of Moses as being the blessings of Abraham."

"What?"

"Get the Bible out of the drawer." Lew got out the Gideon Bible and Dan continued. "Good. Now turn to Deuteronomy 28."

"I know the place. That's where all the blessings and curses are."

"Right," said Dan, "but who were they given to?"

"Moses."

"Right again. Oh you're so smart," Dan said with a twinkle in his eyes. "A lot like your brother, y'know?"

"Cute. Go on."

"Okay, go to Genesis 12, verses 2 and 3," Dan directed. "What d'you find?"

Lew read a few lines and said, "God tellin' Abram to leave his country, people, his father's house and go to the land God would show him."

"Right, but it's nothing like the wording in Deuteronomy, is it?"

"Go on."

"In Deuteronomy," Dan explained, "Moses is told if he'll do, then God'll do, and if he doesn't do, then these curses will be on him. Right?"

"Yeah, so?"

"In Genesis, there is nothing of that kind mentioned," Dan pointed out. "God simply said 'Leave your home and leave your country and I will make you into a great nation and I will bless you; I will make your name great, and you will be a blessing. I will bless those who bless you, and whoever curses you I will curse; and all peoples on earth will be blessed through you.' That's salvation, right there, in the very first book of the Bible we have salvation. And he wasn't talking to Moses. He was speaking Abram, or Abraham, the father of many nations. What did Abram have to do to receive all of this? Nothing except get out of where he was and believe God, which he did and God in effect said, 'That's right'. There was no performing, showing God how good he was, was not required. Only Believing."

"Yeah, I see what you mean," said Lew. "This is beginning to answer a lot of questions I've had the last few months. It clears up my thinkin' and makes all this about worship fall into place. I now see why satan is so dead set against us worshiping. He remembers what real worship is and can't afford to let us find out, because when we do, we won't need to be bothered by him again. It's not really 'doing' as in performing, but rather 'being' in God's presence in obedience, and that obedience is not a 'chore' as a performance would be, but a joy and privilege to be with our Father. Cupcake is not performing, he is just being."

"There's something else I've recently seen," Dan said, changing the subject.

"Oh? What's that?"

"I've seen who's gonna be taken and who's gonna be left."

"You mean in the rapture?"

"Yeah," Dan answered. "However," he continued, "I really don't think there is going to be a rapture in the way we've been taught."

"Oh? Explain yourself," Lew asked.

While all this conversation was taking place, the naastis were having a fit, but they could not invade the hospital because the 653rd Intercept Group was flying cover for Roi and Rapha while they were giving the two brothers more and more revelation. Nadia, on orders from UNICINC, had personally instructed them to give Lew and Dan the answers to every question they had.

UNICINC had taken Advocate, Nadia and Obed into confidence and told them there was no time to waste. Obed had then asked UNICINC about the time table of future events, and he had been told to show the secret to any Vertical that was interested in such things. UNICINC could evade that question no matter how it was worded. According to the local scuttle-butt even Advocate himself could not get that answer out of UNICINC. However, Obed noticed, UNICINC had said there was a secret, and he remembered the conversation Advocate had had with His disciples just before that day had happened.

# 7

# HERE?

OR three days Word had been helping Frenchy clean and stretch furs. The two had put together a caribou stew and made fresh bread earlier in the day and Word had been answering some of Frenchy's questions. Questions which led Word to think Frenchy might be ready to ask The Question. Word had prayed about this day many times and the Lord had explained it to him in such a simple way, he thought he would try to explain it the same way to Frenchy. *'Maybe today is the day,'* he thought.

"In time," was the response he received in his heart. He then got another idea and asked.

"Does an orange tree make oranges because it's an orange tree, or is it an orange tree because it makes oranges?"

"What?" Frenchy asked. The question had come from way past the left field fence and caught Frenchy completely off guard. "That's a good one. I'll have to think on that awhile." *'Strange question,'* he thought, *'what's that got to do with God and stuff?'*

"I s'pose," he finally said, "it makes oranges because it's an orange tree. If it were a lemon tree it would make lemons."

"Right. Here's another one. Is it a zebra because it has stripes or does it have stripes because it's a zebra?"

Following the same logic Frenchy answered, "it has stripes because it's a zebra."

"Right again. Now, is a person a sinner because he's sinned, or does he sin because he's a sinner?"

"Well, he must sin because he's a sinner." They had just finished removing the last of the skins from the stretching frames and planned to take them to Fairbanks in a few days. Even though it was only three o'clock in the afternoon, it was almost dark. "Aren't you getting' hungry?" he went on, changing the subject and not wanting to talk about religion, or any anything like that. "We still have plenty of stew and don't forget that fresh bread."

"Now that you mention it, I do have an empty spot in the mid-section. You're right, by the way. People sin because they're sinners. How'd they get that way?"

"They were born that way," Frenchy curtly replied. "But I don't want no more God talk. I've been burned enough by Christians. I moved out here to get away from those wussie creeps and don't care if I never meet another one."

"I'm really sorry you've been hurt, but it was people, not Jesus, that hurt you."

"That's a high and mighty platitude, but I really don't give a dad-gummed rip, and I'd appreciate it if you'd leave me alone about it. Don't get me wrong, I'm really glad for the help on these furs, but if it means havin' to listen to this God crap, then I'd just as soon do'em by m'self, thank you very much."

*"Boy,"* Word thought, *"must've been some kind of conflict to have left those kinds of scars."* 'Father,' he prayed silently, 'how can I help him?'

"You intercede and let me handle it," Father responded in Word's spirit.

Like a submarine gliding through the quiet, black sea, the aroma of caribou stew and homemade bread slid through the walls of the cabin adding to the surrounding smells of trees and wood smoke. The stove, an elaborately simple affair made from a converted fifty-five gallon drum, was the only heat source for the cabin, and that proved handier than a handle on an axe. It was always ready for cooking. In the winter at least. In the summer Frenchy did his cooking in the great outdoors. Earlier that morning Frenchy had put the stew pot on the back of the stove to keep it warm, and Word had made a couple loaves of honey wheat bread.

Frenchy did not like being cramped, so he had built his cabin as a two story affair. A rarity in Interior Alaska. The first floor was his main living area with a kitchen in one corner. He'd made his furniture using what was available and, while not fancy, it was quite comfortable. Each step to the upper level was a single log running through the exterior wall, which meant there were also stairs on the ouside to the second floor. There was a deck on the second floor surrounding the cabin. A couple of Frenchy's friends had scoffed at the idea while he was building it, but when he finished he thought he had detected more than just a twinge of jealousy in their eyes and voices. '*Eat your hearts out,*' he'd thought as he had nailed the sign NOWHERE over the front door. '*Since I live in Nowhere, Alaska, I'd better be comfortable.*'

The second floor meant a lot more work and time, but it had been well worth the effort. It became his Ham shack, his amateur radio room, and the deck was just frosting on the cake. His call sign was KL07AJ, and on the log wall above the desk was a large world map with pins sticking in the places he'd talked to.

Word continued with the change of subject and said, "certainly was strange how Tourist showed up."

"Yeah, it was. Don't make sense at all," Frenchy replied, thinking back to the day before. "One second I'as under that tree, and the next Tourist-type is over there pickin' up the tree and pitchin' it like he'd been practicin' for the Tree Toss in the Olympics. You got any ideas?"

"Well, not really. Unless..." he trailed off.

"Unless? Unless what?"

Word wondered how he could tell him that Tourist might have been an Angel. "Oh... I was just thinkin..." Word said, deciding to be straight forward.

"Yeah?" Frenchy asked. "Hope you don't strain somethin'"

"Thanks! What a pal! Anyway, you s'pose Tourist might have been an angel?"

"What! An angel!? Come on." Frenchy could not believe what he'd just heard. "You're kiddin', right? An angel? Here? Now? C'mon! I think you did strain somethin'. How you figure he was an angel?"

"Well, think about. If I heard you right, Tourist-type, as you call him, just sorta materialized right before your eyes, picked up a tree, and who knows how much that thing weighs, threw the tree off to one side and when he'd finished what he came to do, he just vanished into thin air. It's the only thing that makes any sense at all. What else could he have been?"

Frenchy thought about that long and hard. '*There was this Tourist-type in blue jeans and a flannel shirt... a flannel shirt for cryin' out loud, not even a wool shirt, and wearing sneakers, no coat, and it's colder than the north-end of a south bound moose, and Tourist doesn't even seem to notice! But why? Why here? Why now? Why would an angel suddenly show up. Is somebody trying to tell me something?'* Frenchy's line of thinking continued along these lines. Killing his father had been the major source of his pain, and the folks in the church had turned against him, and he even thought God had turned on him, and, as a consequence, he had chosen to not associate with Christians any longer.

"You can't trust this guy," thordan snarled, stabbing his claws into Frenchy's head. "He's one of those Christians," he sneered. "Besides, God don't want nothin' to do with the likes of you anymore. If you'll remember, you killed your own father!"

Frenchy still recognized God and wanted desperately to be able to have the kind of relationship he had once had with Him, but he didn't see how God would want him after everything that had happened. Still, though, there was that nagging feeling deep inside of wanting to be in God's good graces once again. Could he dare trust this guy? There was no way he could know about all that had happened to him, so maybe he could. But, still, he didn't think he could stand any more hurt and decided to keep his distance. At least for the time being.

"Yeah, I guess it could have been an angel," Frenchy commented, "but why here? Why now?

# 8

# HAMS

**B**IRDS and feathers. Computers and software. Trains and tracks. Mining and Leadville. If one was thought, the other was brought to mind. That's the way it seemed to be. First it was silver, then it was Molly B., or Aunt Molly, or Molly B. Denim. Taken from molybdenite and wulfenite, the common name was molybdenum, it was mined out of the mountain at the Climax Molybdenum Mine, just a few miles east of Leadville, Colorado.

Leadville's boardwalk was long ago replaced with cement. Longer on wear, but shorter on atmosphere, which was short enough, given Leadville's 10,152 feet above sea level. 14,433 foot Mt. Elbert filled the western horizon and Mt. Sherman's 14,036 feet was on the east. Coloradans called them fourteeners. Any mountain over 14,000 feet was a fourteener. Leadville, brisk in the summer, was flat cold the rest of the year. For Leadville locals there are four definite seasons, June, July, August and Winter.

The town, although not built to be romantic, had a certain romance attached to it, as did the other towns of the early mining era. Cripple Creek, Fairplay, Ouray, Central City, Alma, Silverton, St. Elmo. The list could go on and on, but either the gold played out, or became too expensive to get out. But, there was still 'gold' in them thar hills, except it was called zinc, lead, some other 'precious metal', or tourism. In Leadville, they called it Molly B. The stuff nuts, bolts, and planes were made of.

For most locals, however, Leadville brought to mind the thought of nachos. Nachos at the Silver Rose Café. The decor of the Silver Rose was definitely 'early mining' with bentwood chairs, oak tables, red and white checkered table cloths, white walls with light blue trim, leaded windows, brass chandeliers, hardwood floors, and the double door entry set in the south-west corner of the building, right on Main Street. The Silver Rose made their nachos by piling tortilla chips on a bed of re-fried beans, smothering that with melted Cheese, Black Olives, Tomatoes, Lettuce, sliced peppers, and a salsa hotter than the space shuttle's exhaust.

"I was hopin' to see you again before headin' out of the area." Lew heard as the door closed. It was Bud and he spoke as he was walking over to the table where Lew was seated. It had been several days since he had last seen him and wanted to touch base at least once more before heading back to Alaska. He planned to check out Union Station in Denver, and then go up to Cheyenne and thought Lew might give him some hints on finding the last remaining steam locomotives on Union Pacific's roster.

"Hi guy?" Lew said, startled to see Bud walking over to his table. "I thought you'd be long gone by now. Not that I wanted you outa here, but I was in Denver for a few days and had no idea how long you planned on bein' around. Pull up a chair and help me with these nachos. What's keepin' ya, anyway?"

"Well, m'friend," Bud began, pulling out a chair and throwing a leg over the back, "I heard about your brother, and I was also wonderin' if you could tell me anything about the two steamers U.P. has. How is your brother, anyway?"

"Oh, he's fine now. Help yourself to the nachos," Lew motioned toward the plate while continuing. "It was touch and go for awhile I guess, but a miracle happened on the operating table and he pulled through just fine. I drove him home three days ago. How'd you hear?"

"I talked to your pastor."

"Oh," Lew said.

With a far away look in his eye, Bud continued, "Fairbanks has a really good place for Mexican food, too. It's called The Lord's Inn. The name of this place has me puzzled, though. The Silver Rose. Any idea where they got that name?"

"The Lord's Inn, huh. There's another interesting name. As for this place, I think," Lew said, with a thoughtful tone, "they named it after the ore, molybdenite, from which they get molybdenum. I guess the ore kinda looks like a blue rose. The café's been here several years, and as far as I'm concerned, as long as they keep making these nachos, it can stay. I make a special trip for nachos at least once a week. Sometimes when we're coming through town we even radio ahead for an order an' somebody brings it to us. I know folks who come in from Denver or Durango just for the nachos."

"I can certainly understand why," Bud said through a mouthful. "These are fit to wrap your mouth around. By the way," he munched, "thanks for the lesson in mineralogy." Changing the subject he continued, "Any idea why anyone would want Dan dead?"

"Just tryin' to answer all the questions of a tourist," Lew said, smiling around a mouthful of nachos. "Nope," Lew crunched, "not really, but we're almost positive of one thing. We think it was a deliberate attack by satan. One of the folks in Dan's church was delivered from the satan-worshiping crowd and we think that's the cause of this harassment. The police don't have much to go on, and the people in the church who were involved with the satan worshipers have checked clean, so the only thing left for us to do is keep prayin'."

"You can count on that. As a matter of fact," Bud responded, "I'm scheduled to call my brother in Alaska tonight, so I'll mention it to him, and he'll get his prayer chain on it. We're not goin' to let old what's his face get the upper hand on this one. I, for one, am fed up with his antics and intend on making sure my angels are kept busy. They may have to put in for hazardous duty pay, but I figure we've got 'em for protection and help so let's keep 'em busy."

"You sound just like my pastor. He sees us as a warring body and gets everybody he can involved in intercession, praise and worship. Tell me more about your brother. You call him Word, right?"

"Right," Bud said. "His name is William Orville Randolf Davis, and because of that we call him Word. I s'pose you'd call him somethin' colorful, like a sourdough, or mountain man, or somethin' colorful like that, but he's just an ordinary Alaskan who likes bein' alone. He lives on his trap line in a cabin he built himself, doesn't mind bein' in town, but prefers bein' alone, and gets to town 'bout every six weeks or so. I really wish you guys could meet up in person sometime."

"Say," Bud continued with a thought in his voice, "I'm camped at the tunnel and I'm goin' to talk with him tonight. Why don't you stop by? I have an extra bed and you're more than welcome to spend the night. That is, if you don't have to get back to Minturn right away. I'd welcome your company."

"Thanks for the offer. You say you're gonna talk with your brother? How you gonna do that? Can't access a cell phone from up here, so Ma Bell must've strung a phone line up there for ya."

"No, no. Nothing so elaborate. We're Hams. Amateur radio operators," Bud explained. "It's almost a necessity for Word. Besides, he's a real electronics nut. I just took it up to be able to keep in touch with him, what with him being out in the bush and me in town, and all. We were really close growing up and we wanna keep it that way."

"You mean you can be assured of makin' contact? I thought amateur radio was almost a hit-and-miss sorta thing?"

"Well, if a guy doesn't have what it takes it would be. But, we learned a long time ago it pays to prepare for the worst conditions. That doesn't just apply to the long, cold winter either. The atmospheric conditions play a big part in the way radio waves work. Sunspot activity, for instance, can effect what happens, and also the Aurora Borealis, the Northern Lights, in Alaska, and the north, especially. Word tells me if there's a lot of Auroral activity, the radio can be totally useless. Also, if a large solar flare lets go it can make the bands totally useless for long distance communication for days. Fortunately, we haven't had any problems like that the past couple months. We're both runnin' pretty high powered rigs and so far, we haven't had any problems. We've kept a regular schedule since I left Fairbanks two months ago. Friday night, 8 o'clock his time. Works great, most of the time. Although we work CW mostly, I'll try and use voice tonight. Since we're up so high it should work. What'ya say?"

"Sounds like fun to me. What's CW?" Lew asked.

"CW? That's Continuous Wave. It means we use morse code," Bud said. "Boy, these nachos are super."

"Yeah. I know." The thought of endless beeps and tweets didn't have much appeal to Lew and he tried to gracefully back out. "You sure you have room enough for me? I don't want to put you out in the cold, so to speak."

Bud was not about to take 'no' for an answer, however, and continued, "Sure I have room for you. I have the sofa-bed, plenty of food, stereo system, Hosanna tapes, classical music, some great classic movies, plenty of fuel for the generator and of course the Ham shack."

"You really know how to rough it don't ya?" Lew kidded and thought of another tactic. "Don't s'pose you have any Bogie movies'?"

"Bogie? You a Bogie nut? Sure. We can watch any Bogie movie we want," Bud said. "as long as it's 'The African Queen', the 'Maltese Falcon', or 'Casablanca'."

Seeing there was no way out, he chuckled "Okay, count me in. Hey, you got any plans between now and then?"

"Not really. I think I've seen about all the railroadin' there is to see around here, and have taken about all the angles. Why? Got somethin' in mind?"

"Have you seen the Molly B'?"

"The Molly What?"

"The Molly B. That's one of the names the locals have for the Climax Molybdenum Mining Company. It's a few miles out of town at the top of Fremont Pass. They're served by the D-S-L-n-P and it's pretty interesting for train nuts."

"Nope, haven't seen it?"

"You wanna see it?"

"Sure. Sounds cool."

"Well, then how 'bout grabbin' some Enchiladas or some-thin' a little more substantial than these nachos and then we'll head on out there?"

"Fine by me. Now, about those Union Pacific locos?"

"Oh yeah. Well, all's I know is they have two of'em, num-ber 844, and a Challenger number 3985, and they keep'em in Cheyenne."

"Yeah, I know all that. But where in Cheyenne? In the roundhouse??

"Yeah, in the roundhouse. At least I think that's where they're kept. When you get to the depot, go to the track side and you'll see it across the tracks. U.P. still uses what's left of it, so you'll see quite a bit of activity around there. Might be a good idea to talk with the Terminal Superintendent and get permission to roam around. As long as you have the railroads' permission to get some pictures, you won't have any trouble. They're pretty hard-nosed when it comes to trespassers."

"You think it would hurt to show'em this,?" Bud asked while pulling an Alaska Railroad Photographer's Identification card out of his wallet.

"Absotively not," Lew exclaimed. "You show'em that and you'll not only get to take some pictures, they're just liable to let you go anywhere you want."

# SCRAMBLE

" **L**OOKS to me like it's another attack prompted by satan. He does a lot of this sort of stuff." A couple of days had gone by and Scott Dennis, the Morning Man, was responding to Xan's questions about the preacher's shooting.

"What do you mean?" Xan knew Scott was a religious kook, but over the years of working together had grown to like him anyway.

"You see, he's always trying to foul up people's lives," Scott continued, "and this is just one of the ways he tries. Another thing that makes me think it was Old Slewfoot is this guy's a pastor, and pastors, especially those who are a threat to satan, are often attacked. Maybe not in such an obvious way, but attacked nonetheless."

"You mean you actually believe all that garbage? I thought you were smarter than that."

"Let me put it this way. I wouldn't be here if I didn't believe that 'garbage', as you so delicately put it."

"What do you mean you wouldn't be here? And don't tell me you think God, or whatever you call it, got you this job. That's a bunch of..."

"No, Scott interrupted, "it's not as simple as getting me a job." He opened the collar of his shirt, showing an ugly red scar running from just below his left ear to the center of his throat. He could still remember the noise of the wreck. "I'm talking about saving my life. If God had not intervened when this happened... well," Scott paused, "it took five hours of surgery and eight pints of blood to get me to the point where I could regroup."

"Look, I m not doubting it took a lot of skill on the part of the surgeons," Xan agreed, "but with all the expertise of the doctors, don't try to tell me God had anything to do with it." Xan was at the point of walking out, but there was something about Scott that made her want to hear more. The something was an aura, or an attitude more than anything else.

"Okay, I won't try to tell you that. However... let me tell you what happened while I was on the table. I never lost consciousness before they put me under, and I was acutely aware of everything that was going on. Xan, I could see the inside of the ambulance, and from the amount of blood on the attendants clothing I knew I was hurt bad. I also heard them on the radio. They didn't expect to make it to the hospital in time.

"When we did, I saw the astonishment on everyone's face. I heard the doubt in their voices. Saw the despair in their eyes. I knew my time was up.

"I didn't even feel it when they put the needle in my arm for the anesthetic, but when I started going under I thought, *'so this is what it's like to die. Not at all what I've heard.'*

"Well, I went through this dark passage-like thing and heard people's voices and felt very hot. Then I saw a bright white light and heard my name. I remember thinking it was the doctor trying to wake me up, but I couldn't move. The voice was unfamiliar but not at all threatening. I tried to answer, but when I opened my mouth nothing came out. Instead, I found myself face to face with a guy that looked like he'd just stepped off a fishing boat. A big dude about six foot four and weighing about two hundred and fifty pounds with an incredibly gentle voice. He said, 'Scott, come here. I want you to see something.' "So I went with him."

"Wait a minute," Xan said, "I don't believe what I'm hearing."

"I'm not asking you to believe it," Scott said. "I'm just telling you what happened." He could see in Xan's eyes a flicker of reception, but he could also sense a real spiritual battle taking place and decided it was time to shut down this conversation and do some serious praying. "We'll talk more later," he said just before keying the mic.

"Magic Ninety-nine. We're gonna Push for a Porsche in Sixty seconds. Stick around." While he pushed the start button to play the commercial, Scott immediately started silent intercession for Xan. *'Father,'* he began, *'I turn Xan over to you right now. Show her what she needs to see. Thank you, sir.'*

| | |
|---|---|
| 2050Z | DSI INTSIG BULLETIN |
| ~ ~ ~ | RE/naasti OPS |
| 469992 | MESSAGE FOLLOWS |

AT 2045Z DSI MONITOR STATION LOVELAND GOLDEN AND
BUCKLEY RECORDED AN EHF TRANSMISSION FROM
NASQUAD EHF FACILITY SEMIVISROKMONT XX

MESSAGE DURATION 1 MINUTE 17 SECONDS 5 ELEMENTS
XX

EHF SIGNAL IS EVALUATED AS "ATTACK AND DESTROY"
TRANSMISSION TO NASQUAD AIR AGENTS IN
SEMIVISROKMONT XX

AT 2039Z A "SPECIAL AGENTS" TRANSMISSION WAS
MADE BY NAASTI HEADQUARTERS INTERNAL TRANS
STATION DENVER AND SATELLITE SIX-SIX-SIX XX

BANDS USED: ELF VLF VHF UHF EHF XX

MESSAGE DURATION 37 SECONDS WITH 2 REPEATS
IDENTICAL CONTENT MADE AT 2034Z AND 2035Z XX

SIGNAL COVERAGE AS FOLLOWS: CENTRAL SQUADRON
AREA ROCKY MOUNTAIN SQUADRON AND DENVER
WING AREA XX

NOTE SOUTHERN SQUADRONS NOT REPEAT NOT
AFFECTED BY THE BROADCAST XX

NUMEROUS ACKNOWLEDGMENT SIGNALS EMANATED
FROM ADDRESS IN AREAS CITED ABOVE XX

BEGINNING AT 2046Z DSI MONITOR STATIONS LOVELAND
GOLDEN AND BUCKLEY RECORDED INCREASED
ELF TRAFFIC AT NASQUAD BASES BUCKLEY AND
LOWRY XX

EVALUATION: A MAJOR UNPLANNED NASQUAD DESTROY
OPERATION HAS BEEN ORDERED WITH ASSETS
REPORTING AVAILABILITY AND STATUS XX

| 2051Z | END BULLETIN |
|---|---|
| ~ ~ ~ | DSI SENDS |
| 469992 | BREAKBREAK |

\* \* \* \* \*

The EFTO message had been formatted and had used the
same abbreviations as the previous one and the watch commander at NORHAF immediately alerted his superior. He
also began the process that would get the 739th Tactical
Fighter Squadron airborne. He hit the button on his con-
sole labeled 'SCRAMBLE' which simultaneously sounded the
Scramble Klaxon in the ready room and opened his communications channel.

"Scramble Eagle Flight. This is not a drill. Repeat. This is
not a drill. Scramble Eagle Flight."

B ud had been quite impressed with the Molly B. From
a distance it reminded him of a model railroad layout,

and he filed that thought in the back of his mind to talk with some friends about modeling it. He had also taken some shots which they could use, if they actually got around to it.

The picture taking time was cut short when the weather closed in and the light shut down, but Bud was so enthralled with the scene they had waited until it was too dark for film before heading back to camp. They got there about seven o'clock or so, and were happily munching their way through pizza, while Humphrey Bogart and Katharine Hepburn were fighting the river, the leaches and the Germans in "The African Queen".

Lew was fascinated with Bud's fifth-wheel rig. While not fancy on the outside, inside were all the comforts of home. Bud said the plain, rather ugly rigs attracted a lot less attention and that suited him just fine because, he said, he couldn't see it when he was driving anyway. He had a fully equipped galley with microwave, conventional oven and range, plenty of cupboards and more than ample counter space. Up two short steps, in the 'nose' of the trailer, was the Ham Shack. Originally a two bedroom layout with one in the 'nose' area and the other in the back with the galley/living area between, Bud had specially modified his by doing away with the usual bedroom stuff in the nose. He explained that the nose, being the farthest place from the generator storage in the rear, would make for more reliable communication.

The main room contained the television, audio/video system control center, a library of books, as well as audio and video tapes, and a hide-a-bed. The rearmost area was Bud's room, with the darkroom/restroom between the galley/living room and the back room. He shot color slides and black and white negatives along with his digital stuff so it was not a full fledged dark room, but adequate for film developing with plenty of room for chemical storage and the negative and slide cataloging. The computer for his digital images sat on a small desk in his bedroom.

"Well, my friend, it's about time to warp some ether." The movie had just ended and they talked while cleaning up the 'theater'.

"Okay. What d'ya mean 'warp ether'?"

"Getting on the air," Bud answered.

"Oh. Why do you call it warping ether?"

"Don't really know for sure, but I guess it goes back to the early days of radio when they called it 'wireless', and the transmitters were tube affairs, not like today's solid state, transistorized stuff, and some of those tubes were filled with ether. To make a tube work an electrical current is passed through it which excites the electrons. I suppose the ether is warped a little in the process."

"Oh, glad I asked," Lew answered, more than a little underwhelmed with the radio stuff. However, the idea of talking all the way to Alaska intrigued him. "It's ten 'til ten. What's that make it in Alaska?"

"It's a two hour difference, so it's almost eight there."

"What do you do to get it working?"

"Nothin', really, since the generator is already online, and the antenna's up. I'll just turn it on and tune it up. Actually, there is very little tune-up involved, 'cause basically, I only use it to talk with Word so I leave it tuned to the same place. I guess I'm not your typical Ham as I don't really use it for a hobby. Some folks really get into it, though. They'll sit and rag-chew for hours on these things. They call it DX-ing, which is trying to talk to Hams in other countries. I guess it's easy to get bit by the bug after receiving a few QSL cards—uh, those are the special postcards that confirm that you actually made contact. I've seen some fancy ones from Africa, South America, the Far East, Russia and several other places, and I suppose trying to collect every possible country can be addictive, but I'd much rather sit and watch trains for hours. They prob'ly don't understand me either, but at least I'm on the right track. What d'ya say we head up to the shack and fire her up?" Bud asked leading the way.

Lew found it to be rather cozy with everything well laid out, and not at all what he had pictured in his mind. Somehow he thought it would be crowded with all sorts of equipment, but there were only two or three things on a rather small table, which was in front of the large window with a chair on either side. As far as Lew could tell, it was a 'den' and Lew couldn't figure why Bud kept calling it a shack. Certainly didn't look like a shack. Bud said that is just what Hams call their radio rooms. He asked about the size of the equipment and Bud told him about everything being solid state, so it took up a lot less room than it would otherwise. He told Lew he was using a 'transceiver', a combination transmitter and receiver contained in one box.

"The beauty of the transceiver," Bud explained, "is once you've tuned in the frequency you want to use, both the transmitter and receiver are matched up. That means a lot less hassles. You don't have to switch between transmit and receive in order to carry on a conversation, a quicker tune-up period, and only one piece of gear to find room for. It makes this room a lot more comfortable to be in."

"You mean everything is right there in that thing?"

"Yup. Let's get started."

While they were talking Bud had been fiddling around with the knobs and buttons and was ready to go. He picked up the mic, pressed the button and began.

"AL07KC, AL07KC, Alpha Lima Zero Seven Kilowatt Charlie, this is KL07PS portable Zero, this is KL07PS portable Zero, Kilowatt Lima Zero Seven Papa Sierra portable Zero. America London Zero Seven Kilowatt Canada, this is Kilowatt Lima Zero Seven Peggy Sue calling on schedule and listening." "Hope he's around," Bud said to Lew after unkeying the mic.

"He should be near his radio shouldn't he?" Lew asked.

"Well, he should. We'll wait a bit and try again." The wait was short lived as Bud's "box" crackled with a response.

"KL07PS portable Zero, Kilowatt Lima Zero Seven Papa Sam portable Zero, this is KL07AJ, Kilowatt Lima Zero Seven Alpha Juliet."

"Wonder who that is," Bud said before keying the mic. "KL07AJ, this is KL07PS portable Zero. I am trying to make a schedule with AL07KC."

"KL07PS portable Zero. I have AL07KC here with me. Standby."

Word had heard the radio bark to life, recognized the call and suddenly remembered he had forgotten, completely forgotten, about his schedule with Bud. A lot had happened the last few days and Friday had simply slipped in unnoticed. Since Frenchy was an active participator in the Alaska nets, his radio was tuned to the Alaska calling frequency and had heard Bud's call sign.

*"Was it possible,"* thought Lew? *"That voice on the radio sure sounds familiar."*

"Hi Bud. We've got a good copy tonight. Would you believe I forgot about you?" Word asked.

"Thanks a bunch," Bud responded. "You forgot about me? That's a fine greeting. What's happenin' anyhow?"

"Well, how much time you got?" Word knew his brother's set up and was referring to the amount of fuel for the generator.

"Enough".

"Okay," Word when on. "You 'member me tellin' you 'bout a guy named Frenchy?"

"Yeah. The guy that lives in Nowhere."

"That's him. Well, he had quite an experience the other day. Seems a tree fell on him and God helped him out."

"Sounds pretty int'restin'. Was that him who answered the call? How did God help him out?"

"Yup, that was him. Bud, I'm tellin' ya, it was a real miracle. I guess he had a bad gash under his arm and God instantly healed him."

Lew could not believe what he was hearing. He had a strange feeling he knew what had happened, but could not explain it.

"For cryin' out loud," Bud asked, "what did he do to the tree to make it fall on him?"

"Nuthin'," Word came back, "that's what's so strange. It just cracked and fell on him. We thought about the cold doin' it, but it was only twenty-three below, so that probably wasn't it. I figure it was old slewfoot messin' around.

"Hmm, does sound kinda weird. How'd he get out? You said God helped him, but how? Exactly."

"Well, now, that's the miracle part. He was lyin' there in the snow trying to figure a way out and all of a sudden there was this tourist-type who simple walked over to the tree, picked it up and threw it off to one side."

"What? Picked it up by himself? Where'd this guy come from, Krypton?"

"Don't know," Word chuckled and continued. "Frenchy had never seen him before and he wasn't dressed for winter. It was like he wasn't prepared to be there, but he was there anyway."

"Hey, hold on a second," Bud contemplated. "How d'you know he was there?"

"He left his tracks, Bud. He was wearing 'Reeboks!'"

"Oh. Guess you gotta be somewhere to leave tracks. Go on," Bud said, as he un-keyed the mic. Glancing down at the floor without thinking, he saw Lew's shoes. Reeboks. White with red stripes. Bud looked at Lew. Lew looked at Bud. The silence was large enough to drive a train through. Abruptly, Lew reached for Bud's coffee cup, grabbed his own and headed to the stairs leading to the galley.

zoltan, Lew's naasti, started inserting thoughts into Lew's brain. "What if what seems to have happened actually happened?" zoltan had his two feet hooked into Lew's side and was using the two claws under his wings to insert thoughts into Lew's mind. Lew thought the thoughts were his and was trying to prolong the process of re-filling the coffee cups and get his mind around what was going on. "How are you going to explain it?" zoltan continued. "Bud'll think you're crazy!

You do know you are crazy, don't you?" Lew tried to think, but knew he had to get back. He was, after all, there to meet Bud's brother over the airwaves.

*"Oh father,"* he prayed, *"what's going on?"*

# EAGLES

Mortal combat between Olam and belial was happening in the skies over Colorado, and belial, Scott's naasti, was putting up a heckofa good fight, and Olam, Scott's angel, was aware of more naastis arriving. He told Scott he needed some help.

As soon as Scott began praying, NORHAF responded by scrambling four of it's Elite Fighters. Eagle Flight of the 739th Air Defense Wing. After take-off, Eagle Flight leveled off at Angels 85 (eighty-five thousand feet) and set up a cruise speed of Zipp 9.5 (ninety-eight percent of the speed of light) and a course which would bring them out of the sun. The members of the 739th ADW (Air Defense Wing), as well as all other ADWs, were actually angels with special abilities and assignments. Protection. Able to change their appearance to any of several configurations, depending on what was required for a particular mission, they had an arsenal of weapons ranging from their own form of hand-to-hand combat to the most imaginative firearms available to anyone, anywhere.

If you will recall the incident Lew had seen on the Christian TV show where a man had been looking for an opportunity to steal a lot of electronic equipment from a parked car, the two men the fellow had seen standing next to the car were members of the 841st Air Defense Wing.

For the operation against belial, Eagle Flight had adopted the appearance of Advanced Tactical Fighters and they resembled F-14 Tomcat fighters with their two vertical stabilizers and adjustable wings, wings that could be set in a "normal" position, or swept back for high speed flight. There were many important differences between an F-14 and a member of an ADW. For one, the ADWs also had the ability to completely fold their wings back against their vertical stabilizers. This gave them the appearance of fat, flat pencils with tail feathers, and allowed them to reach unbelievable speeds. In addition, they could maintain altitudes far above anything any air force in the world could put in the air.

After being scrambled, the flight leader received detailed information and instructions about Scott's request and learned that sapphira, Xan's naasti, was about to join belial. As they approached the Denver skies from the south they slowed to Mach 2.5 (two and a half times the speed of sound) and dropped to Angels 45 (forty-five thousand feet).

"Eagle One to Flight. sapphira is on her way. Two and Four, you're on top. Three, you're on me. It's in and out, hot and fast. I'll draw belial's fire and you nab him. Set all weapons for Extended Nerve Desensitizing, repeat, all weapons on Extended Nerve Desensitizing. Do not, repeat, do not use the Kill mode. We are authorized for Desensitize only. Repeat... Desensitize only. Use END only! Two, maintain contact with HQ. Four watch for bogies. Everyone copy?' In order to keep the radio chatter to a minimum, only the position each pilot maintained in the formation confirmed an order. The other three pilots responded with only their 'slot' number.

"Two."

"Three."

"Four."

"Okay," radioed Eagle One, "here we go. Three, let's get'em. Olam," he then said to Scott's angel, "we're here." He heard the pilot in number three slot respond "Three" as he retracted his wings against his vertical stabilizers, peeled to his left out of formation, and set up a power dive putting belial in his sights.

"Roger, Eagle one. I'll put you in the sun," Olam responded as Eagle Three also retracted his wings and rolled to his right into position behind Eagle One. Olam then maneuvered belial around so he was facing the sun, blinded. At that instant, Eagle One flashed by with cannons blazing and made a hard left, climbing turn, and slowed his ascent. belial took the bait and broke off his attack on Olam to concentrate on this new-comer. He lasted all of two seconds before Eagle Three nailed him with a cannon shell and he spun head over heels out of control in a spinning nose dive to the ground. He moved no more. He wasn't dead, but he wasn't a threat either. As Eagle One watched the engagement between Eagle Three and belial on his scope he extended his wings to get maximum lift and climbed back to forty-five thousand feet.

Just as Eagle Three opened fire, eagle Four spotted sap-phira trying to close on Three's tail and called, "One. sap-phira's on Three's six." Eagle One simultaneously arched his back and folded his wings against his twin tail and went into a tight inside loop and rolled into a steep power dive.

Three looked and picked up sapphira in the Rear-Facing Radar, the RFR, and, keying his microphone said to his leader, "Flag Time." Code for the maneuver they'd practiced to perfection.

While he rolled into a gentle, climbing right turn, letting sapphira get closer, he switched his RFR to receive his opponent's target-lock signal, and keep a close watch on his RFR. His own target-lock light came on as sapphira's target-lock was activated. At that instant, he chopped his throttle to idle, extended his wings and flaps, and fired a burst of cannon. The result was an immediate drop in air speed from roughly fifteen hundred miles per hour to around one hundred fifty, and a wall of END shells extended in front of him. In order to avoid a collision, sapphira yanked back on her stick. She missed but roared right through the shells that ripped her from nose to tail. The read-out reassuringly flashed the letters "END" as Three's radar signaled a disable, and sapphira joined belial in a smoking, non-moving heap on the Colorado landscape.

Two notified HQ of the action, while One and Three joined up and made a slow pass over the smoking hulks of the two naastis.

"Gotcha!" One yelled to them as he pulled out of his dive and hovered over the two smoking masses. "Time's almost up."

Three added, "And there's not thing one you can do about it."

Anger and rage welled and boiled in sapphira and belial, but they responded with nothing more than a glare. They also began trembling at what was about happen. Not only had they been disabled by the angels, they knew lucifer would want know why they had permitted it.

Eagle One opened his mic and said, "Eagles take Angels 130," the order for all four angels to join up at one hundred thirty thousand feet.

As Eagle Flight joined up they changed from fighter/intercept to surveillance and early warning. They throttled back to a leisurely eight-five knots. From 130,000 feet with a speed of about a hundred miles per hour, the earth below them did not appear to move at all and they could oversee Scott, Xan, Olam and Elyon while their radars enabled them to see far past the distant horizon.

Headquarters expected an all out naasti reprisal and ordered Eagle Flight to observe radio silence, activate stealth procedures and be prepared for anything. Any further communication from Eagle Flight to HQ would be done via Thought Processors. Of course if HQ wanted them somewhere else in a hurry, a normal radio channel would be opened. Using the Thought Processors would mean the boys in NORHAF Communications would have their work cut out for them as the TPs were only as effective as the prayer life of the earthbound Intercessors. UNICINC had invested a lot of time in that area, however, and the Verticals had begun to get the idea that intercession was more than getting together at 'prayer meetings'. It had taken a long time, but thankfully, humans were finally beginning to see that not only could they intercede anywhere, anytime, it was expected of them.

THE conversation had just stopped. It had not happened in a rude way, but it was, nonetheless, over. Suddenly. Xan was mentally re-playing, again, the conversation she had had with Scott. She had never encountered anything, or anyone, quite like Scott, and normally she would have been put off and quite upset by someone just refusing to talk with her, but for some reason, she didn't feel that way. Only confused as to the 'why' of it. He hadn't seemed mad or agitated, except there had been a complete change in his attitude that he could not, or would not, justify. He had simply stopped talking about it.

It was now 12:40 p.m.on Friday, a week and a half later, and Scott would not say anything more about the story of the preacher getting shot. She had asked about it several times during the past ten days, but could not get him to talk about it at all. He had stopped talking about it, but she could not stop thinking about it, and that was what she did during most of her off hours.

It had not taken her a great deal of time to realize a major 'benny' that comes with Denver—the close proximity to the extraordinary Rocky Mountains, The Rockies. The station occupied the entire seventh floor of a high-rise just off Interstate 25 in the extreme south part of the Metro Area, and looking at the 'hills' out the west windows had, more than once, enticed her into taking a drive before heading home.

This week-end was no exception and she had planned in advance on not going home. A change or two of clothes were neatly packed in a bag she put behind the driver's seat, and on her way out of town she stopped at a toot-n-cash and got some spending money. Highway 285 west was the first leg of her loop and from there, well, time would tell.

If she had a hobby, it was driving. Just driving. Anywhere, anytime, any distance. As she headed west she looked in her rear view mirror and saw the Metro Area duck down behind the front range, and Buena Vista popped into her minds eye. That was to be her first stop, except for a piece of pie in Bailey. She had inherited her mother's metabolism and could eat just about anything she wanted. She had a definite 'tooth' for pie and ice cream.

Since moving to the Denver area she had been to Buena Vista several times and had found a place with good Oriental food and that would be as good a place as any to plan the rest of her week-end. Maybe she would spend some time in Leadville, too. Scott had told her about the nachos at the 'Blue Rose' and filed that thought for future reference.

*'What a day,'* she thought while making her way through the gears. *'Just look at that crystal clear sky. There's not a cloud to be seen, the car's as smooth as a Compact Disc, and we're playing all the right stuff. This music wouldn't be any better if I'd programmed it myself.'*

While descending the steep hill just outside Bailey she tickled the gas of her Audi TT Coupe just enough to bring the revs up to match the transmission and deftly caught third gear. While in the apex of the sweeping right turn she shifted into second and grabbed a toe-full of binders to slow for the town.

Bailey. A sleepy, short, pit stop of a town with a café which offered the best pie she'd ever eaten. However, while savoring the freshly ground coffee and enjoying a slice of Blueberry Pie ala mode, that troublesome story invaded her thoughts again. *'Why would anyone shoot a preacher? That seems a bit extreme,'* she commented mentally. 'An attack by satan' was what Scott had said it was, and although she had not understood exactly what he meant, he did, at least, have an explanation, and an explanation of any kind was more than she had. Maybe she would make a few calls when she got back to town. Just to ease her own mind.

"Gentlemen, here are copies of the intercepts which have come in during the last twenty-four hours". UNICINC was speaking to Advocate and COMHAFs Nadia and Obed. The four of them were having a Top Secret, totally secure conference, and all of the 'intercepts' were transmissions from naasti Headquarters to the individual units which had taken part in the involvement.

"You will notice," UNICINC continued, "there has been increased activity in the Rocky Mountain and Alaska Divisions. You are to be commended on bringing your Verticals to the realization of the importance of intercession, worship, and prayer. Our success is directly proportional to the amount of support we have, and that support depends on the intercessors.

"You will also be pleased to know the 739th Rocky Mountain has been quite active and prosperous the last few hours. The vertical 'Dan Andrews' is recovering nicely from his latest attack, and 'Xan Franklin' is being helped by Elyon, who has shown the Minturn prayer group her need for guidance. I want Rohi to help Elyon in her preparation. Be especially aware of jezebel, as our latest information indicates she is extraordinarily agitated, or, to be more accurate, she is extremely mad at Xan's interest in getting to the bottom of the attack on 'Dan'. Elyon has been instructed to answer every question she has. jezebel launched an offensive against 'Xan', the 739th responded and now sapphira and belial are in END status. Needless to say naasti is quite upset, and we are quite tickled. Elyon has accomplished much in Xan's life". There was a ripple of laughter when UNICINC had said naasti was upset. "Any questions?"

"No sir," the three replied in unison.

"Very good. Nadia, Obed, excuse us, please."

"Yes, sir," both responded and left.

After they were out of the room, Advocate and UNICINC went to what looked like a wall paneled in Mother of Pearl, and as they approached it, it began to separate in the middle with both halves sliding back to reveal a panorama of the entire universe. There were thought controlled solenoids along the bottom which could bring anything, or anyone, from anywhere, anytime, into sharp focus, while the 'subject' was never aware of the 'surveillance'. However, if necessary, either UNICINC or Advocate could speak directly to that person, or persons. In fact, they had done that many times. They also took particular pleasure in watching several groups of Verticals which met, in earth time, every seven days for a period of a couple earth hours. The Verticals called themselves churches, but both Advocate and UNICINC simply referred to them as part of their body. However, as much as they enjoyed observing the groups, they were ecstatic when a single Vertical asked Him to accompany them.

As Advocate was admiring the view, UNICINC put His arm around Him and pressed something into His hand. Advocate looked at it. It began: EYES ONLY: FIRST NEWMAN. When he read its contents, His heart almost stopped. It would have if it could have. He was holding 'The Timetable', and the date of writing, in the upper right corner, was 111. As their calendar is not divided into human months, only 24 hour periods, it would be: the First Period (the first twenty-four hours—a human day) of the First year, of the First Day (the first thousand years) after Christ's death and resurrection.

UNICINC knew what He was thinking and spoke, "That date is the beginning of the new time. That is, the time which began at your re-birth. To use this, simply scan your eyes down the page."

Advocate tried it and what appeared to be an ordinary piece of paper showed every event in time in the minutest of detail, with the scenes moving past quite rapidly until Advocate 'thought' stopped them and then they progressed in real time. When He had seen enough of an event He found He only needed to shift His gaze slightly and the scene would continue until he thought stopped it at another point in time. He also observed that the date changed to coincide with what was happening. Discovering that, He thought ahead to His Departure date.

"I wondered how long that would take," UNICINC said.

Advocate had been lost in His thoughts and the remark startled Him. "Oh, uh, right. Just checking."

"You will notice I have not put it in yet. However, I will tell you this. I've instructed Nadia and Obed to reveal the secret to any Vertical who wants to know."

"You mean what I told the disciples outside Jerusalem?"

"Yes."

"I see."

"It will be within the year." UNICINC saw the thought forming and added, "Not one of our years".

"I thought the time was getting close."

"Try as I might," UNICINC began, "I admit to having a little trouble keeping the lid on this one. I saw Gabriel working on his trumpet a short while ago."

"Sir," Advocate began, "I..."

"You don't," UNICINC cut-off, "need to call me 'Sir' when we're alone. What you did changed all that, and you and the Verticals are the same now."

"Oh, okay, Dad," Advocate said, "I was wondering..."

"In time, Son. In time."

# 11

# TENNESSEE PASS

L EW was praying while carrying two cups of coffee back
to the ham shack, but he still had no idea what would
happen when he spoke with Word and was wondering if
Frenchy would recognize his voice. He even wondered if he
really remembered Frenchy's voice or it if had all been a trick
his mind was playing on him. *'Oh, Lord'* he prayed, *'what,
exactly, is going on? Is this some kind of cruel joke?'*

Word was speaking as Lew stopped at the shack door,
"You say he's there now?'

"Yeah. He just went to refill our coffee," Bud replied to
Word and then spoke a little louder so Lew could hear, "Hey
Lew. You gonna be much longer?"

"Oh... uh... no," Lew stammered. *'Hey, God, I need some
help. Now!'* Lew was about to panic as he went to his chair in
the shack.

"This is KL07PS Portable Zero," Bud said, identifying
the station.

"This is KL07AJ," Word answered, as Lew sat down in
the shack.

Bud handed the mic to Lew and said, "Here, put the mic
close to your lips and press the button when you want to talk,
and release it when you want to listen."

"I don't know what to say," Lew countered.

"Try 'Hello'," Bud stated with a twinkle in his eye, "it's always worked for me."

Taking the mic from Bud and putting it to his mouth, Lew pressed the button and tentatively said, "Uh, hello, uh, Word? Uh, this is... Lew."

They didn't hear anything and Lew wondered, hoped, if God had shut down their power or something, and then he heard Bud telling him to release the mic button. When he did, he caught the last part of Word's statement.

"Ask him to repeat," Bud advised.

Lew tried again. "Uh, I forgot to let go of the button. Would you repeat, please?" He then made a point of releasing the button.

"No problem," he heard Word answer. "I remember my first time trying to talk on one of these things. Don't let it scare ya. It doesn't bite unless you stick your finger inside it." His chuckling could be heard before he unkeyed his mic.

*'If he only knew,'* Lew thought as he pushed the button again. "Oh... uh... Thanks. I've never done this before. I don't know what to say."

When he first heard Lew's voice, Frenchy thought it sounded familiar, but could not put his finger on exactly where he might have heard it. Then again, he reasoned, maybe it was just the radio playing tricks on his ears.

"Well," Word picked up, "tell me about Colorado, or what you do for a living, or how you happened to meet my brother."

"Oh, okay," Lew began, "let's try Colorado first. I live in a little burg called Minturn. It's just down the freeway from Vail. You've heard of Vail?"

"Vail? Is that where they ski?"

"Yeah," Lew chuckled, "you could say that. Anyhow, Minturn is just a small dot of a town on the road map, but it's a major dot on the map of the Denver Salt Lake and Pacific Railroad. I run trains over the mountains to Salida and back. How 'bout yourself," he asked, realizing this ham stuff wasn't so tough after all.

"Oh I just keep to myself mostly. I got a few dogs and run a trap line in the winter and try and make enough money so's I can play when it's daylight, which is all summer. I 'magine you'n Bud have quite a bit to talk about, seein's how he's such a train nut."

"Oh yeah, we have. Matter of fact, we're right next to the tracks at the top of a mountain as we speak."

"How'd you run into him, anyhow?"

"Um... let's see," Lew thought out loud. "It's been kinda hectic the last few days. Oh yeah, I remember. I met him at the fillin' station. I saw his Alaska license plates, we started talking, and here we are. He says you really know how to pray and have a good understanding of worship."

"Well, I don't know if I have a good understanding of worship or not, but I do know I'd rather be with God, and do what He wants me to, more than anyone, or anything, else."

"Y'know," Lew continued with a thought in his voice, "the next time you're with Him, would you mind talkin' to Him 'bout my brother?"

"No problem. anything specific," Word asked, "or just in general?"

"Well, he was shot a few days ago. He's out of danger now, at least medically speaking, but he's working with some people who have been involved in satan worship and we feel they're not finished with him yet."

"KL07AJ," Word said, identifying the station. "Is he a pastor or somethin'. You'd better I.D. the station. Bud'll tell you what to say."

Bud pointed to the black plastic call sign badge on the transceiver and said, "Just read this and add Portable Zero to it."

Lew read, "KL07PS, Portable Zero," and continued. "Yes. He pastors a church in one of the Denver suburbs."

"You bet I'll pray for him," Word answered. Lew could tell by the tone in his voice that he was serious when it came to prayer. "How seriously was he hurt?"

"Well, it would have been disastrous if God had not intervened. I guess there was a lot of internal damage and they were ready to take out his spleen, but God had other plans and healed him right there on the table."

"Wow! That sounds like a God thing. Glad he's okay now. You can count on me praying for him, and the people he's helping."

"Great. Thanks a bunch, Word. I'm gonna put Bud back on. Nice meetin' ya and I hope we can chat again sometime."

"Fine business, Lew. You oughta plan on makin' a trip up here sometime. Seven three Lew."

Lew handed the mic back to Bud and asked what 'seven three' meant. "That's Ham-talk for 'best regards'. Be glad he didn't say 'eight eight' to ya. That means 'hugs and kisses'." They both grinned as Bud keyed the mic, "I'm back, buddy. Hey, why're you at Frenchy's anyhow?"

"Oh... didn't I tell you what happened?"

"Yeah, you did, but why are you there now?"

"Well... we got here a couple days ago and I figured he could use some help with his furs, so I stuck around for awhile."

"Oh. Well, have a good time. I guess we'd better pull the plug for now. If Frenchy's not in ear-shot tell'im me'n Lew're prayin' for'im."

"Fine business, Bud. I'll be waitin' for your call next week."

"Boy, Word, I sure hope you don't forget me again," Bud taunted.

"Nah, I won't. Seven three, KL07AJ, out."

"See ya, pal. Seven three, KL07PS Portable Zero, out."

As they were signing off both men heard a steady, low-pitched growl drifting through the night. "Sounds like an east bound coal drag's workin' his way through the Esses," Lew said. "He usually has about six units on the point with another four, at least, pushing on his rear-end, kinda like my train the other day. The helpers'll drop off on the fly when they get up here. You ever see a helper drop off like that?"

"Nope," Bud said. "All I do is take pictures and I've only seen'em stop to cut out a helper. Why don't they stop to drop off?"

"Well, it seems the bean counters in Denver have convinced the wheels in Denver that it saves'em a couple minutes and a few bucks. You know, the fuel savings of not having to start the train again. It's quite an operation to watch. Just hope it's not too dark to see it"

"How do they do it?"

"Well, it's gonna be easier if you see it, so let's head on out and I'll tell you on the way," Lew said while grabbing his jacket.

"Sounds fine by me," Bud said, shutting down the radio and pulling on a sweatshirt.

As they left the fifth-wheeler both grabbed a piece of pizza and stepped out into the brisk, high altitude night, under a sky as clear as Waterford Crystal. There wasn't a breath of a breeze and the moonlight reflecting off the snow made it bright enough to see. The scene reminded Bud of nights under the Northern Lights, and the stillness served to magnify the distant rumbling on the other side of the mountain. A falling sat streaked across the western sky.

"Now, the helper," Lew said around a mouthful of pepperoni and Italian sausage as they were making their way toward the tracks, "has his air tied into the train and he is coupled onto the rear end of the caboose. What this means is somebody's got to be out there to close the air brake, both on the helper unit and on the caboose, and pull the pin on the coupler. That somebody is the fireman on the helper and the rear end Brakeman on the train. They'll both go out to their respective platforms and when the proper time comes, they'll make certain the helper is pushing and then they'll first shut off the air and then the Brakeman will pull the pin. Some crews run a rope from the cab door to the knuckle release, allowing them to release on the fly after shoving coal drags over the pass. Not quite kosher, but it happens."

"Why does he make sure the helper is actually pushing?" Bud interrupted.

"Well, if he wasn't pushing there could be some pressure on the coupler, and if that were the case then neither one could release the pin. Anyway, once the pin's pulled the fireman will signal to the helper who'll back out of his throttle a notch to slowly uncouple for the train. Then, when the break's complete, the Brakeman'll signal to the helper hogger, who'll radio the head end hogger, and then, as they say, 'it's all downhill' from there."

"Sounds interesting. Speaking of hogheads, or hoggers. You have any idea why engineers are called that?"

"Well, here's what I've heard." Lew answered. "I've heard a locomotive called a hog, and the person that is in charge of a locomotive would be the head, therefore, a hoghead is a person in charge of a locomotive. Here's one for you. Brakemen are still called 'snakes.' You know why?"

"No idea."

"Cause they do so much roamin' around on the ground."

"You ever work helper service?"

"Oh yeah. I'as in helper service the first two years I was here. It's sorta fun the first couple weeks, but it gets rather boring seein' the same ole trees sixteen or twenty times a day. I like bein' on the road, but it gets to be a drag, too. S'pose everything does after awhile."

"Yeah, I guess you're right, but I think it'd take me longer than a couple weeks to get bored runnin' trains. Hey Lew, does the Engineer on the helper run his units from the train end or his other end?"

"From his power's rear end. In other words, he goes backwards up the hill. That way they save time by not having to stop and switch cabs for the trip down the mountain."

Just as Lew was finishing the explanation the block signal facing the south changed to red, which meant the coal train was two blocks away, about two miles. "What you been telling me about railroads," Bud said, "is kinda like the church. At least how it should be."

"Yeah? How you figure?"

"Well, think with me here. The cars and the units are coupled together to form one unit of however many cars and locomotives are together."

"Yeah, okay. But I still don't follow you."

"Just suppose the cars represent the people, the locomotive, or locomotives, represent the staff, and the Engineer represents the pastor. Now, ya see Lew, as long as the cars are coupled together and the air brakes are operational, it's a train. The Engineer controls the train, but the Conductor is the Boss of the train and tells the Engineer what to do and where to go and what to do regarding the individual cars. Right so far?"

"Yep. Go on."

"Okay. Who owns the train."

"Well, the railroad."

"Right. For illustration purposes the railroad represents God."

"Okay."

"Right. Let's stay on that track. The people are the cars, the staff is the set of locomotives, the pastor is the Engineer, and Jesus is the Conductor. The Conductor tells the Engineer what to do, and if a church is set up as it should be, then the pastor runs the church under Jesus' direction from Father God, just like Jesus. He said he only did what the Father told Him to do.

"Now... have you ever heard a coal car say to the locomotive 'I want to be a box car?', of course not. However, I've heard lots of folks say they didn't like the job they 'had' to do in the church, and if they push it far enough they cause strife and division in the local church."

"Yeah. I see what you mean. That's, uh..." Lew thought out loud, "something to ponder."

"Now. Here's what I'm seein'. When the entire body of Christ sees who owns the Church, and who's in charge, then churches all over the world will begin to do what God tells them, not necessarily what man tells them. And when that happens, it won't be long before Jesus will come back," Bud said.

"That's what the monkey said," Lew remarked.

"Huh?"

"That's what the monkey said."

"What'ya mean, 'that's what the monkey said'?"

"Yeah. when he caught his tail in the lawn mower he said, 'won't be long now'."

"AARRGGHH!! Lew! That's terrible!" Bud exclaimed. Then a thought flashed through his head. "I suppose you're gonna tell me the monkey went to Sears then?"

"Sears? Why Sears?"

"It's a retail store isn't it?"

12

# GIZMO

ACH bend brought Xan closer to the visually immeasurable expanse of Colorado known as South Park. An area of the state known for its cattle, its cold, its lofty mountains, its stark reality, its striking beauty, and its ability to make looky-loos out of ordinary people. The magic of South Park had once again trapped an unwary traveler.

Standing at 10,000 feet above sea level, just west of the summit of Kenosha Pass, Xan could see a dot on the landscape a thousand feet below. The dot was the 'town' of Jefferson, which, in another time, was a helper station on the long forgotten Denver & South Park Narrow Gauge Railroad. Only a convenience store on the east edge of South Park was what Jefferson would be for Xan.

Stretching seemingly to Eternity itself, South Park was beautifully dangerous. The weather could change from serene to tempestuous in a matter of minutes. On the day of Xan's trip, however, serenity was the forecast, and the horizon, an illusive seventy miles to the west, looked more like twenty-five or thirty. From Xan's vantage point, the rim of the world was actually the west edge of South Park with the mighty collegiate mountains, Mt. Harvard, Mt. Yale and Mt. Princeton, thrusting their sheer magnificence toward the planets. All were fourteeners and appeared to be only an arm's reach away. As the sun slipped slowly closer to the jagged tops of the collegiates the winter's chill told her it was time to get back in the car, so into her TT she climbed and continued toward Buena Vista.

About fifty minutes later she rounded a sweeping left-hand bend and began to ascend an escarpment which ended in a righthander at the summit of Trout Creek Pass. Being late in the afternoon she was prepared for the sun to come blazing into her eyes as she rounded the curve and had pulled the sun visor as low as she dared. She loved to hear the engine hum it's higher tones and had down-shifted into third gear. Approaching the right-hander she backed out of the gas and set up for the corner. When she reached the apex her eyes caught a glimpse of a shiny something just outside the white line marking the right shoulder and made a minute correction to place it just outside her tires. At the precise instant her tires passed the shiny object, the sun slammed into her eyes, momentarily blinding her. Having the car under complete control, she lifted her left hand to block the light while continuing to steer with her right.

Expecting her hand to provide some relief, she was quite amazed when it didn't. At that moment an eastbound semi was rounding the same curve and they met. They didn't collide, but the sudden appearance of the truck was enough to distract her attention for just an instant, and in that instant she found herself completely out of control and heading for the right hand shoulder, which, she noticed was covered with loose gravel and a snow berm of about 3 feet high. As she hit the gravel, she slid, spun, and found herself back on the pavement, and with tires squealing in protest she knew she was heading toward the opposite side of the road. As the tires hit the gravel on the left shoulder, the car went into a spin. She saw the sky spinning, the mountain turning, and felt a sharp jolt as the car shuddered wildly to a stop, headed in the opposite direction.

As she sat there a moment or two to regain her composure something directly in front of her grabbed her attention. A bright, silver, shining object, not unlike what she had just seen beside the road was hovering directly over the hood of her TT. She blinked her eyes to get a better focus, and saw it was moving. Continuing to watch it as it got closer to the windshield and came over the top of her car, it stopped directly over roof. The object didn't appear to be much more than three feet in diameter, but she felt herself being drawn through the roof of her car and into the interior of whatever it was above her. She wondered how she was going to fit through the open door of the 'thing', and saw what appeared to be a control room. As she went through the door, she turned and saw herself in her car. *'This is weird,'* she thought, watching the door close.

L EW kept thinking about the radio call to Alaska. For some reason he could not explain, Frenchy's voice kept ringing and echoing in his ears. Neither could he explain the feeling of having been in Alaska and helping Frenchy get out from under that tree. He was sure there were several reasons he could not believe it. For one, he knew he was not strong enough to have lifted that tree all by himself. Two, things like that just don't happen. Or do they? Three... well he could not think of a third reason, but that did not change his mind or keep those thoughts from invading his privacy. Bud and Lew were back in the main room and Lew asked, "Isn't there someplace in the Bible where someone was taken from one place and put in another?"

"Well," Bud began thoughtfully, "what about in Acts where Philip was told to meet the eunuch, and he does, then Philip was suddenly taken away and the eunuch never saw him again?"

"Oh yeah. Wonder what the eunuch thought about that?"

"Never mind the eunuch. What about Philip? How do you suppose he felt?"

"Oh, I kinda think I have an idea of how he felt."

"Really," Bud said in a half-hearted, joking tone. He then looked at Lew and saw a very serious look in Lew's eyes. Changing his tone he said, "And how would you know that?"

"Well... I don't really know how I know, but I think I know."

"Just how are you going to explain this one?" Rapha, Lew's angel was talking to Tsidkenu, Bud's angel.

"I am just going to let them think it through for themselves," Tsidkenu answered.

"Oh?" Bud asked thoughtfully. "Exactly what are you saying, or trying to say?"

"I think I'm saying..." Lew paused, then continued, "Hmm... how can I put this so you won't think I'm some kind of nut?"

"Too late for that," Bud joked.

"Right. Thanks. Um... I think I was in Alaska and helped Frenchy out from under that tree."

"Interesting."

"Yeah. Interesting."

"And you think that because?"

"Well, first it was his voice. It sounded, um, familiar like. Like I'd heard it somewhere before."

"Yeah..."

"Then he started telling you what had happened. At that point I began to wonder and as you two were talking I realized that I knew what he was going to say, before he said it. Hey," Lew asked in mid sentence, "am I crazy?"

"What?! You, Lew Andrews, asking me if you're crazy? Look who's driven a pick-up all the way from Alaska, in the middle of winter, draggin' a fifth wheeler, chasin' trains, traipsin' around the mountains with somebody I don't even really know. You ask me if you're crazy?! Come on, gimme a break."

"Well, you gotta admit, hearing a voice on a short wave radio that sounds like you've heard it before and knowing what that voice is going to say before it says it, is a little out of the ordinary."

"Out of the ordinary, yes. Peculiar? Absolutely! But Crazy? No, Lew, I don't think that qualifies as making you crazy."

"Well, it may not make me crazy, m'friend, but it sure is drivin' me up the wall."

Rapha and Tsidkenu, were sitting on top of Bud's fifth wheel. "Do you suppose," Rapha asked Tsidkenu, "you should at least give Lew a hint that he's on the right track?"

"'On the right track', "you're even beginning to pun like him," Tsidkenu kidded.

"Okay, okay, bad choice of words, I admit, but he is getting a little, uh, what do they say," Rapha said while thinking, "uh, oh yeah, up tight. He is getting a little up tight."

"Yes, I suppose you're right. Maybe we should let them know a little bit more. You want to tell Lew, or do you want me to tell Bud?"

"Na, you go ahead and tell Bud. Ya know? This is gonna make for interesting talk back at Headquarters."

"Why should it drive you up the wall?" Bud asked. "You think God's not big enough to take you to Alaska if He wants to?"

"No, no. It's not that. It's... uh... well... I mean why would He want me in Alaska? What'd I do to deserve that?"

"Man, I don't know why. If you're going to ask questions like that, why did he put Philip with the eunuch? Come on, don't get lost in those kinds of questions. God does what He does, and sometimes, a lot of times, it doesn't make a lick of sense to us. Look at the Apostle Paul. As I understand him," Bud went on, "he seems like he was very much a red-blooded human and I suppose when he found himself in any of the predicaments he found himself in, he probably asked himself why would God put him in a situation like he was in. Or John, on Patmos Island. There he was, you talk about being in the middle of nowhere, I don't think there is any place closer to nowhere and yet look at what he wrote."

"Yeah, I know," Lew agreed, "but those guys were disciples and apostles. You know, they'd either walked with Jesus, or had seen him up close and personal."

"True. Very true. But. Haven't you walked with Jesus?" Bud asked, rather pointedly. "Isn't He your personal savior?"

"Well, yeah, but, isn't that a little different?"

"Oh yeah? How you figure it was any different?"

"Well…" Lew's mind galloped through his life and everything he'd ever read or been taught about God and Jesus, trying to make some sense of all this, "I don't know. It's just that I don't even think I'm anything like Paul, or John, or Peter, or any of those guys in the Bible. I mean, sure Jesus is my personal savior, and I love him with all my heart, and would do anything for him, but I can't figure why he'd put me in Alaska."

"So, what's the beef?" Bud reasoned. "So He put you in Alaska for a little while. Big deal. You helped someone get out of a predicament, and saw God's power at work. Sounds to me like that's a pretty neat experience."

"Easy for you to say," Lew said, thinking about the whole thing. "But, I guess when I look at it like that, it really isn't such a big deal, and I certainly did see God do some pretty amazing stuff. I mean, look at that tree."

"Tree nothin'!"

"Look at your trip! How far you figure it is from here to Alaska? Three thousand miles? And how long did it take you to get there, do what needed to be done, and get back here."

"Yeah. I hadn't thought about that. I don't have a clue how long it took, but it couldn't have been much more than three or four minutes, 'cause I remember seein' Smitty's light coming through the trees just on the other side of the tunnel, and then he waved to me as he went by. So all of that must have happened in the amount of time it would have taken him to bring his train from the tunnel to where I was parked.

That's about 5 minutes. Five minutes! You mean, I went to Alaska and back in less than five minutes?"

"Yep," Bud exclaimed, "that's what it looks like to me."

A s she surveyed her surroundings, Xan saw a chair behind a desk, and on the desk there was something that looked like an ordinary piece of paper. She walked over to the desk and picked up the paper and read:

Alexandra Marie Franklin.

Born, 05/18/51.

Reborn, ??/??/??

Encounters: 45,109,753.

Results: negative, 99.9991%, positive 0.0009%.

At this point she stopped reading and the paper began to show familiar events in her life. She saw herself in front of the first radio station where she worked. There was her graduation from high school. She was proudly wearing the cap and gown her father said she would never achieve. She saw herself as a child of six learning to ride her bicycle. She saw a child she knew was her mother, although she didn't know how she knew. Then the events began to progress more rapidly, still in reverse, and suddenly she found herself on a dusty road leading into an ancient city. Coming out of the city was a massive group of people and she heard angry voices shouting obscenities. There were men carrying spears and she saw a figure in the center of the mob who appeared to be bent over with a heavy weight. She realized the weight was a rough hewn beam of wood and the figure was a horribly beaten man. He was stark naked, bleeding from numerous wounds, and almost to the point of losing consciousness. His dark brown hair was matted with dried blood. She saw thorns driven into his entire scalp and the blood from the wounds had run onto his face and beard. His face was swollen beyond recognition from severe beatings and his beard having been ripped out of his face, and his back was one mass of bloody meat. The scene reminded her of an animal which had just been skinned, except it was still bleeding. That meant only one thing. He was still alive. His back had been skinned to the bone, yet he was still alive enough to carry a massive timber.

Then the scene changed. Suddenly. This same man was looking down at her, but she could not see from where. He looked directly into her eyes and spoke in a calm, gentle voice that was racked with pain, "Xan," He said, "I have done this for you."

Then He looked around, gave one final gasp and said, "it is finished." With those words, his head slumped forward onto his chest, which gave one final, painful heave, and the death rattle echoed over all creation.

"MAC?"
"Yes."
"This is Dan."

"Well, hi there," Mac said, wondering when he would hear from Dan. "Somehow I thought you were going to call. What's on your mind?"

"Well, I know this is short notice," Dan began, "seein' it's Thursday, but could you come over and teach us about spiritual warfare this weekend?"

"Interesting."

"How so?"

"Well, it's strange you should ask, Dan. I was just now trying to figure out how to get over there. I think I can get someone to cover for me. I'll check around."

"That sounds like a plan. You remember how to get to our house?" Dan asked.

"Well, yeah. You still live near the Federal Center, don't you?"

"Oh yeah, we haven't moved."

"Great! When do you want us to come over? We don't want to impose on you guys, so we'll just get a motel room. How soon do you want us?"

"Impose! Don't be ridiculous, Mac. You'll stay with us! As for when, anytime you're ready, just head on over."

"Are you sure? I mean it's alright with us to stay in a motel."

"Sure, I'm sure. How long can you stay?"

"Well, okay, but I don't know how long we'll be able to stay. I'm not sure what 'the boss' has planned. I'll talk to her and let you know when we get there. How's that?"

"Sounds fine to me."

"Okay. I'll get a cover for Sunday, talk it over with Sharon and get back with you. We might even be able to come on over this afternoon."

"That would be great."

"Oh, wait a second. Sharon just walked in. Let me talk to her and call you right back."

"Sounds good. Talk to you in a few."

As he hung up the phone he was more sure than before that they needed to be at Dan's for the week-end and said, "Honey-bunch, that was Dan on the phone and he asked if we could come over for a few days. He wants me to teach about Spiritual Warfare. You have any pressing plans that can't be changed?"

"Not really," Sharon replied. "How soon do you want to leave?"

"Well, how about as soon as we can get some things together? That alright with you?"

"Sure. Let's grab some burgers on the way out of town and head for the hills."

One thing among many things Mac appreciated in his wife was her ability to listen to God on the spur of the moment, as this was not the first time a 'spur of the moment trip' had rearranged their schedule. He then picked up the phone.

Dan answered, "Hello."

"Hey, Dan it's me. We're gonna grab some burgers on the way out of town and hit the road. We should be there in a couple hours or so. Don't expect us 'til you see the whites of our eyes."

"You got it, m'friend. Thanks for comin'. I'm lookin' forward to it. Drive safe," Dan said, as he started to hang up.

"Will do," Mac said. "See ya."


A VERY puzzled Xan found herself back in her car. The 'gizmo' was nowhere to be seen, and from her vantage point on the hill she could see for several miles back the way she had come, and in the distance was the truck that had distracted her attention. She thought it would have taken it about five or six minutes to get that far away. That meant she'd been in the 'gizmo' about that long, although it had seemed like a lifetime. Her lifetime.

Remembering the sudden stop, she got out of the car to inspect the damage. To her surprise, there was none. There was nothing broken. Nothing scratched. Not even a dent. Her car was in the snow berm, but nothing was broken, or even scratched as far as she could tell. She recalled thinking when she was slammed to a stop that she had rammed backwards into a big rock or tree, and that something was going to be broken back there. But the rear-end of the car was in the snow and there was no rock, no tree, no highway guard, no damage. Nothing. A puzzled Ms. Franklin got back in her car, shifted into first gear, checked very carefully for traffic, made a U-turn to put her in the direction of Buena Vista, and headed west once again.

All the while she thought about what had happened. The image of that man looking down at her, speaking directly to her, was burned with laser clarity into her minds eye. He had actually spoken to her, by name. Why? Who was he?

"It was Jesus," Elyon, her angel, said.

'Unless,' she thought, 'it could have been that guy Jesus that Scott told me about. But then, why would He talk to me like that. Unless...' She just couldn't figure it out.

All the way to Buena Vista she thought about this experience. It was such intense thinking she had even turned off the CD player, and as she pulled into Buena Vista she thought the first thing to do would be to grab something to eat, then get a room.

The Missing Spoon was her intended target so she stopped. The waitress came to her table to take her order. As she began to order it hit her. She could not speak. Absolutely could not get out a single sound.

# KNIFE

WORD took off his snowshoes and hung them on hooks just to the right of the cabin door. He had been checking his traps and putzing around in his storage shack. It was about four thirty in the afternoon, about an hour after sunset. "I'm home," he hollered as he walked in the door, but there was no answer. Checking through the cabin he found it empty. He went out around back.

Rounding the corner of the house he saw something in one of the trees but the sun had already dipped below the horizon and he was not able to see clearly. He walked closer. The closer he got the more the form took on a human shape. As he got to the base he could clearly see what it was. The sudden realization overwhelmed him.

"Barbara!" he screamed. He started clawing his way to his wife. "Barbara, what are you doing... what have you done... I'll get you down... Barbara!... why?... Oh God, why? Why Barbara??" He secured himself between some branches and reached for the knife he carried around his waist. It was gone! Then he remembered he hadn't taken it with him that morning. checking his pants pockets, he discovered he didn't have his pocket knife either.

He made a mad scramble down the tree breaking several limbs and almost a leg when he fell the last eight feet. As he dashed to the house to find a knife a myriad of questions ran through his mind. "Why? What did I do? What made her snap like this? Why? WHY!?" But, there was no answer.

He barged into the cabin, furiously looking for a knife, a saw, anything sharp. His eyes landed on a razor blade by the sink. Grabbing it without thinking and putting in an outside pocket of his parka he made a mad dash back to the tree, getting to her as fast as he could. She had tied a length of clothesline around her neck, and as he saw her blue, distorted, bloated face, his futility came out in a gut-wrenching scream, "Barbara, NOOOOO!"

Frenchy woke suddenly, startled by a scream he knew was not his. Raising up on one elbow to listen he was able to pinpoint it as coming from above. But he could not figure why Word would be screaming the way he was. He got off the couch into almost total darkness. There was no moon and the room was lit only by the stars and the Northern Lights. The clock next to the bed read 1:35 a.m. As he slipped into his moose hide moccasins and headed for the stairs he again heard the gut-wrenching scream. *'Wonder what's buggin' him,'* he thought on his way up. He went past the troubled form on the bed and turned on the lamp over the desk. That didn't even wake the troubled man, and Frenchy could not decide whether he should wake him or not. The decision was made for him when a wild-eyed Word sat straight up in bed.

Not visible to Frenchy, kije was sitting on Word's head with his tail wrapped around Word's neck and his claws driven into the side of Word's head, filling his brain with pictures.

Rubbing his eyes, Word saw Frenchy.

"You okay?" asked Frenchy.

"Uh... what?" Word was desperately trying to forget what had awakened him. "Uh... yeah. I guess so."

"You were screaming like somebody was beatin' the livin' crap outa you or somethin'."

"Oh... oh, uh, yeah. Guess you could say that," Word mumbled, trying to focus.

Frenchy went down to the sink and filled a glass with water. "Here," he said as he was returning to Word's bed side, "have a drink."

"Uh... yeah... thanks."

"You want to talk about it?" Frenchy could see Word was definitely shook up about something.

"Uh... no..." Word then thought, *'Satan you're up to your no-good tricks again and I'm not about to let you win this time.'* Determined not to let satan get by with his tricks again, Word went on. "Uh... yeah. Why not? Put on some coffee and we'll talk. This could take awhile."


T HE smell of freshly brewed coffee woke Lew. Momentarily disoriented he opened his eyes to the familiar sound of diesel locomotives grinding through the tunnel and was brought back to reality. Sitting on the edge of the sofa-bed he pulled on his socks, stumbled to the stove and poured himself a cup. The sunlight was streaming through the window and the clock on the microwave told him it was 7:18.

"Must be Henry Meyer and the GM Special," he said aloud as he took his coffee outside. Sure enough, Henry Meyer was in the hoghead's seat. Henry was surprised to see his friend coming out of a fifth-wheel trailer at the top of Tennessee Pass and he gave a friendly 'toot toot' on his horn. Lew returned a big wave. Bud returned from his morning hike just in time to witness the proceedings.

"Friend of yours?" he asked.

"Yup. Henry Meyer. One of the best hoggers on the D-S-L-n-P. You give him a train runnin' late and he'll do his darnedest to get her back on schedule. He's an old steam head, and those guys don't like runnin' late."

"You mean he used to run steam locomotives? Sounds like a proverbial Casey Jones to me."

"Yup," Lew chuckled. "Pretty much. But Ole Henry knows when to get his hand outa the throttle. Something Ole Casey shoulda done."

"Sounds like maybe Mr. Jones shoulda taken some lessons from Mr. Meyer."

As the train rumbled past the conversation of the night before continued. "I been thinkin' about your five minute visit to The Last Frontier," Bud said. "How'd you like to take some time off and drive back up there with me?"

"Bud, there's nothin' I'd rather do, but I'm gonna have to think on it awhile. Thanks just the same."

"Sure. No problem. If you should change your mind, the offer's always open. Thought anymore about your adventure?"

"Yeah, I have. Still can't figure it though."

"What's to figure?" Bud asked.

"Yeah I know... but still."

"It does kinda boggle the mind, I'll give you that. I can only imagine how I'd feel if it happened to me. However, with what's gone on in the former Soviet Union, and what's goin' on here in America, I'm beginning to think this kind of thing is going to become more commonplace. I mean, when folks begin to understand exactly what worship and intercession and obedience are all about, I think we're going to find out about a lot of folks taking unplanned excursions."

"Yeah, I can see your point. We really are going to have to be serious about God and His things in the next few years. Especially if the Rapture doesn't happen just like we've got it planned out."

"You been thinkin' about that, too?"

"Yeah. I have," Lew answered. "But what I've been thinkin' I don't think the church, quote unquote, wants to hear. What about you? You think there is going to be a rapture?"

"Nope, can't say that I do," Bud countered. "At least not quite the way we've been taught. Something is definitely going to happen, otherwise Paul would not have told us what he did."

"You mean about the dead in Christ rising first?"

"Right. Then there's what Jesus taught."

"What Jesus taught? Refresh my memory. What did Jesus teach?"

"Remember, I'm just thinking out loud here. I can't prove any of it. Of course, nobody can really prove any of their theories. Sure, lots of folks have lots of ideas about the rapture and when it's gonna happen, but none of those theories can be proven, beyond a shadow of a doubt. I'm not a pre-tribber, or a mid-tribber, or even a post- tribber. I guess you'd call me a pan-tribber."

"Pan-tribber?" Lew questioned.

"Sure. It'll all pan out in the end."

"Aha. Sounds like a cop-out to me."

"So what did Jesus say?"

"He said," Bud continued, "in Matthew 'as it was in the days of Noah, so shall it be when the Son of Man returns.' That's my paraphrase."

"Oh yeah. I remember that."

"Right. What happened to Noah and his family? Did they go anywhere?"

"Only into the ark."

"Right. Did they leave the earth?"

"Um... no they didn't."

"Precisely. Now, combine a couple lines of thinking. The majority of the church world has thought the dead in Christ are those Christians who have died, physically. However, as I see it, it occurs to me that the same guy that wrote 'the dead in Christ shall rise first' also wrote, 'I die every day' and he also said, 'count yourselves dead to sin but alive to God in Christ Jesus' and, 'if anyone is in Christ, he is a new creation.' I'm not quite sure what's going to happen, or how, or when, but I really think Paul was not only taking about the Christians who have died, physically, when he talked about the dead in Christ rising first."

"Who, then, do you think he is talking about?" Lew queried, truly involved in this line of thought.

"It's gotta be those Christians who have really sold out to God. Those who have laid down their lives for God by giving themselves to His work, over and above their own selfish desires and ambitions. Somebody once said that Christianity is free, but being a disciple will cost you everything you have. I think those are the folks Paul is talking about rising first. Then, you add to that what Jesus said about things being the way they were when the flood hit. As far as I can tell, Noah's ark did not fly, and his family did not leave the earth, but they were protected from the flood and it's effects.

"And, speaking of the flood," Bud took a swig of coffee as he continued, "have you ever stopped to think about what it must have been like in the ark while it was raining and storming for forty days and forty nights?"

"Um... no, not really. Why?"

"Well, Lew, think about it for a bit. First of all, let's be really conservative. I'm not sure how high Mount Ararat was at the time of the flood, but I know it's seventeen thousand feet today. So, let's just figure, for the sake of conversation, let's say it was only ten thousand feet high at the time of the flood. And also, for the sake of this conversation, let's say Noah and crew started out at sea level. Okay, the water rose over ten thousand feet in forty twenty-four hour periods. Let's do the math... ten-thousand divided by forty equals two hundred fifty. That means the water would have had to have risen at least two hundred fifty feet per twenty-four hour period. Let's do that math... two-hundred fifty divided by 24 equals ten point four. That's almost ten and a half feet per hour! Can you imagine what kind of storm that would've been?!"

"Well, yeah... but aren't you forgetting that it wasn't just a rain storm?"

"No. I haven't forgotten that, and that's my point! The rain combined with the water erupting from the earth itself must've made for one heckofa rough ride."

"Then, you're saying we're in for a rough ride like Noah had?"

"Yup! I think there's gonna be a whole lota shakin' going on. In the church and in the world. I just can't prove it."


SOMEHOW, through much note writing and pointing to items listed in the menu, Xan was able to make her choices known to the waitress. Xan was shaken to the core at not being able to speak, but at the same time she was experiencing a calmness about the whole thing. Fortunately, the waitress didn't say anything about her lack of speech.

She savored an extraordinary plate of Peking Duck in plum sauce, prefaced by a delicious bowl of hot and sour soup and a pot of freshly brewed Green Tea. She then paid her bill and went to the motel just across the street, still puzzled about her lack of voice. She figured it must be some kind of laryngitis that would go away as quickly as it had come. However, that statement, *'I have done this for you,'* was still ringing in her ears.

The next day dawned bright and clear. She brushed about an inch of fresh, dry, powdery snow off her car, and headed north toward Leadville.

As she topped off the gas tank she noticed she still had no voice, but other than that she felt great. In her element once again she saw the Independence Pass sign a few miles north of Granite and made a mental note to take that road someday. She knew it went over to Aspen, but had never driven it.

The sign reminded her about the reports she had read about a bicycle race going over the pass. She couldn't remember all the details, but the thought of riding a bike over Independence Pass from Aspen to Vail was just overwhelming to her. While thinking about those racers that strange 'encounter' of the day before again worked its way into her head. What could it mean, *'I've done this for you?'*

She arrived in Leadville about noon and looked up the Blue Rose Café. Sure enough, everything Scott had told her about it was true. If anything, he had understated it. Her plate of nachos hit her spot and was a great break in her day.

After eating she climbed into her car and headed north out of town. When she reached the junction of Highways 24 and 91, with Highway 24 angling left toward Redcliffe and Minturn, and Highway 91 angling right to Fremont Pass and Dillon, she made a snap decision and went left.

As she drove along she listened to CD's and tried not to think about anything in particular. She crossed an overpass, putting the train tracks on her right, and admired the incredible country around her. A small stream connected the few lakes in a high mountain meadow, and the whole picture was framed by majestic peaks. Off to the right she saw the railroad tracks lead into a tunnel and hoped she would have one, too. The further she drove, however, the more apparent it became that the highway went over the mountain while the train went through it.

Just as she approached the final curve climbing the last bit of the hill, she notice a pick-up/fifth-wheel combination waiting to pull out onto the road. There was a Jeep behind. Still a little jumpy after having had her transportation jerked around the day before, she thought they might try and pull out in front of her. However, when they made no move she went on. As she went by she noticed the orange and blue Alaska license of the front of the pick-up. *'Long ways from home,'* she thought. A few miles on down the road she saw the highway ahead of her curve over a very high bridge. Always interested in the unusual, she crossed the bridge and pulled into the parking area on the left side of the road. As she was taking in the scene she saw the fifth-wheeler and the Jeep cross the bridge. But, they did not stop and continued on past the turnout without slowing.

She walked over to the edge and saw an exit from the road she had just been on that led down the hill and under the bridge. Her curiosity piqued, she got back into her car and headed back to the road and down the hill. On reaching the bottom she discovered the road went under the highway. Awed by the sight ahead of her she once again pulled over to the side of the road. Looking toward the west she saw the highway bridge, a very high arched affair, spanning the canyon with the train tracks at the bottom. A train was coming toward her, struggling uphill through the cut. All of this was set against the backdrop of the incredible Rocky Mountains. A perfect picture. She was not so much interested in trains as she was in unusual photographs, and this was definitely something she had never seen before. She took several shots to make sure she got what she was looking for. She didn't know what she was looking for, but wanted to make sure she got it anyway. What she got, however, was not what she expected.

When the train had passed she returned to her car and proceeded toward Minturn.

A few miles down the road a sign point to the left announcing Battle Mountain. *'Interesting name,'* she thought while driving around a right hand curve, down and around into the sweeping left hander. Coming out of the left hand corner she pulled into the scenic overlook on her left, and there in front of her stood Battle Mountain, a small town perched precariously on the side of the rugged chunk of granite where she had been driving. *'Only in Colorado,'* she thought. This too deserved some serious picture taking. All this time she remained aware of not being able to talk, but with no one to talk to anyway it didn't matter.

After a few more picture stops she rounded the right hand curve over the train tracks just south of Minturn and decided it was time for a coffee break.

Entering the town she saw what looked like a great place for coffee. June's Café. *'Aha,'* she thought, *'another of that famous, national chain of eateries. Café. This one's run by June. Just what I'm looking for.'* She found a parking spot, went inside, and took a seat by the window on the side away from the trains.

When the waitress asked for her order she momentarily forgot her predicament and tried to speak. Of course nothing came out. However, a lady across the aisle saw her frustration and offered to help.

"Hi," she said, "I'm Verna Philips. Mind if I help?"

Xan shook her head 'no' and, getting a napkin wrote, "Thanks. I'm Xan Franklin" she wrote, motioning for the stranger to have a seat.

"I hear you have laryngitis," Verna said. "By the way, how do you pronounce your name?"

Xan smiled and wrote, "Z A N. Guess I do have laryngitis."

"WHAT you are saying, then," Dan said to Mac, "is that God is not interested in performance. Right?" Mac had arrived at Dan's about an hour before and while their wives were putzing around in the kitchen, the guys talked shop.

"Yes," Mac replied. "He want us. Not what we do. You see, many people think they have to do something for God, when God has already done all that needed to be done. Realizing what lucifer was going to do, God made a way for Mankind to be restored to his intended place. So, he sent His Son, Jesus. Question for ya. Was Jesus God or Man?"

"Well, He was both," Dan answered.

"Right. Another question. Did He do what He did as God or as man?"

"Hmm... good question. Well," Dan thought out loud, "I suppose he did what He did as a man."

"Exactly. If He had done those things as God we would not be able to do the same things, and He told us that the things He did we would do, and even greater. So, He had to do them as a man. Think about this: What did Jesus do?"

"Uh... I suppose you mean something besides the obvious of raising the dead, healing the sick, causing the blind to see, turning the water into wine, et cetera et cetera."

"Yes. What did Jesus do? He was very specific."

"Well, let's see," Dan thought for a minute and then answered, "He said he only did what the Father told him to do."

"Exactly! He only did what the Father told Him to do. And... he did it as a man."

"Go on," Dan prompted, "I think I see where you're headed."

"He said we would do greater things, but what He did was only what the Father told Him. So, it seems to me that we only need to do what Father God tells us to do. Nothing more. Nothing less."

"Yes... and if we do something for God, even though it is for God, if He hasn't told us to do it, then we're doing it because we think it needs to be done. Right?"

"Right! And it's not going to happen, no matter how hard we try. We must make certain we only do what He tells us to do."

"I gotcha. Go on."

"Well, Jesus asked the Father, in the garden, if there was another way. Right?"

"Yeah... go on."

"But there wasn't, and He said, again my paraphrase, 'what do you want?' It was at that point that Jesus made the decision to die, as a man, so that Mankind would have a way to get back into fellowship, as well as relationship, with God. We, men, have labeled it 'salvation.' When we realize, fully, the implications of that, then we will truly worship Father God. You see, worship is more than singing or dancing or waving flags or shouting or being quiet or any of the other things man has devised. Worship is paying homage to, reverencing, and being with someone you love. That's how it should be with God."

"Then," Dan asked, "what can we do?"

"Nothing. Absolutely nothing," Mac replied. "God has already done it. Paul the Apostle saw this and cautioned the

Galatians against trying to do something. He said, 'Don't mix anything with the gospel, for in so doing you will dilute the power of the cross.' When Jesus died, His executioners had not killed him. Jesus gave up his life. Willingly. Just before He died, He said, 'It is finished,' meaning the way for Mankind to get back into relationship and fellowship with Father God was finally finished. Then, three days later, Jesus became the 'firstborn of many brethren.' That means there are a lot more like Him. Just like Him. Folks who no longer fear death, knowing it is only the body that will be silenced. The spirit has been re-born to never die again.

"When a person knows this," Mac continued, warming to his topic, "I mean really knows in his 'knower', his intuition, his heart, then worship becomes spontaneous. That person doesn't have to 'practice' praise and worship. Do you realize we don't have praise and worship practice anymore?"

"You don't?" Dan asked. "I thought that's what you did on Tuesday nights."

"Used to. Not anymore. We have music practice, but not praise and worship practice. If a person has to practice praise and worship they have made it a performance and they do not fully comprehend what Jesus did."

"Interesting."

Just then Donna called, "You guys want something to eat, or are you just going to sit out there and talk shop all day?"

# MINTURN

'**D**EAR *God, help!*' Word prayed in his spirit.
kije tried with all his strength but could not keep his claws in Word's head, and as he was trying to jab them back in something grabbed his head and threw him against the hard wall of the cabin. Nissi then pounced on him and clamped a huge hand over kije's mouth. Struggle as he might, kije was unable to break free.

"Yeah! A pot of coffee sounds like a great idea," Frenchy said as the two men headed down the stairs.

"It was Barbara," Word said in almost a whisper.

"What? Did you say something?"

"It was Barbara,' Word repeated a little louder.

"Barbara? Who's Barbara?" Frenchy did know what he expected Word to say, but it was definitely not the name of a woman.

"My wife," Word answered, a tone of finality in his voice.

"Wife? Did you say 'wife'? As in married?" Frenchy almost shouted. "I didn't know you're married!"

kije tried to scream at Word but Nissi had wrapped kije's wings over his mouth and Nissi was sitting on him. He thought the very life was going to be squeezed out of him. Nissi bounced a couple times just for good measure.

thordan had not faired much better. Jireh had grabbed thordan's tail and wrapped it around his head and over his mouth, making sure his measly little wings had gotten tied up, too. Jireh sat on the window sill and dribbled thordan like a basketball.

"I'm not. I was, but I'm not."

"But..."

"She hung herself." Word was speaking so quietly Frenchy had to strain to hear him. There was more despair than sound or words in his voice.

"She what?" Frenchy thought he had heard Word say his wife had hung herself. "Did you say she hung herself?"

"Yeah," Word answered with an anguished hush that was barely more than a whisper as he got to his feet and began pacing.

"Oh," Frenchy responded. "Guess that would tend to give a feller nightmares. Sorry guy."

"Yeah," Word nodded out loud, remembering and pacing. "I came in one afternoon and found her in a tree. I reached for my knife to cut her down and remembered I hadn't taken it with me that day, so I scrambled around all over everywhere tryin' to find it, but couldn't. Then I saw a razor blade by the sink. I didn't even think about looking in the drawers, I just grabbed it and climbed the tree and started cuttin' her down."

"OH!" Frenchy exclaimed. He didn't know what else to say. What else could he say? He could not believe this would have happened to anyone, much less to a guy like Word. He wondered how a guy could love a God that killed his wife.

"I really bloodied my hands that day," Word continued. "I could hardly carry her body once I got it down. I called Bud and he brought out a State Trooper and they helped me bury her. She's right out there," Word motioned behind the cabin.

"How come you didn't have a knife with you?"

"I've asked myself that hundreds and hundreds, prob'ly thousands of times, and I can't give myself, or anyone else, a good answer. I just don't know. Got up that mornin' knowin' I wasn't goin' out on the trap line and for some reason didn't strap it on. I told myself that day I would never again leave the house without a knife. Fat lota good that does now."

*That's why he always has at least two knives with him,'* Frenchy thought. "Wow! Some kinda load! I thought you didn't have any problems, bein' a Christian an'all. How can you love a God that would do that to ya?"

"Huh? What?" Word asked. "Oh," he continued, realizing where that thought came from. "God didn't do it. satan did."

"What? satan did?"

"Yeah! That's why I hate him so much. Besides, just 'cause I'm a Christian don't mean my life's a downhill sled ride."

"Well, how you figure satan killed her?"

"For one thing, Frenchy, God's not in the business of killin' people. He's in the business of savin' 'em. satan's the one who came to kill, steal and destroy. Not God."

"Yeah, sure. I've heard all that before, but since my wife left me I just can't believe it.

"What if Word is right," Jireh asked Frenchy. Frenchy thought the thought was his own. "If he is," Jirreh continued, "then maybe..." Frenchy began speaking out loud, "...satan caused me to kill my dad. Unless..." he said while refilling their cups, and thinking out loud.

"Unless what?" Word asked.

"Unless satan caused me to kill my dad," Frenchy answered.

Alaska may have a lot of miles in it but not a lot of folks. Things get around and Word knew about Frenchy killing his father. "You mean you thought God had done that?"

"Well... when all my so-called friends at church turned against me and treated me like I was the culprit, it did make me wonder."

"Yeah, I know what you mean. But..." Word paused, "people aren't our enemies. satan is."

"Yeah... maybe," Frenchy reasoned. "At least, lookin' at it that way makes a lot more sense. Is that why you can go on even though you've got this terrible, hurting memory haunting you?"

"Sure. I mean, the way I figure it's like this. I been tellin' you a whole bunch of stuff about God and things. Right?"

"Yeah."

"Well, satan doesn't know everything, but he does have ears and hears just about everything. So, it only makes sense that he would know what's been goin' on 'round here, and doesn't like it. So, he sent one of his henchmen to hassle me." Changing gears, he continued, "satan, you're a lousy, no good, stinkin', rotten, defeated creep and in Jesus' Name I'm puttin' you on notice right now that I'm claiming Frenchy as one of ours, and there's not a thing you can do about it. Frenchy," he said, returning the conversation to him, "I want you, right now, to tell God exactly how you feel about Him."

"Mac and Sharon are back," Dan called to Donna when the doorbell rang. Mac and Sharon had gone to the nearby shopping mall to look around and relax a bit. As he opened the door he saw it wasn't Mac and the... .22-caliber bullet exited the muzzle of the silencer striking Dan in the middle of the forehead. He was dead before he hit the floor.

Donna had heard Dan say they had returned and then heard the front door open. Then there was a thump followed by silence. A cold chill ran through her.

"Dan," she called, "is everything all right?" She had been in the kitchen and grabbed a towel on her way to the door. Rounding the corner she saw Dan's body lying in the doorway.

"Dan!" she screamed. "Dan! Oh, God, no!" As she knelt by his body she heard tires squealing in front and looked out the door, but the tears made it impossible to see anything. "Dan!" she yelled again.


"WHAT brings you to this neck of the mountains, anyway?" asked Verna.

"Out for the weekend," Xan wrote. "Nice little town."

"I like it," Verna replied. "Lived here all my life. Known June since she was a baby. By the way, your voice loss is just temporary. You know that, don t you?"

"Hope so," Xan wrote. "All of a sudden."

"I thought so. You met someone, didn't you?"

"You know?"

"Well, Xan, let s just say news travels fast in these parts."

"Explain," Xan penned.

"Okay. But, before I do, correct me if I'm wrong about this. You lost your voice after seeing something that looked like a flying saucer. Right?"

Xan nodded head with in inquiring expression.

"Okay. What you saw was not something from outer space. Unless you think God is in outer space."

"God?" she wrote. "No thanks," she penned and began to get up to leave, but something in Verna's eyes made her stop and think.

"Don't leave," Elyon, Xan's angel, said. "Look at the peace in her eyes. You have nothing to be afraid of. Surely, you don't think this little old lady can hurt you. What harm will it do to listen to her?" Sitting in the booth next to her, Elyon is unseen.

When she looked into Verna s eyes she saw peace and contentment like she had never seen before and something told her to sit down and listen. After a few seconds she sat back down and wrote, "Okay, I'll listen."

"You see," Verna continued, "God does some strange things sometimes. This is one of those times. He wants you, Xan. He has tried many, many times to get you to see Him as He really is, but you've refused. If He has gone to the trouble of making a flying saucer just for you, the least you can do is listen to him. Agreed?"

"You're serious, aren't you," Xan wrote.

"Yes, Xan. I am. Very serious. Why don't you tell me what you saw?"

"No," she wrote. "You tell me." *If he can send me a flying saucer he can tell this woman what I saw,* Xan thought to herself.

"Okay, if that's the way you want it." '*Father,*' she prayed inside, '*you gotta help me here. Thanks.*'

Deum, Verna's angel, began telling her what had happened, and Verna simply said what Deum told her.

"There was a thing that looked like a flying saucer by the side of the road and you swerved to miss it, lost control of your car, spun around and ended up on the wrong side of the road, heading back the way you'd come. It then rose up over your car and you were drawn inside it."

By this time Xan really was speechless. She saw herself sitting in a little café in a little town in the mountains of Colorado, and a lady she'd never seen before in her life was telling her what happened to her less than twenty-four hours ago.

'*Impossible,*' she thought, '*I didn't tell anybody. I haven't seen anybody, except the lady in the restaurant, the desk clerk at the motel, and the guy at the filling station. Since I have not been talking I would have had to write this down, and I certainly did not do that.*'

"Once inside," Xan heard Verna continue, "you were shown a man being crucified. That man was Jesus, and He said something to you. I don't know what He said, but it was to you, and for you. How'm I doin' so far?"

"OK." she wrote, still not believing what she was hearing.

"How about that," Elyon said, "pretty good, huh? How do you suppose she knows all that?"

Xan thought, '*was this lady psychic or something?*' "Go on," she motioned.

"Okay. Then you got back into your car, drove on to Buena Vista, probably spent the night there, and drove on over here today. I don't know anything more than that, Verna said, but the important thing is this. God has something special lined up for you. If, and it's a big if, if, you believe what you've seen and heard. Out of curiosity, would you mind telling me what He said to you?"

Xan thought about telling Verna, and after what seemed like a long commercial, she wrote, "I've done this for you. And, it is finished."

"Do you know what that means?"

Xan shook her head no.

"God was showing you," Verna answered, "in a way only He can, that what Jesus did on Calvary was for you, personally."

"What was finished?"

"The process of getting mankind back into relationship with God."

"What?" Xan wrote as a waitress came up to the table.

"Hi, Verna," the waitress said, "who's your friend?"

"Sally, I'd like you to meet Xan. Xan, Sally."

Xan smiled and nodded her head in greeting.

"Nice meetin' ya, Xan. You guys want more coffee? And how 'bout some muffins? Hank made a really good batch this morning. They're honey-n-bran. I think there's a couple left if you want'em. I'll be glad ta zap'em in the nuker for ya."

"That would be nice," Verna said. "This is the gal I told you about."

"Oh. Nice to meet you. Verna's really nice. She can help you with your voice problem, too. I'll be right back with the muffins," Sally said, heading for the kitchen.

"How," Xan wrote, "did she know?"

"Well," Verna went on, "Sally's my best friend and a good prayer buddy. I told her what I saw during the night."

"What you saw?"

"Yes. I had this dream and you were in it. I didn't know your name, but I recognized you when you came in."

"Dream?" Xan wrote. "Doing?"

"Yes," Verna replied. "You weren't doing anything. I just saw you and knew I would meet you sometime. I didn't know it was going to be today. Me being here is just part of my daily routine. I always come over and chat with Sally and the gang, and you just happened to come in today."

"Oh," she wrote.


A FTER the conversation about the rapture, Bud and Lew had struck camp and headed to Minturn. They pulled into the parking lot at the train yards and Lew took Bud with him to check the duty roster. Lew was to drive a hot shot to Pueblo, so they said their good byes. Bud said he was going to stick around Minturn awhile and then head for Denver a little later that afternoon.

About an hour and a half later Lew was taking his train out of the Tennessee Pass tunnel and he eased his throttle out a notch and set up some braking to let his helper drop off. After the helper signaled him the All Clear, he released the brakes a little and let his speed creep up to ten miles per hour. With over eighty-five hundred tons of dead weight behind him, he didn't want the whole thing getting away from him. What he was not counting on was a signal test. Unfortunately, the dispatcher had been in the mood to exert his authority, and with

Lew less than a mile from the signal he turned off the light in the signal. The signal was mounted on the highway bridge over his track. When the light suddenly went dark, Lew reflexively threw the train into Emergency Stop and the maximum amount of braking that could be applied, was applied. In the days before computers, Emergency Stop clamped on all the brakes, on all the wheels, and all the Engineer and Fireman could do was hang on and hope to get stopped before running the signal, or worse. However, the new computerized systems in the newer locomotives kept the wheels from slipping, and the dynamic brakes from overheating. He still had nothing to do but hang-on and ride it to a stop, but the new gadgetry gave him at least a little hope he'd get stopped before the signal. That little hope was not enough and he found himself, and his train, sliding, grinding, and squeaking.

The Book of Rules said if he came upon a blank signal, that is one not lit, he was to stop short of the signal and send the head-end Brakeman ahead of the train on foot. The Brakeman was to walk to the next lighted signal and the Engineer would bring the train at walking speed one quarter of mile behind the Brakeman.

However, the more than eight thousand tons on a downhill grade did not want to be stopped, and Lew and his tonnage slid squeaking past the signal, finally coming to a stop about a hundred yards too far. He sent his Brakeman ahead on foot and followed according to the rules to the next signal. When they got there Lew saw the company pick-up and knew he'd been had.

As he climbed down out of his cab, the replacement Engineer walked up to him and said, "Hope you haven't used your job insurance. You're gonna need it."

And need it he would. When he got back to Minturn and spoke with his boss he found he'd been given a two month unpaid vacation. Fortunately he had not touched his job insurance money since he hired on and had plenty to sustain him for the next sixty days.

Before going home he stopped at the yard office and picked up his check. It just happened to be pay day. As he drove into his driveway Cupcake was waiting for him, and before he had even stopped the Jeep, Cupcake was all over him.

"Settle down, boy," Lew managed between licks, "I'll have plenty of time to spend with you for the next couple months. It seems that so-and-so dispatcher has just had some fun at my expense."

Of course Cupcake could not understand exactly what his master was saying, but he could tell something was not quite right.

Having put some things together Lew picked up the phone to call Pastor Mac, and then remembered, as he heard Mac's phone ringing, that Mac had gone to Denver for the weekend. He hung up, grabbed his stuff and threw it, along with a big bag of dog food, in the Jeep. He didn't need to tell Cupcake to get in. Then he backed out of the driveway and headed for Interstate 70.

"SIR, we have a problem." The Watch Commander was speaking as he approached Lieutenant Colonel Ben-David.

"What sort of problem," Nadia asked.

"There has been an unauthorized Termination Operation against a Vertical in the Rocky Mountain Sector," the WatCom responded, handing the terminal to Nadia. "We have been ordered to engage a Discontinuance Procedure against the naastis."

Taking the communique from the WatCom, Nadia read:

\* \* \* \* \* \*

EyesOnly
COMNORHAF
EFTO

\* \* \* \* \* \*

| 2120Z | DSI INTSIG BULLETIN |
|---|---|
| ~ ~ ~ | RE/naasti OPS |
| 469993 | MESSAGE FOLLOWS |

AT 2115Z DSI MONITOR STATIONS LOVELAND GOLDEN AND BUCKLEY RECORDED AN EHF TRANSMISSION FROM NASQUAD EHF FACILITY SEMIVISROKMONT XX

MESSAGE DURATION 1 MINUTE 7 SECONDS EHF SIGNAL EVALUATED AS "TERMINATION CONFIRMED" TRANSMISSION TO NASQUAD AIR AGENTS IN SEMIVISROKMONT XX

AT 2110Z A "SPECIAL AGENTS" TRANSMISSION WAS MADE BY NAASTI HEADQUARTERS INTERNAL TRANS STATION DENVER AND SATELLITE SIX-SIX-SIX XX

BANDS USED: ELF VLF VHF UHF EHF XX MESSAGE DURATION 37 SECONDS WITH 2 REPEATS IDENTICAL CONTENT MADE AT 2112Z AND 2113Z XX

SIGNAL COVERAGE AS FOLLOWS: NORTHERN
    SQUADRON AREA ROCKY MOUNTAIN SQUADRON
    XX

NOTE SOUTHERN SQUADRONS NOT REPEAT NOT
    AFFECTED BY THIS BROADCAST XX

NUMEROUS ACKNOWLEDGMENT SIGNALS EMANATED
    FROM ADRESSES IN AREAS CITED ABOVE XX ORIGIN
    AND TRAFFIC ANALYSIS TO FOLLOW XX

ANALYSIS: AN UNAUTHORIZED NASQUAD TERMINATION
    XX

INSTRUCTIONS: VECTOR INTERCEPT TO LAST KNOWN
    COORDINATE OF TERMINATOR(S) AND ENGAGE
    DISCONTINUATION PROCEDURE XX

2120Z                                    END BULLETIN

~ ~ ~                                      DSI SENDS

469993                                    BREAKBREAK

                    * * * * *


"Thanks, Chief," Nadia said after reading the EFTO
Message. Then Nadia changed his communicator to the frequency for DSI.

"DSI. Do you have the coordinates of this termination?"

"Aye, sir," DSI responded. "One zero five point zero eight
West, by three niner point four three North."

"Thank you, DSI." Nadia then changed to the frequency
for Combat Information Center, 'CIC'.

"CIC, aye," came the response through Nadia's headphones.
Nadia asked, "Which 739th flights are on Alert Status?"

"Sir," the voice in Nadia s headphones was strictly business, "the 739th has the Hawks, the Eagles, the Doves, and the Falcons on Alert Status."

"Excellent," Nadia began. "Vector the Doves and the Hawks to one zero five point zero eight West, by three niner point four three North. Have them proceed at maximum speed and scan all frequencies for Nasquad Terminators. Engage and destroy. Repeat, engage and destroy."

"Aye, aye, sir," CIC responded. "Doves and Hawks are to engage and destroy," he repeated and then directed his attention to Air Operations. "AirOps, scramble the Doves and the Hawks to one zero five point zero eight West, by three niner point four three North. Proceed at maximum speed, scan all frequencies for Nasquad Terminators. Engage and destroy. Repeat, engage and destroy."

"Aye, aye, sir," AirOps responded. He then punched 105.08W, and 39.43N into his Global Positioning System, and since the precise locations of both flights of Elite Fighters were known, the correct heading for each showed up instantly on his flight control board. Each angel also had his own GPS and the AirOps Communications Computer fed the coordinates to the pilots' computers as they were being read by AirOps, and an Estimated Time En route was inserted into the pilot's full-color, three dimensional moving map.

With his In-flight Communicator in hand he keyed the push-to-talk button and said, "Dove One. Hawk One. This is AirOps. Do you copy."

"Dove One, copy. Heading 272, ETE 10 seconds."

"Hawk One, copy. Heading 225, ETE 15 seconds."

"That is correct, gentlemen. Proceed at maximum speed to one zero five point zero eight by three niner point four three. Scan all frequencies for Nasquad Terminators. Engage and destroy. Repeat, engage and destroy."

"Aye, sir," Dove One responded. "Dove One copies engage and destroy Nasquad Terminators at one zero five point zero eight by three niner point four three."

"Aye, sir," Hawk One responded. "Hawk One copies engage and destroy Nasquad Terminators at one zero five point zero eight by three niner point four three.

"Dove One, Hawk One, that is affirmative." Ops said to the leaders of the two flights. "You're on the screen. Keep your heads up and knock'em dead. Ops out."

The Air Operations Officer then rekeyed to CIC. "Doves and Hawks are proceeding to engage the Terminators. It's on the screen."

"DEAR God," Lew prayed out loud, "help me find Bud."

By this time he had gone the block and a half to the highway. June's Café was directly in front of him, and while checking for traffic he also checked the parking lot for Bud's rig on the very slim chance he was there. Not seeing it, or any traffic, he pulled out and went to the bank to deposit his check, then headed for Denver. He remembered Bud telling him he wanted to check out Union Station and decided that would be the first place to look.

# HURRY

"WHAT else?" Xan wrote.

"Not much, really," Verna said, "but I would like to ask you a question."

Xan penned, "O K."

"When, are you going to give your life to God?"

"What?" Xan wrote in oversize letters.

"Give your life to God. That's what this whole experience is all about. God wants you. And He wants you to serve Him with your whole self. When are you going to make Him your partner?"

"Well," Xan began writing, "I really don't think..."

"Xan, what DO you think?" Verna interrupted. "Do you think you just happened to lose your voice? Do you think I just happen to know all this about you? Do you think all this is just coincidence?"

"Don't know what to think," Xan penned.

"Well, then why don't you stop thinking and begin doing?" Verna could be a little direct at times.

"Do?" Xan wrote, "what do I do?"

"First of all," Verna advised, "stop doubting and begin believing."

"Believe? Believe what? What do you mean?"

"In your heart of hearts you know what I mean. What you saw while you were in that space ship thingy was God telling you that He sent His Son Jesus for you, personally. Don't you see? God loves you so much that He made a very special attempt to show you that Jesus died for you."

Xan had to think awhile before beginning to write once again. She thought about all the times people had talked with her about God, and remembered the paper thing had something about forty-something million times on it. She just couldn't believe what was happening to her. If what Verna was telling her was the truth, and she certainly had hit her 'adventure' on the head so she didn't have any reason to doubt her, but if it were true and God really had made that 'thing' just for her, then she decided it must be true and this was the thing to do. Finally, she wrote, "You're right."

"Okay," Verna began, "let's get on with it. Pray with me. Father God..."

"Father God..." Xan mouthed,

"Please accept me as one of your own..." Verna prayed,

"Please accept me as one of your own..." Xan mouthed,

Verna continued, "I believe Jesus was who He said He was..."

"I believe," Xan said, beginning to feel sound in her throat, "Jesus was who He said He was..." with each word her voice became stronger.

"... and I confess that He is Lord..."

"... and I confess that He is Lord..." her voice becoming even stronger...

"... and I ask you Father to adopt me as one of your children..."

"... and I ask you Father to adopt me as one of your children..." by this time Xan was speaking normally, and she felt the weight of years of searching falling from her shoulder, and she realized, for the first time, that God Himself was becoming real to her.

"Father God, teach me your ways..."

"Father God," Xan prayed, "teach me your ways..."

"And help me to understand your Word ..." Verna continued.

"And help me to understand your Word ..." Xan felt all the pressure of unforgiven sin lift from her shoulders. She was completely overwhelmed at the thought of God, the Creator of the universe, being so concerned about her as to send her His own Flying Saucer to show her how important she was to Him. The realization was so immense she just lost the ability to speak, again. She could not even think. All she could do was thank Him for what he had done, and she vaguely heard Verna's continuing prayer.

"Father God, I thank you for Xan and for bringing her into my life. She is a precious child, Father, and I ask in Jesus name that you put someone into her life that can, and will, answer her questions. I also ask for a hedge around her. Father, I ask for special protection for Xan. Please don't let anything come her way that would convince her that what was done here today was not real. Father, I put my shield of faith between Xan and whatever satan and his cohorts would throw at her until such time her faith is strong enough on it's own to effectively resist the fiery darts of ole what's his face.

"Boy, that guy's in a hurry," Sharon exclaimed to Mac as they were heading back to Dan and Donna's house. They had gone to the grocery store in the mall about a mile away and were about two blocks away when someone in a junky lookin, white van tore past them in the opposite direction. They noticed it because the guy was driving so fast. If they had not been so preoccupied with what they were doing they would have heard the warnings from their angels.

"Mac," Adon said, "there's a problem at Dan's house. He has been killed and his killer just went past you in that van." Noticing that Mac was not listening, Adon contacted Headquarters.

"Yeah," Mac agreed, as he turned the corner onto Dan's street, "wonder what got into him? Sure am glad this kind of thing doesn't happen often at home."

"Yeah," Sharon replied. "The high schoolers feeling their cheerios on Saturday nights is enough for me."

As they pulled into Dan's driveway Sharon said, "Well, we're back. Did you and Dan have anything you needed to talk about before tomorrow?"

"Um..." Mac thought out loud, "not a whole lot. I imagine he'll handle the service and turn it over to me for the sermon, but I don't know for sure. Why do you ask?"

"Oh," Sharon said, while getting a bag of groceries out of the back seat, "it's such a nice evening how 'bout you and Dan fire up the Barby, and Donna and I'll get the steaks ready?"

They had parked in the driveway in front of the open garage door.

"Sounds like a plan to me," Mac replied as they were going through the garage to the kitchen door. Holding the door for Sharon he shouted, "Hey you guys, we're back."

"OH, Sharon!" Donna screamed from the front door, "they've killed him!"

Sharon put her bag on the counter and was on her way to the front room when she heard Donna screaming. "Donna!" she called, "where are you?"

"I'm..." Donna cried through her tears, "... at the front door. They've killed Dan! Oh, Sharon... why'd they do this? What did he ever do to them? What am I goin' to do without him? Why? WHY!?"

Mac saw Donna holding Dan's lifeless, bloody head in her lap as they reached her and one glance told him there was no hope. "I'll call the police," he said, going to get the phone from the top of the television. As he dialed 9-1-1 he said to Sharon, "Try to get her somewhere else."

"Okay," Sharon nodded. "Donna, let's go to the couch. We can't do him any good now."

"NO! Sharon... they didn't have to kill him! Oh Dan!" Donna was crying as Sharon tried to get her to her feet.

"Hello?" Mac was saying into the phone. "Hello? Yes. Listen, I'm calling to report a murder."

"Yes, sir," said the voice on the other end of the phone, "has someone been killed?"

"Yes. Yes! You gotta get somebody over here right away!" Mac responded.

"Are you the only one there?" the voice asked.

"No," Mac answered, "my wife is here and also the victim's wife."

"I see," said the voice. "What is the address?"

"Oh... um..." the question had surprised Mac. His thoughts turned to Donna and Sharon, "Oh... yeah. Um..." it's eight ninety-eight South Swadley."

"Eight ninety-eight South Swadley," the voice said. "Please stay on the line, sir, while I get an officer on the way."

"Okay... please hurry."

"Yes, sir, we will. Just don't hang up the phone."

"Okay, I won't." Mac then walked over and sat on the couch next to Sharon and Donna. "I've got 9-1-1 on the line. They're sending someone," he said putting his only arm around Donna and holding the phone with his shoulder. Then the voice was back.

"Sir?"

"Yes!" Mac answered, getting the phone back in his hand.

"An officer is on the way."

"Oh thank you!"

"Sir, how many people are there with you?"

"Only two. My wife and the victim's wife."

"Did you see who did this?"

"No, sir, I didn't. We'd just returned from the store when we found him. When is the officer going to get here?"

"Sir," the voice said, "he's on his way. Are you sure there is no one else with you?"

"Yes, sir. I think we're the only ones here. Do you want me to meet the officer in the driveway?"

"Please don't hang up sir!"

"No, no, I won't. I'm on a cordless phone and can meet him in the driveway if that'll help him find the place."

"That would be fine, sir. If you'll tell me what you're wearing I'll let the officer know what to look for."

"Oh, uh, yeah," Mac said, trying to think, "...Um, I've got on blue jeans and a sweatshirt."

"Blue jeans and a sweatshirt. Anything else?"

"Oh, yeah. I only have one arm."

"Say that again, sir."

"I only have one arm," Mac responded.

"Okay. A one-armed man in blue jeans and a sweatshirt. I'll relay that information. Can you go to the driveway now?"

"Sure. I'm on my way."

Then he said to Sharon, "I'm going out to the driveway and meet the police. They're almost here," Sharon nodded her acknowledgment.

"Sir," the voice said.

"Yes..."

"The officer said he's less than two blocks away. Are you in the driveway?"

"Almost. I'm just a few steps away," Mac said, runnin. "My car is a blue sedan in the driveway."

"Yes, sir. A blue sedan in the driveway."

"That's right. I'm almost to the street now... oh, I see the lights now." He then waved his arm to get the officer's attention.

The officer nosed his car diagonally across the driveway behind Mac's car and with the front end pointed toward the house and the driver's door on the far side away from the house. Mac was at his door as he stopped and said, "Hello. I'm Reverend MacIntyre. I'm the one who called 9-1-1. In fact, they're still on the phone."

"Please, sir, get down beside the car," the officer instructed. He was not taking any chances on getting himself or any one else hurt. He could see that Mac did not have any weapons as he only had one hand and the phone was in it. "Who's in the house?"

"Only my wife and the victim's wife, plus the victim."

"Only two people plus the victim. You sure?"

"Yes, sir. Since you're here can I hang up the phone?"

"Go ahead," the officer responded, opening the door and getting out. "Did you see anyone else?"

"No sir. We'd just got back from the store and walked in when Donna, that's Dan's wife, called to us saying Dan had been shot."

"So, as far as you know, your wife and the victim's wife are the only ones alive in the house?"

"Yes sir," Mac answered as he saw two other units, the first with a lone officer, the second with two officers, pull up and stop.

"What do you have, Jerry?" the driver of the first said through the open window on the passenger side of his car to the officer with Mac.

"Hi Tom. This is Reverend MacIntyre. He placed the call to 9-1-1. He says his wife and the victim's wife are the only ones alive in the house."

"Okay," he said, getting out of the car. "Bill, you take the left, Skip you take the right. Cover me. I'm going to the front door. Jerry, you stay with the reverend here."

Using Mac's car as a shield the officer known as Tom worked his way to the open garage door with his service revolver drawn. He then proceeded to crouch low and work his way to the front door, being careful to stay beneath the window. When he got to the door he knocked and said, "Hello inside. This is Officer O'Dell with the Lakewood Police Department. Is anyone in there?"

"Yes," Sharon answered, "Donna and I are here."

"Are you okay ma'am?" Officer O'Dell asked.

"Yes, we're fine."

"Is there anyone else with you?"

"No sir, we're the only ones."

"Okay, ma'am, I'm going to come in." Opening the door he saw Dan's lifeless form at his feet and the two women sitting on the couch. As Officer O'Dell opened the door, the officer who had been covering the left side of the house worked his way to the porch and was immediately followed by the other officer. Once they were inside, the officer with Mac began questioning him.


XAN and Verna had spent most of the day at June's, and it had been a day neither would be likely to forget anytime soon. As she drove I-70 back to Denver her mind replayed the many times that God had spoken to her and she had rejected Him. She hadn't known that being a Christian was not a religious experience. She had thought going to church was good enough. Not that she went to church, but that is what she thought. Her ex, she remembered, had been one of those gung-ho Christian types and she had gotten fed-up with what she called his churchiness. However, she was learning, that coming into a relationship, a very personal relationship with Jesus Christ Himself, was a lot more to her liking. As she had prayed with Verna she felt God enfold her in His arms and draw her close to Him. It was what she had wanted her own father to do, but he had always been too busy. As she thought about her life, the lyrics of the old song *The Cat's In The Cradle* rolled around in her mind.

*"Yeah,"* she thought, *"story of my life."*

She knew her own father had been disappointed when she arrived. He had made it very plain throughout her life that he had wanted a son, and on more than one occasion she had been told that she was an accident, and that it would have been much better for all concerned if she had never been born in the first place. The fact that she had not been a boy had created a Grand Canyon sized gulf. A gulf that nothing had ever been able to span. How she had longed for her father to tell her he loved her. But, to her recollection, it had never happened. Then, while praying with Verna, it was as though God Himself had taken her in His arms and erased all the horrible memories she had of her father, and replaced them with so much love she didn't think she could hold it in.

She also did not know what was going on directly over her head. If she had, she would have probably wrecked the car, because directly above her diablo and quirk were in a deep discussion.

"Where in the atmosphere was sapphira?" diablo demanded.

"Sir," quirk began, "Olam the angel had some help from a flight of Elite Fighters because the human, Scott, called for reinforcements."

"Elite Fighters!?" screamed diablo. "Are you sure they were Elite Fighters?"

"Yes, sir. There were four of them. I watched the battle on the scope and saw the whole thing. Two of them covered from altitude, while the other two broke up the attack on Olam. The first one drew belial's fire and the second one got him. Then sapphira tried to get on the second one's tail but he pulled a maneuver none of us had ever seen, and he got her."

"This can't be!" shrieked diablo. "The Elite Fighters aren't operational yet. What happened to belial and sapphira?!"

"They can't move, sir," quirk explained. He wasn't about to tell his Superior Officer that the Elite Fighters had been operational for centuries, as he remembered watching four Elite Fighters bring down the walls of Jericho. He just continued the conversation, "They are still alive, but they can't move. I don't understand it sir. We have communication with them, but they can't move."

"Well," it was diablo's turn to do some explaining, "if it means what I think it means, there is not much time left. I've heard about a weapon they supposedly have. I don't think it exists, you understand, but just suppose they do have it, then that would explain why belial and sapphira can't move. It's called the Extended Nerve Desensitizer. There are no known blocking techniques, and it moves at the speed of light so it can't be outrun. That's what I've heard, but you know how rumors are, don't you quirk."

"Oh... uh... yeah, er, yes, sir." quirk did not want to disagree with his boss. Even though he had seen the same information, and knew the weapon did exist, he was not going to point out that it did, because diablo had been relatively calm toward him since he'd sent thordan and kije back to earth. "I know how the rumor mill works. It's just fantasy, sir. I mean, how could they have such a weapon? We're the ones with the great destructive powers."

"Yes, quirk, you're right. But, just the same, we must not allow this new Vertical to learn The Code, or get involved with the Praying People. And whatever happens, we must, you hear me," diablo's anger had suddenly welled up, and quirk found himself dangling upside down from diablo's hand, "we must prevent her from talking with that Scott character about the recent Termination Exercise."

"Uh... gag... gurgle... yes ... gag... sir." diablo could see how quirk's head just flopped around. It reminded him of a kid's paddle ball, and that's just what he was doing with quirk while talking to him.

"Now, ole creepy quirk." diablo knew quirk hated being called creepy. "creepy, creepy quirk. I like that. But, maybe I'll change your name 'cause of how your head's moving around these days. How about Head-Bangin' quirk? That's got a nice ring to it. Anyway, I'll think of that later, creepy. In the meantime, here's what we're going to do. With belial and sapphira disabled for who knows how long, we can't afford to let the little lady have any contact with that Scott twerp. So, what we do is get her outa Denver. Far, far away from Denver. Like, um..." diablo continued bouncing quirk while he thought, "how about London, or Sydney, or some outa the way place in Alaska or Siberia. Yeah! That's it! She hates it when it's cold, so's we put her in the ice box. We'll freeze our little pipsqueak radio announcer. Yeah, and she hates the Ruskies, too, so let's put her in Moscow! Yeah," diablo said, and gave quirk an extra hard bounce, "Moscow. Let's see how Little Miss Christian likes freezin' to death with the Russians."

diablo had bounced quirk so far quirk thought he was going to be stretched in two, but then he saw himself heading back toward diablo. diablo saw him coming and got ready.

"Yeah, ya sick, twisted freak, it's OFF to Moscow with her."

diablo had timed what he said to match quirk's return, and just as he said 'off' quirk had gotten back within striking distance and diablo had used his hand like a racquetball racket and quirk found himself flying out to space. So far out in space he thought he was going to put another crater on the moon. Instead, he was able to stop his flight, and having regained some kind of control, he headed back to diablo.

diablo then grabbed him and began dribbling him like a basketball and chanting like a little kid, "Xan's goin' to Moscow, Xan's goin' to Moscow."

quirk was thinking, *I give the guy my life and all I get is ten thousand years as a bouncing ball.*

Then diablo had another thought and caught quirk and was holding him like a soccer ball.

"No, creepy, our little lady loves big cities. We'll put her as far away from Moscow as we can find. Yeah, that's it! You, you creepy little henchman, your assignment is to find a place for the lady. A very cold place, a very long ways from Denver, and a very long ways from a big city. She must not have any contact with any of the Christian sissies, either. You understand me?"

"Oh, yeth thir," quirk said, even though the words didn't come out too well because of having been bounced around so much. "A vewy cold plathe, a long wayth fwom Denvuh wif none ob thothe Chrithianth anywhere clothe. Yeth, thir. I underthtand compwetwey."

"You'd better understand," diablo said, going into another rage, "you foul smellin', stupid talkin', creepy lookin', head floppin', no good, fire breathin' Christian getter. Now, get out there and get busy getting her outa Denver." diablo then dropped quirk and kicked him in the direction of Colorado's capitol.

# 16

# PROMOTIONS

"**S**COTT," Xan said, "it was absolutely amazing. There I was not able to say a word and was trying to have a conversation with a perfect stranger." Scott and Xan were in the Main Control room at KMGC Radio and had just finished the last of seven drawings to give away a Porsche. Since they now had about ten minutes of uninterrupted music, there was a few minutes to talk. She had already told Scott about becoming a Christian. However, how Verna had known the things she knew about her was still something she could not understand. "Scott," she continued, "this lady knew things about me that no one could have know. It was... uh..."

"A miracle?" Scott interjected.

"Yeah! That's what it was. A miracle. You can't believe it."

"Oh?" Scott said, a question mark in his voice. "I kinda think I can. If you'll remember I tried to tell you about a miracle."

"Oh... yeah. You did, didn't you? Hey, I'm sorry for the way I acted. It's just..."

"Fuhgedaboudit," Scott interrupted, trying out his New York accent. "I knew what was happening."

"Is that why you wouldn't talk about it? Pretty good, by the way."

"Thanks! Sure it was. I knew if I pursued it it would turn you off completely. I also knew it was going to take something pretty drastic to get your attention. You see, in our business where we talk for a living, it's pretty hard for God to get us to shut-up long enough to hear Him. But, He knows what He's doing and He knows exactly how to get our attention. Even if He has to shut us up, or make us blind, to do it."

"What do you mean, make us blind? Am I going to go blind?"

"No, no. You're not going to go blind. At least I don't think so. But there was this guy in the Bible that was on his way to get a list of Christians in a town called Damascus."

"Get a list?" Xan interrupted. "What kind of list?"

"A list of names," Scott answered.

"Names? Why names?"

"Well, you might say he was taking names and kicking butt, because he was going to get all those whose names were on the list and take them to Jerusalem, and when he got them to Jerusalem he was going to have them fed to the lions."

"Feed'em to the lions? Are you sure?"

"Sure I'm sure."

"Yuk!"

"Yeah... yuk! Anyway, he was on his way to Damascus and God stopped him in his tracks. I mean, God flat knocked him off his transportation. Not only that, He blinded the guy."

"Blinded him?!" Xan exclaimed.

"Yep. Made him blind as a bat for three days. Then, as if that wasn't enough, he sent him to the house of one of the Christians he was going to round up."

"You serious?"

"As serious as an FCC inspection."

"So, what did the Christian guy do?"

"Well, Xan, he wasn't too happy about the whole idea. In fact, he tried talkin' God out of it. But, sometimes, God can be kinda stubborn."

"Don't I know it."

"Right. Anyway, the guys that were with this blind guy led him by the hand to the house of the Christian, and I imagine they had pretty much the same conversation as you and your friend in Minturn. Well, after three days this blind guy could see again."

"That's pretty amazing."

"Well, yeah, it is. But that's not all. That same guy went on to write most of the books in the New Testament."

"Really?" Xan asked.

"Yep. You can look it up and read it for yourself when you get home. It's in the book of Acts in your Bible. That's in the New Testament right after the Gospel of John. It's in chapter nine. In fact, the entire book of Acts is a really good read."

"Ax you say?"

"You got it."

"Ax. Like what you cut wood with?"

"Uh... no. You don't got it. It's Acts, as in doing something."

"Oh! As in acts of a play?"

"Now, you've got it. Only in this case it's the Acts of the Apostles."

"The Acts of the Apostles? Apostles? What are apostles?"

"Apostles are those people who are sent from God with a special message. The apostles the book of Acts talks about, were the folks that traveled around with Jesus, plus a few others of that time."

"Aha... sounds interesting."

"It is, Xan. In fact the fellow I was just telling you about became one of those apostles."

"Hmm. I think I'm going to have to find out more about this guy. What's his name, anyway?"

"Paul. It started out being Saul, but it was changed to Paul." Then, glancing at the clock he said, "Time to get back to work. You got the winning number?"

"Me?! You know I'm not eligible to win?"

"No! That's not what I meant. Do you know where the number is?"

"It's prob'ly in the daybook," Xan said matter-of-factly, referring to the book that contained all the live copy for the day and was on the copy stand in front of Scott.

"Oh... yeah. Why didn't I think of that," Scott replied as he turned to the section for the eight o'clock hour.

"Probably cause you're just an announcer."

"Now cut that out," Scott said in a perfect imitation of Jack Benny. As he found the page with the winning number, he put on his headphones and shifted into practice before going live with the winning number. "And the winning number is," Scott said, getting his brain in gear for the live break, "P31860. That's it, boys-n-girls, P, as in papa, P31860 is the winning Porsche number. Oh, I'm such a nice guy. I bought this thing outa my own pocket, y'know? NOT!"

For as long as Xan had been in broadcasting she still could not get over how the announcer-types could carry on a conversation with nobody. Scott had tried to explain to her that it was nothing more than picturing one person in the mind's eye and speaking with that person. Sounded easy, but when she tried it she found it was not a stroll in the park, and decided she'd stick to the hard-core, copy-in-your-face way a newsperson was able to do their job. As she was going through the door between the control room and the news room she heard the monitor speakers go dead, which meant Scott had turned on his mic and was ready to go live.

She walked into her office just as Scott began speaking, "Yes, sir, boys-n-girls. We've got a brand spankin', shiny new, red Porsche for the lucky person in our Push for a Porsche contest. So, keep your hands on the wheel and off the radio and I'll be right back with the winning number."


A s Lew was descending the hill just east of the Mt. Vernon turn-off on I-70 he was wondering how he was going to find Bud. Knowing Bud wanted see the Union Pacific yards, he thought the best place to look would be the area around Union Station. Since he didn't live in the Denver Metro Area he had to do some serious thinking about which way would be the best way to get where he wanted to be from where he was. His first thought was to go into town on Sixth Avenue and get off on Kalamath and that's where he wasn't sure.

"Take Sixth to the Valley," prompted Rapha, Lew s angel.

*"I ll take Sixth to the Valley,"* he thought the thought was his. I-25 was also known as the Valley Highway, or the Valley for short.

Then Rapha spoke again, "Take the Valley north to the Auraria exit."

*"That s it! The Valley to Auraria... Auraria to Market, left on Market and left again on 17th to Union Station.* Good idea, Father," Lew said out loud, "thanks a bunch!"

He thought Bud's rig should not be too difficult to spot as there would probably not be many like it down by the station, early in the evening. His mind drifted off to the old song he'd heard on the old Victrola as a kid, and he changed the words to fit the occasion.

As he pulled into the parking lot he saw very few signs of trains. "Hey, cupcake, where'd the trains go?" He decided to have a look around anyway.

"Okay, ole buddy," he said as Cupcake jumped out of the Jeep, "I'm gonna need your help findin' Bud. Let's see what's goin' on. Now you mind your manners," he said as they were walking.

"Woof, woof," Cupcake said.

"Let's go up this way," he continued, motioning to his right, "and see if we can scare up somebody who might've seen Bud." They first crossed the tracks headed north under the 20th Street viaduct toward Coors Stadium. Cupcake, having grown up around trains, and being a well-mannered pooch, stayed right with Lew.

Oh, how Lew wished he could have seen this place back in the late '40's and early '50's when the Union Pacific was running their daily passengers. As a kid, even though the Great Northern ran in Seattle, the fancy yellow Streamliners of the Union Pacific grabbed his fancy, and the Union Pacific, the

U.P., became his railroad of choice. He saved everything he could get his hands on that concerned the U.P.

His uncle, a conductor for the U.P. out of Portland, had given Lew a set of Union Pacific timetables for his birthday one year. Lew thought he had died and gone to heaven when he opened his gift. He had even tried talking his teacher into letting him do a book report on the Wyoming Division Timetable, but she said no. That did not dissuade him from reading them however, and it wasn't long until he had the complete set of five timetables almost memorized.

All of the railroads of the time named their passenger trains and Union Pacific had the City series: the one that went to Los Angeles and called that depot home was the City of Los Angeles, the one that called Denver home the City of Denver, the one that was named for the City of Roses, the City of Portland, the train his uncle worked for so many years, and the one that made it's home in St. Louis the City of St. Louis. As he was walking over the ground that had once vibrated to the passing 'City' trains, Lew's mind conjured up what it must have been like. He remembered seeing pictures of the westbound City of St. Louis leaving Denver for the west coast. It had three locomotives, three or four baggage cars, five or six coaches, at least five Pullman cars, plus a diner and a square-tailed observation dome-car bringing up the rear, and he used his mind's eye to see one of U.P.'s finest leaving Denver and he wished with everything in his being that he could have, just once, ridden one of U.P's city trains.

That was not to be, however, so he resumed his looking for his friend from Alaska.

" I DON'T really think that God wants to know how I feel toward him," Frenchy said.

"Why? Are you mad at him, or somethin?" Word asked.

"Well... yeah. I am kinda mad at him. I mean I kinda understand what you've been tellin' me about satan bein' the one that killed your wife an' all, but I think I've done too much for Him to want to know how I feel."

"What ya mean, you've done too much for Him to want to know how you feel? You think he doesn't know already?"

"No, that's not it," Frenchy said.

"Well, what is it, then?"

Nissi then said to Word, "He's afraid he'll start cussing at God."

"You think God doesn't know you want to cuss Him out?" Word asked.

"What!?" exclaimed Frenchy, surprised that Word knew what was going around in his head.

"I think you're afraid to cuss God out. You're prob'ly afraid He'll knock you over dead, or somethin, if you start tellin' Him how you really feel, cuz you know once you get started you'll just fly off the handle and start cussin' a blue streak and say whatever comes into your head. But, let me tell ya somethin'. That's okay. God knows what's inside, and there's nothin' he's never heard before anyway. So it's okay to yell at Him."

"Are you sure?" Frenchy asked. He'd never heard it was okay to really let God know what was going on inside.

"Sure, am. Look, if you keep it inside, ole what's-his-face can, and will, use it against ya. But, if you let it out in the open where God and everybody can hear it, then it's not a secret any more. And if it's not a secret, there's no reason for satan, or anybody else, to go blabbin' it around."

"Huh! I for sure ain't never heard anybody say anything like that before. Don't sound, um..." Frenchy was trying to think of the right word when Word spoke...

"Religious?" Word asked.

"Uh... yeah. That's it. Don't sound religious enough."

"Guess what, m'friend?"

"What?"

"It ain't s'posed to be religious. I haven't been talkin' 'bout gettin' religion. I'm talkin' 'bout creating a relationship with the God of the universe, your Heavenly Father. I'm talkin' 'bout being able to call God, Dad."

"What? I thought we've been talkin' 'bout religion."

"Actually," Word continued, "we've been talkin' 'bout a relationship. I know about you and your dad. It's common knowledge in these parts. What I'm tellin' you is this. You can have the same kind of relationship, and the same kind of fellowship with the God of the universe as you wanted to have with your own dad."

"You are serious, aren't you?"

"As serious as sixty below."

"Well, I thought God was only gonna rip me a new one if I didn't do right. And, on top of all that, I'd see the folks in the church sayin' one thing on Sunday and living somethin' else the rest of the week. Man, I gotta tell ya, I don't want nothin' to do with a bunch of hypocrites. They say one thing and do another. I mean, you can't trust 'em as far as you can throw a moose."

"Believe me, I know what you mean."

Nissi then said to Word, "He's mad at himself for turning his back on God, but won't admit it to himself. Ask him about that."

"But," Word went on, "let me ask you a question."

"Yeah?" Frenchy asked, only half interested. He really didn't want anyone looking too deep inside. "What's the question?"

"You're not really mad at God, are ya?"

"What ya mean I'm not mad a God. You're damn right I'm mad at God."

"Aren't you really mad at yourself 'cause you turned your back on God when you killed your father?" Word asked.

The remark stopped Frenchy cold. He demanded, "What? How'd you know about that?"

"Never mind the how. Isn't that what's really going on here?"

Frenchy's heart was pierced to the quick. He knew what Word had asked was the absolute truth, and that knowledge triggered something so deep down inside that all he felt like doing was crying like a baby. But he wouldn't do that. Men don't cry. Especially Alaska men who live alone, in the bush, on a trap line in the middle of Nowhere. That's what he thought when he felt the piercing in his heart, but then he heard Word saying something else.

"God knows you didn't want to turn your back on Him," Word went on. "He knows how you really feel, deep down inside. He knows you want to have fellowship with Him again. He also knows how hard it is to admit that to yourself. Frenchy... God knows!"

Frenchy felt Word looking at him and thought he was trying to stare a hole through him and he turned to stare back at Word, but when he did, all he saw was compassion and caring in Word's eyes. That was all it took. Frenchy LeBlanc, tough, Alaska, trapper, John Patrick "Frenchy" LeBlanc could control his emotions no longer. The years of bitterness, the years of hatred toward the folks at his former church, the hatred toward himself, it all came gushing out, and all 347 pounds of his 6 foot 7 inch frame fell to his knees.

"HEY, Cupcake," the voice said behind Lew. "What are you doin here?"

Turning around, Lew saw Bud coming out of Union Station. They had been looking for Bud for about 45 minutes and were walking on one of the platforms between the tracks.

"Well, howdy!" Lew answered. "I've been lookin' for you, actually."

"Well, here I am. But I thought you had to go back to work."

"Well..." Lew drew out the word in a rather high-pitched voice, paused and continued, "I did go back to work, but it seems I was the victim of a cruel dispatcher's joke."

"Joke? What kind of a joke?"

"The kind of joke that can get a guy fired."

"I don't follow you."

"Well, Bud, dispatchers can test us head-end crews anytime they want. The one on duty did and I didn't pass his test, so here I am."

"What kind of test?"

"Oh, it was one of those signal tests. I'd had a test less than two weeks ago and wasn't countin' on another one so soon and I must've let my guard down."

"What's a signal test?" Bud asked as they were walking along the platform with Cupcake staying close to his master.

"Well, the signals are ultimately controlled by the dispatcher, and the Book of Rules says that if I come up on a signal that's not lit I'm supposed to stop my train before I get to the un-lit signal and let the head-end brakeman proceed on foot to the next lighted signal, while I follow him with the train. Well, the dispatcher turned out a signal just after I'd dropped off my helper on the other side of the Tennessee Pass tunnel. I was rolling about ten or so miles an hour and was about a half mile from the signal when he turned it off. However, going downhill, ten miles an hour was too fast to stop the load I had in the half a mile."

"Well," Bud picked up, "didn't the dispatcher know the distance was too short?"

"Of course he did, and at the hearing it'll all come out in the wash and I'll get all my regular pay. However, in the meantime, I've got a sixty day vacation. So, did you find out what you needed about U.P. s steamers?" Lew asked, changing the subject.

"Nope. I haven't seen anyone around here, 'cept for the folks in the station. The only thing they know about is Amtrak. Hey, since you got a couple months off, how 'bout you 'n' Cupcake here comin' back to Alaska with me?"

"Oh wow! Hmm... golly... gee..." Lew kidded, "I thought you'd never ask. When do we leave? I think I'll talk to Mac about leaving Cupcake with him, though."

"Well, I'm ready when you are. I was headed to my house on wheels when I saw you guys."

"How 'bout we head over to Dan's then and see what's goin' on? Where's your house on wheels, anyway? I looked for it when I got here, but didn't see it."

"That's a great idea. I was hoping I'd get to meet him. By the way. Why do you call your dog Cupcake?"

"Well... I was watchin M*A*S*H one night and there was this dog. A big, beautiful, German shepherd that had been wounded. His name was Corporal Cupcake. I thought at the time that if I ever had a dog worthy of the name, he'd get it."

"Well, I'll be," Bud responded. "You gotta admit it's kinda unusual name for a two hundred pound brute of a dog."

"Yeah, I s'pose it is. Then again, you gotta admit Cupcake is an unusual brute of a dog."

"Yep, you got that right. He is a fantastic animal. Oh... I parked my rig in the big parking lot on the other side of the building." The three friends had walked around the south end of the Union Station building and were heading toward U.P.'s old freight house.

"Oh," Lew said, motioning with his hand for Bud to follow him, "let's go to my Jeep and I'll give you a lift to your buggy. That is if you don't mind sharing space with Cupcake for a block or two."

"Sounds good by me. I been luggin' this camera stuff around and it's startin' to get heavy. I'd appreciate the lift." As Lew and Cupcake took Bud to his rig they decided that Bud would follow Lew to Dan's house.

"NADIA," Adon said.

"Nadia here."

"Nadia, I have a positive ID on the Terminator of the human Dan Andrews."

"Good work!" Nadia then said into his communicator, "CIC."

"CIC, aye."

"Monitor Tac One."

"Aye, sir," CIC responded, changing frequencies.

"Okay, Adon. What'd ya have?"

"Nadia," Adon began, "the terminator's in a junky looking white van. Colorado license AP thirty-one oh five. That's Colorado license Andrew Peter three one zero five. He's just turned west onto Sixth Avenue from Union Boulevard. Let's knock him off. We don't want a repeat in Minturn."

"Great! CIC, you got that?"

"CIC, aye. Junky white van, Colorado license Andrew Peter three one zero five, headed west on Sixth Avenue at Union Boulevard.

"That's affirmative. You have your orders."

"CIC, aye." Combat Information Center then directed his transmission to the Doves and Hawks. "Doves and Hawks."

"Dove."

"Hawk."

"Positive ID on the Terminator. He's in a junky white van, Colorado license Andrew Peter three one zero five, turning west on Sixth Avenue off Union Boulevard. Carry out previous orders."

Dove and Hawk had converged on the coordinates given them previously, and when the license number came in verbally, it had also gone into the on-board combat computer, which had processed the information and performed a vehicle search of all vehicles with in a one mile radius of the coordinates. It had begun searching for the license even as the digits were being read, and by the time the last digit had been spoken by CIC the on-board computers had found the van, and marked it on each pilot's moving map.

"Dove. Junky white van, Colorado license Andrew Peter three one zero five, west on Sixth Avenue from Union Boulevard. I have him in sight."

"Affirmative, Dove," the leader of Hawk Flight said. "He's in front of us moving at over 70 miles per hour. We're fanning out. Two go left. Three go right. Four get on his tail, I'm getting on his roof."

"Hawk," Dove leader said, "I have him in sight. We'll swing around in front of him to cover you guys."

The killer made a hard left turn from Union Boulevard onto Sixth Avenue directly in front of a Colorado State Patrolman, who was southbound on Union Boulevard at the time. Seeing the white van squealing around the corner, the patrolman hit his lights and began closing the distance. The killer was driving no ordinary van, and as soon as he saw the patrolman's lights he tromped down on the gas to avoid getting picked up. Not only was he high on crack at the time, he also had other illegal and several weapons with him.

When the patrolman saw the van speed up he knew it wasn't going to be just another day at the office and picked up the microphone. Switching his radio to the universal channel which was monitored by all the various police departments in the Denver Metro Area, he keyed his mic and spoke,

"This is CHP, five echo seven. I am in high speed pursuit of a white van westbound on Sixth Avenue just west of Union Boulevard, license Able Papa three one zero five."

"CHP five echo seven, the is Lakewood one delta six. I am at Isabell Street and Sixth. Do you need assistance?"

"One delta six, this is five echo seven. That is affirmative. He's in the left lane and we are runnin' over ninety. There's very little traffic."

"Okay, five echo seven, I am on the on-ramp and I have you in sight."

When the killer saw the Lakewood cop pull onto the freeway ahead of him, he suddenly swerved to the right to try and ram the newcomer. At that instant the Lakewood cop's angel reached into the fuel injection system of the engine and shut it down. Simultaneously, Hawk One, flying directly over the van, reached down and moved the van to the left. The resultant loss of speed of the cop's car, and the help from Hawk One was just enough to allow the van to narrowly miss hitting the cop's car. The Lakewood cop had no idea why his engine had cut-out just when he needed it, but when he saw the van swerve in front of him, he was sure glad it had. Then, as suddenly as the engine had stumbled, it caught, smoothed out and ran like a charm.

"Hawk to CIC. Our boy just tried to ram the Lakewood officer who joined the chase at Isabell Street. He missed and is still proceeding west on Sixth. I'll change the light at Sixth and Colfax and see if he'll take the ramp to I-70. Going this fast, a Mark IV-A will cause him to loose control. Dove. Slow traffic on I-70 westbound."

"I don't know what this guy's running in that van," said the Colorado Highway Patrolman into his microphone, "but it sure is a lot faster than it looks. One delta six, are you still with us?"

"Yeah," the Lakewood officer replied, "I'm still here. My engine cut out at the last second."

"It looks like he's taking Highway 6 west. I hope the light holds green for him."

The killer could see he had two pursuers and began swerving back and forth across the three lanes of the freeway. However, he had no idea his human pursuers had help from the finest fliers in existence.

Sixth Avenue intersected with West Colfax just west of the I-70 cut-off, and the killer saw the light turn amber for him and made the snap decision to take the I-70 cut-off. He was traveling about a hundred miles per hour when he entered the ramp, and although he got on his brakes as hard as possible without sliding the tires, he was still going too fast, and the van began leaning dangerously to it's right.

"This is five echo seven," the highway patrolman said, trying to remain calm while driving over 90 miles per hour. "Our boy's takin' I-70! He's goin' way too fast for the ramp! I think he's goin' over!"

"Dove here. We're slowing traffic on I-70 westbound."

At that point the four Elite Fighters of Dove Flight simultaneously shut down the air supply of all vehicles on I-70 between 38th on the north and the Morrison cut-off on the south. Since every vehicle was affected the same way, at the same time, the drivers were unaware of anything unusual going on.

"Okay, three," Hawk One said into his mic, "keep him on the road. We don't want him falling on the eastbound traffic below. Four. Drop back and take him out."

The pilot in the number Three slot matched the speed of the van and flew with his left wing touching the right side of the van, holding the van on it's wheels.

"That's it, buddy," the angel in number four slot said to himself, "just a couple more seconds." Hawk Four had a target lock on the killer and was waiting for the vehicle to clear the overpass over Sixth Avenue before sending his missile on it's way. As the van exited the bridge Hawk Four squeezed the trigger on his control yoke. If the projectile had been visible to humans it would have looked like five darts heading for the van. Four of the darts had been sent toward the tires on the van, and the fifth had a lock on the driver's heart. All five darts struck their intended targets together. The result was devastating.

"Oh, my God," said the highway patrolman who was right behind the van, "he lost it. He's goin over the side! Denver dispatch, we're gonna need an ambulance at the west end of the on-ramp to I-70 westbound from Sixth Avenue westbound. We have a rollover."

Since the Lakewood officer was behind the highway patrolman he had a better view of what happened, and also more time to slow down. He was able to stop about 50 feet past the end of the guard rail.

"Hawk to CIC. Terminator destroyed."

"CIC. Good work Hawk. Nice touch on the cars, Dove. Okay, you guys, it's Angels 100. Maintain surveillance."

Both flights responded and headed for 100,000 feet above sea level.


SCOTT was on the air with the winner of the Porsche when Xan saw Gene Bailie, general manager of KMGC radio, motioning to her through the window of the news room door. As she went into the hall and followed him toward his office she had no idea what he wanted. A chat with The Big Guy, with no immediate supervisor in sight, could mean anything.

"Xan," he began while walking toward his office, "I've been listening to the morning show, and I'm very impressed with the way you, Scott, and Rodger have blended into a team on the air."

"Thanks, Skipper," she said. No one at KMGC considered themselves as working for Gene Bailie, but as working with him. Everybody liked Gene. "You got my Porsche yet?" she asked with a twinkle in her eye.

"How'd you know that's what I wanted to talk to you about?" Gene countered as they went into his office. Walking behind his desk he continued, "I hope you like red."

"I don't care what color it is," she said, "just as long as it's a Porsche."

"Well," Gene went on, "I'm glad for that." He reached into the lower left-hand drawer of his desk, pulled out a blue, foil-covered box about the size of a loaf of bread, handed it to her and said, "Here. This is for you."

Beginning to unwrap the gift her curiosity was at a peak. "What's this for, anyhow?"

"Well, Xan, I tell you what. We all know how much you like sports cars, and how much you like to drive. We also know red is your favorite color so we all went together and got you a little something for your birthday."

"Birthday?!" she exclaimed. Taking the last of the paper off the gift she immediately recognized a die-cast scale model of a red Porsche 911 Carrera. She couldn't believe her eyes. She looked up and saw the gleam in Gene's eyes a second before she heard the whole crew, who had assembled in the office without her knowing it, burst into a rousing, off-key, exuberant chorus of Happy Birthday . It was her birthday, but she had told no one, and did not expect anyone to know. She had not, however, counted on the sneakiness of Carol, the office manager.

Turning around, she felt her face get as red as the model she was holding and was speechless. Again. As the crew continued their collaborative effort at music making she tried to come up with a clever response, but her mind was as blank as a newly erased reel of audio tape.

"Thanx, guys," she began as they finished, "that was really awful," she said, laughingly. "I could tell it was from the heart."

"Yeah," a salesman piped-up good-naturedly as everyone crowded around her, "it had to be from our heart. We can't sing a lick."

"Please, everybody," Scott said, entering the room, "keep your day jobs. And you, Ms. Franklin, I'd like to wish Happy Birthday to Denver's Number One Newsperson," he said, giving her a big hug while everyone burst into applause.

"Hey, Scott," Gene queried, "who's minding the store?"

"It's on auto-pilot," Scott replied, referring to the computer system.

"Ah good," Gene began, "then we have all the time we need. Now that I have everyone's attention, I have a few things on my mind, so let's head into sales where there's more room."

As everyone made themselves comfortable on chairs, tables, desks, floor, anything they could sit on, Gene began.

"As you no doubt know, we had a few entries in the Addy Awards at the Colorado Broadcasters Association Convention last week in Pueblo. What you don't know is, I got to bring home two First Place Trophies." At this news the entire room broke into 'nice work's', 'way to go's', 'good spot's', 'bravo's', and a rousing round of applause for the entire staff.

As the room quieted to a dull roar Gene continued. "Dick Phelps, front and center."

As Dick, a long, lanky, red-haired fellow who ran his life as though he didn't have a care in the world moved to the front of the room, Gene proceeded. "Dick, for your series of spots for Wheels Unlimited, here is a First Place Trophy."

Dick had produced an exceptional series of commercials for the car dealer whom everyone had said would never advertise on radio. Not only had he sold them on using radio, he had also talked them into doing the Push For A Porsche Promotion, which had been responsible for making them the number one Porsche dealer in America. As he took the trophy, Dick's grin was as wide as America itself.

"Hey guys," Dick began, holding the trophy, "this belongs to all of us. I couldn't have sold Wheels if there had not been a production staff and air staff to back me up. We also had to have terrific support from you, Carol, and your staff in traffic. I know scheduling all those live breaks was a nightmare. Thanx a bunch. All of you!"

When the applause had died down a bit, Gene announced the second award.

"Charlie Delaney, gitcher bod up here." As Charlie, the dapper Production Manager from Sydney, Australia, whom everyone in Denver considered the best in the business, made his way to the front Gene said, "Charlie, for your work on the Colorado Air account, you also received a First Place Trophy."

Colorado Air was a new account. It was their first year in business and had decided to go with radio as their only advertising medium. To the folks in the know, it had been a chancy decision. However, what the folks in the know didn't know was the entire board of directors of Colorado Air were retired radio people, and had, unknown to the KMGC staff, carefully screened the radio stations in the entire Rocky Mountain West for the best staff of people. They had very little trouble finding KMGC, and when the names 'Gene Bailie' and 'Charlie Delaney' popped up, their decision was made. KMGC would handle all of the copywriting, production, and distribution for the new airline.

"Well, mates," Charlie articulated in his inimitable accent, "we really got the blokes off the ground, didn't we?" Once again the room was a ruckus with laughter, cheers, whistles, applause, and good natured kidding all around.

As the noise once again decreased to a more tolerable level Gene said, "Now. As most of you know, the Spectrum Group, our parent company, has purchased another station. This new one is in Juneau, Alaska. But, what most of you do not know is, we will be sending some of our KMGC crew to Juneau to run our new baby. It's a ten thousand watt FM and the call letters will be changed to KMJK, Magic 98. With some of our people heading to The Last Frontier we can only imagine what the papers are going to be saying about us. However, as Spectrum has done in the past, none of you will be out of a job, and some of you are in for promotions.

"I know we'll all miss the folks that are moving, but I also hope you'll be pleased to know that with this new acquisition, Spectrum has begun a sort of time-share with our other stations. I'll explain this a little later. First, about the promotions.

"Okay, first of all, Scott Dennis will be the Program Director, Jack Marshall will be the General Manager, Xan Franklin will get to go back to her cave, as she calls it, as she will be the Production Manager, and Dick Phelps will be the Sales Manager. We've found a fellow broadcaster who has been working for the Juneau paper for the past good while and he's agreed to be our News Director. The rest of the staff will be comprised of the folks who are presently at the station and who decide to come aboard the Spectrum ship."

As the announcements were made the room once again erupted into cheers and whistles and wishes of good luck.

"Okay," Gene continued as the conversations quieted, "about this time-sharing whatchamacallit. What it amounts to is you'll be able to trade positions with someone in one of our other stations for a semi-extended period of time. Say a month or so."

"Does this mean we can go to Hawaii and get paid for it?" George Forbes, an Account Executive, asked.

"You bet, George. And not only Hawaii, but also Florida, Chicago, New York, Frisco, and now, Alaska. We've worked a deal with Colorado Air, who has worked a deal with Alaska Airlines, so we'll even be able to pay your airfare. How's that grab ya?"

"Great!" came a reply from the front.

"Like a hairy hand in the dark," somebody said from the back of the room.

"Oh yeah? How do you know what Harry's hand feels like in the dark?" somebody else kidded back. The resultant laughter and kidding was deafening.

"Okay, everyone. Anymore questions?" Gene asked.

There were none and the impromptu meeting was officially over.


"HEY, your buddy Mac's here," Lew said to Cupcake as he pulled in Dan's driveway. As he got out of his Jeep he motioned to Bud to park his outfit in the vacant lot next to Dan's garage.

"Isn't this your pastor's car?" Bud asked Lew as the two were walking toward the front door.

"Yeah, it is. He came over to spend the week-end with Dan and Donna. I think he's speaking Sunday." As he was want to do at Dan's house he took Bud with him around to the back door, thinking everyone would be on the patio.

Seeing no one, Lew knocked on the sliding door. "Wonder where everyone is?" he asked, looking through the door. He didn't see anyone and checking the door, he found it locked, which only served to remind him once again why he didn't like the big city. "What ya wanna do now?"

"Well, I'm kinda hungry. How 'bout we get a bite to eat? There's gotta be a decent place close."

"Oh yeah, plenty of em. Whatcha in the mood for? There's a pretty good Mexican place, and several eat-n-run joints."

"Okay. I haven't had Mexican since the other day at the Blue Rose."

"Fine by me. Let's check out Jose O'Shea's."

"Jose O'Shea?" Bud asked incredulously. "Where's he from? Southern Ireland?"

"Cute. Not a clue, but it's pretty good food, from what I hear."

"Well, I'm game if you are. You wanna leave Cupcake here in the trailer?"

"Oh, I don't think that's necessary." The two friends were walking back toward their vehicles and Lew continued. "He's been with me before, and I've got a leash in the Jeep. However, there's only the driver's seat, and the small jump seat in the back."

"Well, I'll just unhook the trailer and we'll take my pick-up. It'll only take a minute. How 'bout that?"

"Sounds good. Need any help?"

"Not really, but if you want, you can crank down the jacks while I un-hook the cables."

"Okay." Bud showed Lew how to lower the jacks and then climbed into the bed of the pick-up.

Just as they finished making sure the trailer wasn't going anywhere they saw a Lakewood Police cruiser turn into the driveway. "Wonder what he wants," Lew said.

"Yeah... Hey... that's Mac in the back seat. And Sharon and Donna, too." 'Oh, Father,' Lew prayed, a dreadful feeling hitting his heart.

As the officer and the others got out of the cruiser Lew could tell all was not well. "Hi, Mac, and all. What's going on? Where's Dan?"

"Hi Lew," Mac said grimly, offering Lew his right hand and motioning the officer to join them, "this is Officer O'Dell. Officer O'Dell, Lew Andrews, Dan's brother. Lew," Mac continued, still shaking his hand, "uh... Lew..."

"It's Dan, isn t it?"

"Uh, yeah, Lew... I'm afraid it is," Mac said as everyone formed a cluster around Lew. It was Sharon who spoke next.

"Lew... um... oh, Lew, I'm so sorry," she stammered into tears.

Officer O'Dell then took over, "Mr. Andrews, I'm very sorry to have to tell you this, but your brother was killed this afternoon."

"Say what?!"

"I'm afraid it's true," Mac said. "Someone came by and killed him here at the house."

## 17

# CLOSED

As soon as his knees hit the ground he knew what he wanted. He also knew he was getting it. All the years, all the pain, all the hurt were somehow being washed away and he felt himself once again being drawn into God's embrace. It was so good to be 'home', back where he had wanted to be for so many years, but had thought he would never be good enough to be there again.

"You are good enough," Frenchy heard through the mist of his feelings, and opening his eyes he saw Word. It was like Word had read his mind and he asked, "How did you know that was what I was thinkin'?"

"Well," Word answered, "some things are pretty much the same for everybody I know, and feeling like we're not good enough for God is just one of those things."

Looking at Word a little closer, Frenchy thought Word was different somehow. At least he looked different, sort of. He no longer struck him as some kind of pushy Christian-type, but as more of a brother. Being the only son he had no idea what a brother was, but Word sure seemed like a brother to him.

In that instant of overwhelming emotions and elation his whole world looked different. It was like dark scales had been taken off his eyes and he was able to see everything much clearer than before. The trees somehow seemed more dazzling, the snow cleaner, the air fresher, but more important, his past life didn't seem to matter as much anymore. It was as though he had been given a whole new outlook on everything.

Overhead and out of sight thordan and kije were fit to be tied, which they probably would be once ole-what's-his-face learned what was happening. However, Jireh and Nissi were keeping them so busy trying to stay alive that they did not have much time to do anything other than take defensive actions.

"thordan," Jireh called.

Just as thordan turned to the sound of his name he was grabbed by two of the biggest hands that had ever grabbed something. It was Jireh, and thordan felt himself being treated like a hacky sack. First Jireh was bouncing him on his knee, then he did several headers with the demon, then he kicked him, full force, into a spruce tree and thordan found himself headed back toward a waiting Jireh, only for the soccer lesson to continue.

kije was not fairing much better, but instead of being used like a soccer ball, Nissi was practicing his slap shots, and kije was the hockey puck.

"OUCH!" kije said as he was slammed into the goal. It was no ordinary net goal. The net felt like it was made of steel mesh and it was stretched so tight the kije just bounced right back to Nissi, who was ready for him and gave him another slap shot to the goal. This happened over and over and kije was wondering if he would ever walk straight again.

Then kije heard Nissi say something to thordan and found himself being traded for a soccer ball and Jireh began giving him a soccer lesson as Nissi began showing thordan how hockey was supposed to be played.

The two naastis were kept so busy trying to protect themselves they completely forgot about what was happening between Frenchy and Word.

"You're right," Frenchy said, "I was thinking I was not good enough. However, for some reason, I don't feel that way now."

"I know what you mean," Word agreed. "I remember when I first became a Christian. The whole thing was almost too much to handle. By the way. Welcome to The Kingdom."

"Yeah? So that's what you call it?" Frenchy asked. "Anyway, besides that, I've just got this incredible feeling of peace and acceptance and happiness and, I don't know, uh... love. I guess I'm feeling love for the first time in a long time. Does that make any kind of sense at all?"

"Yup. The Kingdom of God. That's what we're living in, and yes your feelings do make sense," Word answered, "makes all kinds of sense. Maybe this will help. If you were able to ask God, face to face, right now, if you had ever sinned, what do you s'pose would be His response?"

"Well, since he cannot lie He would probably tell me that I had, but that He had forgiven me."

"Good thought, but wrong."

"Wrong?"

"Yup, wrong."

"Well, then, what would He say?"

"He'd say He doesn't remember."

"Doesn't remember? How you figure he doesn't remember? I thought He knew everything. So how can he not remember something?"

"Well, it says in the Bible that He casts our sins into the deepest part of the deepest sea, and throws them as far as the east is from the west and will not remember them."

"Hmm... that's cool."

"Yeah, it is, but it says He will not remember them. Emphasis on the will. He will not. Not does not, or cannot, or should not, but will not. He chooses to not remember them. That's the really cool part."

"Uh, yeah," Frenchy agreed, "that is really cool. Wow! That's really somethin'! He will not remember my sins! How cool is that?"

"Precisely! And if He won't, you shouldn't!"

"Now, that's some kinda somethin' to think about."


THE pain for Lew was almost unbearable, but being on the road for several days headed to Alaska, was proving to be a huge help. He was glad and grateful that his family and friends had convinced him to take advantage of his time off and go to Alaska for a change of scenery. Mac and Sharon had volunteered to take care of Cupcake for as long as necessary. He just could not understand why anyone would want to kill Dan.

'Why would anyone want to kill him,' he asked, not really out loud, but Bud heard something and asked...

"What? You say something?"

"Huh... what?"

"I thought I heard you say something," Bud said.

"Oh, uh... I was just thinking about Dan. I must have been thinking out loud. I wonder why anyone would want him dead."

"Um... I don't know... but you do realize," Bud began, "our fight is not against people and things. Right?"

"Yeah. Of course. But..."

"But what?"

"But... um... I really miss my brother and I don't understand why he has to be dead. All he ever wanted to do was help people, and now..." Lew's voice trailed off.

"Uh... right," Bud stammered, "look... uh... Lew... I know I don't know what you're going through, but I do know you're not going through it alone."

"Yeah... I know... and I really appreciate all the support you've been to me and Donna, but... it's just..."

"No, Lew, this is not about me or Mac or anyone else. I'm talking about somebody higher and more powerful."

"Yeah, I know, but it seems like I've been hung out to dry... alone."

The alone sounded extremely final. Since leaving Denver, Bud and Lew had not really talked about it. Bud had known it would come out sometime. Just not how or when, and he decided to let Lew talk about it on his terms and in his time and not rush or pressure.

Lew, Mac and Sharon, Bud, Jon Wolfe (Dan's Music Director) had all helped Donna the best they could, and she had finally decided to go to Minturn, for a while anyway. She might make her home there, but when Lew left Denver a week ago, she was still undecided, but at least she knew what she had to do with the file she had been keeping until the right time presented itself, and had given it to Bud to give to Lew when he felt the time was right. At least she wasn't rushing things. Everyone was encouraging her to take her time, and he was glad she was going to stay with Mac and Sharon. That thought, more than anything else, eased his mind as he and Bud were a couple days out of Bellingham. Their destination on this leg of the trip was Skagway, Alaska, in what was proving to be a storm of some duration. It had been raining when they arrived in Bellingham and it was still raining, with no end in sight.

The *M/V Columbia*, an ocean-going vehicle ferry and part of the Alaska Marine Highway System, is more than just a ferryboat. The *Columbia's* amenities include a hot-food cafeteria; sit-down restaurant and dining room; cocktail lounge and bar; solarium; forward, aft, movie, and business lounges; gift shop; 45 four-berth cabins; and 59 two-berth cabins. Bud and Lew were sharing one of the outside two-berth cabins, which means they have a porthole, a window, in their cabin. Porthole or not, neither man liked being cooped up in their cabin and were in the forward observation lounge watching the scenery, what they could see of it, the other passengers, and were generally bored out of their minds.

Lew was watching one young boy in particular. He looked to be about eight or nine, maybe ten, and had been out on the deck for the past hour or so, along with several other passengers who did not seem the least bit bothered by the inclement weather. His curiosity finally got the better of him and he decided to talk to him.

"I think I'll take a walk and get some air."

"You're gonna get wet," Bud responded. "Oh, by the way, I have something for you. Remind me when we get to Skagway and I'll give it to ya. It's in the rig and I can't get to it right now."

"Yeah, well, when in Rome," Lew said as he got up to leave. His mind was preoccupied with thoughts of his brother as he walked out onto the deck and headed forward and joined the group of what he supposed were locals. Since this was not tourist season there probably were not very many tourists so he thought they must be locals. He found his way over to where the boy was standing and began a conversation.

"Excuse me," Lew started.

"Uh, yes sir," the boy replied.

"Do you mind if I ask you a few questions?"

Looking around to see who was speaking, the boy also caught his father's eye, who gave him a go ahead nod of his head. "Um. Sure. I guess that'd be alright."

"Does it ever stop," Lew asked?

"Excuse me?" the boy replied.

"Does it ever stop?" Lew repeated?

"Um... does what ever stop?"

"The rain. We left Bellingham two days ago and it was raining. When my buddy and I drove into Bellingham it was raining. It rained all the time we were there, and it's been raining ever since we left there, and I'm just curious. Does it ever stop raining?"

"Oh. Gee, I'm sorry, mister. I don't really know."

"You don't know? Surely," Lew persisted, somewhat amazed that a boy that appeared to be about eight or nine years old, of apparently average intelligence, and quite aware

of his surroundings, would not know if it ever stopped raining, "you must know if it ever stops raining."

"Gee, I'm sorry mister. I just don't know. I'm only nine
years old."


"SCOTT, look at this," Xan said, handing the photograph to Scott. "I took it on my last week-end trip."
"Do you know what you have here?"

"Well, it looks like a cross in a mountain, but I don't
remember seeing it."

"Exactly. It's the Mount of the Holy Cross and there are
only two places in Colorado where it's visible. One is from
the top of Shrine Pass, the other is from the road to Redcliffe.
Looks like this one was taken from the road, and if you weren't
looking for it you probably wouldn't see it. However, a camera sees everything that's there, but our eye only sees what it's
looking for."

Since the announcement of the promotions, the four
weeks it had taken to get everything together had gone by
very quickly for both Xan and Scott. At this moment Xan and
Scott were on an Alaska Airlines flight to Juneau. They had
changed planes in Seattle and Xan had read and dozed all the
way from Denver. She finally decided to retrieve her pictures
from her carry-on.

Xan had become increasingly excited about heading for
Juneau. Excited to begin a new position, to be traveling, and
excited to be seeing some new country. Although Alaska, per
se, was not high on her must see list, anywhere new held an
attraction for her.

Scott, on the other hand, was looking forward to being in Alaska. He didn't know much about Juneau, other than it was the capital and he thought there were glaciers nearby. However, he was going to Alaska, a place he had thought many times about visiting. He was not so sure about living there, however. He was hoping Juneau, being in the southeast part of the state, would not be quite as cold and dark as he had heard it could be in other areas. *'However, all things considered,'* he thought, *'it wouldn't be such a bad gig. It's Alaska! Such a deal!"*

"ANCHORAGE center, this is Alaska 67."

"Alaska 67, this is Anchorage Center. Go ahead."

"Anchorage Center, we understand the weather in Juneau is below our landing minimums."

"That is affirmative, Alaska 67."

"What does it look like from your end?"

"Sir, the weather moved in about 90 minutes ago and has been deteriorating since that time, and it does not show any signs of lifting any time soon."

"Okay then, we request to hold at our IAF until the weather lifts to minimums, or forty-five minutes. If the weather hasn't raised in forty-five minutes we request clearance to Anchorage."

"Alaska 67, this is Anchorage Center. You are cleared to hold at your Initial Approach Fix for up to forty-five minutes. However, sir, we also advise that Anchorage has become marginal and is falling. We will advise, but at this moment we advise vectoring for Fairbanks."

"Roger, Anchorage Center. We'll hang in there for a bit longer and talk to our people. Alaska 67 out."

"Roger, Alaska 67. Awaiting your call as to Anchorage or Fairbanks. Anchorage Center out."

Switching his microphone to the intercom setting, the Captain of Alaska Airlines flight 67 began to address his passengers.

"This is your Captain speaking. Welcome to Alaska, ladies and gentlemen. We have just crossed into Alaska air space, and there is good news and bad news."

A collective groan murmured through the passengers, and the captain continued.

"If you could see through the heavy fog and rain layer below us you could see the lights of Ketchikan. However, we won't be seeing Ketchikan's lights and we probably won't be seeing Juneau's lights either. Up here we're pretty much controlled by the weather and what I have to tell you is not one of my favorite things, and that brings me to the Good News, Bad News.

"We have just received an update from Anchorage Center, and because of that major storm which is covering the entire Inside Passage and partially into the Interior, the Juneau airport is temporarily below minimums. That means we can't land there. That's the bad news. The good news we have plenty of fuel. The other bad news, unfortunately, is the weather in Anchorage is not much better. The other good news is Fairbanks is looking good. So, the folks in Anchortown are keeping an eye on things and we'll let you know as soon as we know what's happening, but at this time it looks like we'll be landing in either Anchorage, or Fairbanks."

Another collective murmur that was more like a groan.

"We realize that is not what you wanted to hear, especially those of you heading for Ketchikan or Juneau. However, we will keep you informed and we apologize for any inconvenience and thank you for your understanding. If you have any questions your flight attendants will be able to help. Again, we apologize for any inconvenience and thank you for flying Alaska Airlines."

"Fairbanks," Xan exclaimed, more than a little taken aback, "isn't that a long ways from Juneau?"

"Uh... yeah," Scott said, "it's a very long ways."

"Well, looks like we're going to see one of those towns. Any ideas as to what are we going to do, or how are we going to get back to Juneau? I wonder how long we'll need to be in Fairbanks?"

"Well, if the weather clears," Scott continued, "and that sounds like it's a big if, we could land in Anchorage and wait for the weather over Juneau to clear. A little better, but still a long ways to Juneau. Otherwise, I guess we don't have much of a choice and we'll get to see Fairbanks. I've heard it's pretty interesting, this time of year."

Turning to his left so he could talk with Jack Marshall in the seat across from him, Scott said, "Sounds like we might not make Juneau without a little detour."

"It certainly does," Jack agreed. "I've always wanted to see Anchorage and I guess I'm going to get my wish on this trip."

Dick Phelps added, as Xan leaned forward to join the conversation, "That's presuming we actually go to Anchorage. The Captain said something about Fairbanks."

"How cold you suppose it is in Fairbanks?" Xan asked.

A Flight Attendant was walking toward the rear of the plane and Jack, sitting on the aisle, said, "S'cuse me ma'am."

"Yes, sir," the attendant replied.

"Since we might be going to Fairbanks we're just wondering if you would know what the temperature is there?"

"Frankly, sir," she began, "I don't have a clue at the moment, but I can ask the Captain and let you know."

"That would be great. Thanks!"

"Not a problem, sir. I'll be right back," and she headed toward the front of the plane.

Flying just outside the windows of the plane quirk and the other naastis heard diablo cackling with glee. "Hey, ole creepy quirk," diablo spoke, "You really outdid yourself."

"Uh, thank you, thir," he responded, not yet recovered from the beating he'd received and also not sure of diablo's mood.

"I told you to send the pip-squeak somewhere cold and not too large, but Juneau, Alaska? Well, that was a stroke of genius," diablo gushed as he gave quirk a hard slap to the back of his head. The slap knocked quirk momentarily off-balance and he had to grab the edge of the wing to avoid being sucked into the engine.

"Oh, well, uh, thank you, Thir!"

# 18

# SKAGWAY

A UGUST 16, 1896. The location was on the banks of a very small creek in the Yukon Territory of northwestern Canada. What happened would change the face of the north, and the world, for years to come. George Carmack, his wife Kate, and Kate's two brothers, Jim and Charlie found gold. In their family the boys were known as Skookum Jim and Tagish Charlie. Skookum means big—he was over 6 feet tall, and Tagish is the village they were from. They found gold, alright. Lots of it. Although George and Company were the ones to find The Strike that made history, there were other prospectors combing the surrounding hills and creeks for the yellow flakes and rocks that would make them rich beyond their wildest dreams, and it wasn't long before there was over a ton of yellow which had to be transported out of the area.

First it was loaded onto boats at Dawson City and floated down the Yukon River to St. Michael, Alaska. There it was put on a steamship bound for warmer climes. Finally, in July 1897, almost a year since it was scooped, dug, and otherwise collected from the earth, the arrival of the magic yellow stuff made headlines when it first arrived in San Francisco. Two days later it arrived in Seattle. The Klondike Gold Rush had begun.

The *M/V Columbia* docked in Skagway at eight o'clock in the morning and about an hour later Lew found himself standing in the middle of Broadway, right next to the main building of the White Pass & Yukon Route. The heart of Skagway, Alaska. He had known about, read about, dreamed about being in Skagway for so many years he could not remember when or how it had all began and it didn't seem real. Yet, there he was, standing in the middle of Broadway. He didn't have to think too hard to conjure up scenes in his mind about what it must have been like so many years earlier. He thought about the railroad tracks running right down the middle of a dirt track that had been named Broadway. Probably pretty close to right under his feet. He saw the Golden North Hotel, with it's dome-shaped turret standing proudly in the Alaskan Sky, as well as it's rumored ghosts, and imagined that just about the only differences between then and now were the train's tracks. They had been removed out of the street, and Broadway, along with the other streets in town, had been paved. However, the sidewalks were still boardwalks and the main form of transportation was still the human foot. '*Some things never change*,' he thought to himself as stood in the middle of the street thinking back a hundred plus years.

Bud and Lew decided to spend a bit of time in this town steeped in history and having parked the rig in the lot next to the depot, they were roaming around, taking in the sights.

"Too bad the train only runs in the summer," Bud broke into Lew's thinking.

"Well, I guess that means I'm just gonna have to come back, doesn't it?" Lew countered.

"Guess it does. We'll still see the White Pass, and maybe even see some of the tracks, if the snow's not too deep."

"Food sound good to ya? I didn't eat on the ferry, did you?" Lew asked. Finally, the trip was doing it's charm and Lew was beginning to be able to put 'those things' in the back of his mind.

"No, I didn't. You must have snuck out before I woke up. Did you have trouble sleeping?"

"No, no, nothing like that. In fact, I had a great night's sleep. I just woke up around five-thirty. I was wide awake and you sounded like you were getting a lot of wood ready for winter," Lew continued, referring to Bud's snoring, "so I just quietly disappeared and left you alone.

"I roamed around the decks watching the sky beginning to get lighter and thinking about what it must have been like during the gold rush. I imagine it probably looked a lot like it does today, except for the pavement and cement."

"Yeah," Bud added, "not much has changed. No more steam engines though. The railroad uses diesels nowadays. They have kept Old Number Seventy-Three, the last steamer, you'll be glad to know. They use it on the weekends. How 'bout we take a gander at the yards and shops on our way out of town?"

"Sounds good, if it's not out of the way, but first I need some grub. My stomach thinks my throats been cut and is beginning to gnaw on my backbone."

"Out of the way? Surely you jest. There is only one road outa town and it goes right by the shops. Nope, it's not outa the way. Now, about breakfast," Bud continued as they walked, "let's turn down the next street and we'll eat at one of the few eatin' houses that stay open all year, and it just happens to be my favorite place in town. The Corner Café."

"The Corner Café, eh? Is that kinda like June's in Minturn?"

"Yup. I think they're part of the same chain," Bud said laughing.

"Well, awright then, what're we waitin' for?"


I T had been a couple days since Frenchy had realized his acceptance back into the family, or the kingdom, as Word had called it. It was about four thirty in the afternoon, almost dark, and they were at Word's place loading both men's furs into Word's truck for the trip to Fairbanks.

"Looks like we're gonna run outa daylight before we get all these furs loaded," Word began, "so how 'bout we grab some grub, get a good night's sleep and head out in the morning?"

"Sounds good to me. I could use a little rest," Frenchy continued. "To tell ya the truth I haven't gotten much sleep the past few nights."

"Oh? Problems?" Word asked.

"Naw... nuthin' like that. Matter o' fact I've been sleepin' like a baby. I just keep thinkin' about how much I've missed being with God, and that keeps me thinkin' about other stuff, and that keeps me thinkin' about all the little details that have happened the last couple weeks, and that keeps me thinkin' about Tourist. That must've been some experience for that guy. I've also been thinkin' 'bout you guys talkin' on the radio the other night. I betcha that was him."

"Who was who?"

"Don't you remember? Your brother had somebody with him. I think his name was Lew, or somethin' like that."

"Oh... yeah, I remember him. Now, you think he was Tourist? Why would you think that? I thought we had just about decided that Tourist was an Angel."

"Yeahbut... I guess he could have been an angel, but... I mean, what if he was a man? What if it was that guy with your brother? Think about it. We had a really good signal. Bud sounded like he was in the next room. Then that other guy got on the radio and his voice sure sounded like Tourist. You suppose it could have been him?" Then realizing what he had just said he went on, "Hold it. Hold it. How could that have been him? How could he have been here and then just a little while later been in Colorado."

"Well," Word went on, "it would not have been the first time, y'know."

"Get out!! Really? It's happened before? Somebody has actually been in two places at the same time?"

"Well, not exactly in two places at the same time, but close. You know, we talked about Tourist being an angel, and he could have been. But I wouldn't put it past God to pull off something like this. In the book of Acts there's the guy that just disappeared."

"Really?"

"Yeah. His name was Philip. It's in the book of Acts. We can find it if you want... anyway, in one verse there's this guy Philip talkin' to a guy about Jesus and in the next verse it says Philip was taken away. In fact, he shows up several miles away. So, yeah, this wouldn't be the first time."

"Now, that's cool."

"So yeah... maybe it was the same guy."


T HE next thing Scott knew he was getting jabbed in the ribs and hearing a voice that sounded way off in the distance, "Scott. You're not going to believe this."

"Huh... what?" he groaned, rubbing the sleep out of his eyes. "I was just checking my eyelids for light leaks. What's up?"

"Right," Xan answered. "Light leaks, eh? For two hours? Right. Listen."

The Captain was speaking over the intercom.

"We have started our descent into Fairbanks and will be landing in about half an hour. At last report they had clear skies and a ground temperature of minus twenty-eight and a calm wind. On the bright side, for those of you who aren't familiar with conditions up here, a calm wind means no wind chill, so it won't be too bad. Also, we have gotten ahead of that storm that is over the entire area south of us, but it's following us and it will hit Fairbanks before noon. That means Fairbanks is going to get more snow. However, on the up side, more snow also means warmer temperatures, so all in all not too bad."

"We're going to Fairbanks and it's twenty-eight degrees below freezin' zero!" Xan was almost screaming.

"Yeah. And?" Scott replied. "What's the big deal. We've got good coats."

"Yeah, but," Xan carried on, "it's minus twenty-eight! Did you get that MINUS part?? It is twenty-eight degrees BELOW zero, and the Captain says it won't be too bad. Won't be too bad?! He must be part polar bear! But I'm a human being, and not an ounce of polar bear!"

"C'mon, Xan, chill out," Scott said, and then realized what he had said, "Oh, sorry. Bad choice of words. Take it easy. We'll be fine."

"We'll be fine? Fine, you say!?" Xan was on the verge of losing control. "Just in case you haven't figured it out by now, I hate it when it's cold!"

"Yeah, well, I'm not too fond of it either. However, I've heard it's not as bad as it sounds. Besides, he also said it's gonna warm up. Did the captain say anything else?"

"Yeah," Xan answered, trying to calm down, "while you were checking your eyelids for light leaks," she said not trying to cover the sarcasm in her voice, "he said that Anchorage was still below minimums, but Fairbanks was clear and calm. That's why they decided to go there. He didn't say anything about the temperature until just now, though. He could've warned us earlier."

"Earlier? Warned us earlier? What good would that have done? It's not like you could have stopped off and bought another coat."

"Yeah, well," Xan began, "it just hit me out of the blue, or dark, whatever, and I wasn't prepared for that kind of news. I'll be alright... I guess."

"Didn't you hear the part about it warming up? Xan, it's going to get warmer"

"Well, I guess anything above twenty-eight below is warmer."

# 19

# FAIRBANKS

B UD and Lew had finished their breakfast and their tour of the shops of the White Pass & Yukon Railroad, 'The Gateway to the Yukon', and they were driving up the White Pass. Looking around Lew could see why the railroad was considered one of the major engineering marvels of the world. Before them rose the massive wall of rock called The Chilkoot Range. The pathway of the road had been determined by the mountain itself and wound its way around and over and through nature's art gallery with its massive granite obstacles that had once been a major stumbling block to the stampeders. The railroad had changed all that, however, but too late for most of the would be rich folks. Although the railroad had begun construction in May of 1898, during the gold rush, it took ten million dollars, twenty-six months and two days of back-breaking labor, and cost the lives of thirty-two men, before the Golden Spike was finally driven at Carcross, Yukon Territory, on July 29, 1900. In those two plus years around thirty thousand stampeders had pulled and dragged and otherwise lugged their one ton—that's two thousand pounds—of supplies that the Canadian government, enforced by the Royal Canadian Mounted Police, required each person to have before they were given permission to proceed into Canada.

The term 'stampeder' is an oxymoron of major proportions, at least in the context of the Klondike Gold Rush. One ton of supplies is a lot, to say the least, and it took many trips up 'the Golden stairs' of the Chilkoot Pass to get that ton of stuff on top. Many trips. Each trip took about six hours, about four hours to go up, carrying or somehow lugging, fifty to sixty pounds, and about two hours to get back down. Then that person would start all over again. Then again, and again, and yet again, for however many trips it took. They were able to make two, maybe three, trips a day. Yes, they were called stampeders, but the stampede moved about as fast as an ice worm going uphill backwards. It was indeed a long, drawn out affair.

On the east side of the valley lay the Chilkat Pass, or the White Pass, as the white man called it. Longer and less steep, it was the route chosen for a railroad. The Chilkoot Pass on the west was shorter, higher and steeper, and it was the one most of the stampeders took to the top. What they would have given to have had the railroad completed rather than just beginning. However, that was not meant to be and when the golden spike was driven at Carcross, it was the completion of one of the most ambitious, most spectacular railways in the world. Indeed, the White Pass & Yukon Route is listed along side the Eiffel Tower, the Panama Canal, and the Statue of Liberty as an International Historical Civil Engineering Landmark.

"Have you ever ridden the train?" Lew asked Bud as they were crossing the Mohr Creek Bridge.

"More than a few times," Bud responded, as he pulled off to the side of the road and stopped. Getting out of the pickup the two men looked back to the bridge they had just crossed. "I just wanted to show you that bridge. It's not like a bridge one would see every day."

"Certainly looks strange to me. It looks kinda like half a suspension bridge.

"Right," Bud continued. "It's supposed to be earthquake proof, or so they tell me. You're right, it does look like half a suspension bridge, and the folks that know these things tell me that's exactly what it is. The up-hill end, the one appears to have no support at all, is actually resting on a shelf-kinda thingy and the down-hill end is able to move with the mountain during a quake."

"Genius," Lew said.

"Alaskan," Bud corrected. "This area of Alaska is a favorite for all of us Davises and we almost always ride the train whenever we're here. Not this trip, though. They haven't even cleared the line of snow. In fact, I hope we can make it."

"You think we might not?"

"Oh, I think we'll be alright. They try and keep the highway open so folks can get into Whitehorse, so I'm bettin' we'll do okay. The railroad, however, is a whole 'nuther story."

"By the way," Lew changed subjects, "why is the town called Skagway?"

"Skagway is a Tlingit word that means 'home of the north wind', Bud answered. "It is said that while in the area a person never breathes the same air twice."

"If today was any example I'd say the folks that named it got it right. So it blows like that all the time, huh?"

"Yup, pretty much," Bud answered.

When they got to the top, elevation 2,888 feet, they were driving on a paved highway between drifts that were well over the top of Bud's rig, and when they got to Fraser, British Columbia, where they crossed into Canada, they found the highway crews had done an amazing job of keeping the snow away from the buildings, and Lew could actually see some of the surrounding country.

"They call this Tormented Valley."

"I can see why," Lew responded, looking around.

"LADIES and gentlemen," the speakers throughout the plane crackled to life, "this is your captain and I would like to be the first to welcome you to the golden heart city of Alaska. We have just touched down in Fairbanks and we're having a heat wave. It is now two twenty-three a.m., the current ground temperature is only eighteen degrees below zero, it is snowing and it looks like there will be another six or so inches on the ground before daylight. For those of you who might be interested, daylight is supposed to happen in about another five hours, around seven thirty.

"On behalf of myself and the entire crew, this is First Officer Gregor MacGregor the Third, thank you for flying Alaska Airlines. Once again, welcome to Fairbanks."

"Well," Scott said, nudging Xan in the arm, "how 'bout that? A heat wave!"

"Um," Xan sleepily responded, "uh, yeah, heat wave. Must be another Alaskan Experience. A heat wave at eighteen degrees below freezin' zero. What did I do to deserve this?"

"Aw, c'mon. It's gonna be okay. Just remember what my granddaddy used to say."

"Yeah? What's that?"

"He used to say, 'Keep your chin up and breathe through your nose. This too shall pass.'"

"Cute," Xan replied. At two thirty in the morning, after having very little, but totally uncomfortable sleep, she was a tad grumpy.

"Hey, Xan," she heard Jack's voice from across the aisle, "did you hear that? We're havin' a heat wave."

"Yeah, yeah... heat wave," Xan responded mostly under her breath. "I'll be glad to find a nice warm room with a bed, and a shower and finally get some real sleep."

"Well," Jack continued, "I'll make a call or two as soon as we get in the terminal and find someplace close. I don't care what it costs, we deserve a nice place. We have no idea how long we're going to be here, so we're going to be comfortable."

"Wow! What a sight!" Lew exclaimed. He and Bud had been traveling for a few hours since leaving Whitehorse and had stopped atop a ridge which gave them a wonderful view of Kluane Lake. It was a gorgeously clear day and the sun sparkling on the snow gave the ground the appearance of being covered with diamonds, and the sun reflecting off the snow made the day so bright, so very bright, both men had donned their sunglasses. "What's the name of this place?" Lew asked.

"That is Kluane Lake."

"How did you say that?"

"Clue-AH-knee," Bud said slowly, being careful to make the AH louder than the rest of the word. "It's a First Nation's word that means 'big fish', and they do get some big ones outa there. From here we can pretty much see the entire length of the lake. Even though it's frozen and covered with snow you can see that it's huge, but wait until we're actually driving beside it. Then you'll really get the impact of how big it really is. They tell me it's about 50 miles long and about 8 miles across. There's a lot more to it than what we're seein' from here.

"Wow. This is purty," Lew said, drawing out the word purty.

"Uh, yep," Bud agreed, "it shore is purty."

"Thanks, by the way, for giving me Dan's file. I had no idea what I would find in it, but, as some wise guy once said, 'Timing is everything.'

"Oh really? Why do you say that?"

"Well, remember the other day we were talking about the flood and the rapture and all that?"

"Yeah... what about it?"

"Well, that's what's in this file. Dan's notes on that very thing. I had no idea he had done so much research on the subject, but what I've been reading has really cleared up a lot of my thinkin'. What he's found really makes a lot of sense."

"Oh?" Bud asked, "how so?"

"Well, Dan didn't see things happening they way we've been taught either."

"Yeah? Go on."

"Okay. Well, he starts out in the 23rd chapter of Matthew where Jesus is talking to the scribes and Pharisees..."

"Those are, were, the religious leaders of the day, right?"

"Right. Anyway, that's where Dan's notes begin and it sounds like Jesus was pretty ticked off at the scribes and the Pharisees."

"Really?" Bud questioned.

"Yeah," Lew continued. "He calls'em hypocrites and fools and blind guides and snakes and a bunch of other things. He even goes so far as to tell the people to do what they say, but not what they do. It's no wonder they wanted to get rid of him.

"Oh really," Bud exclaimed. "Where's this?"

"The twenty-third chapter of Matthew. But the real meat of what Jesus taught, and what Dan has seen, picks up in the twenty-fourth chapter where Jesus is having a private conversation with the disciples."

"Private?"

"Yeah," Lew continued. "That's the whole crux of the matter. What Jesus was telling the disciples was meant for them and for their time. Dan has researched this out and found that this discussion between Jesus and the disciples was just that. Between Jesus and the disciples. Some of the events Jesus talks about were to happen in the lifetime of the disciples, and some others were to happen at a future time. Which is not what we've been taught."

"I think I'm beginning to understand. We've been taught those events were going to happen sometime in our future."

"Right. What Dan has found is this... most of those events have already happened, and some of them will happen in the future."

"Like in Noah's time where Jesus talks about things happening like they did in Noah's time shows us that we, the Christians or the church, are not the ones that will be taken away."

"Right. That's still in the future. Here's a question for ya."

"Okay, shoot. But first, take a look at that." Bud said pointing out the front window toward the right.

What Lew saw was almost more than he could take. "What am I looking at?"

"That, m'friend, is Kluane Lake and we just crossed a river. Slim's River by name. It flows into the lake when they're not frozen. Off to the right is the lake. Doesn't look much like a lake today as it's all frozen over, but trust me it's the lake we saw from the top of the hill a few miles back."

The only thought Lew could bring to the front of his mouth was, "Wow. That's a huge lake. I mean, when you told me about it I tried to imagine it, but now that I see it it's almost indescribable. I bet it's just spectacular in the summer when all the ice is gone."

"Yup. Spectacular is only one of the descriptions of this place. Today the river is all frozen over and covered with snow so you can't get the impact of the colors. In the summer the river looks like chocolate milk, due to all the silt from the glacier that feeds it, but once that water gets into the lake and has a chance to settle down, all that silt goes to the bottom and the lake has that gorgeous blue color of the glaciers."

"Slim's River, eh? Guess there's a story there."

"Naw, ya think?"

"Cute."

"Well, there was this prospector..." Bud began.

"Named Slim. Right?"

"Close, but no cigar. His mule's name was Slim. Before you ask, I don't know why he called his mule Slim. Anyway, one spring, so the story goes, during breakup, the two got a little too close to the river, Slim lost his footing, and the prospector lost Slim."

"Hold it, hold it, hold it," Lew interrupted. "What's breakup?"

"Breakup? That's what we call it when all the ice and snow from winter start thawin' out and movin' out. Some years it's a real mess, and other years not so much."

"Oh. Okay, go ahead. That part about the mule and the prospector. Interesting. Sad, but interesting that we remember the mule but not the man. Anybody know the man's name?"

"Well, if anyone does know his name I haven't heard. That doesn't mean he's totally unknown, just that I don't know his name. Yeah, interesting."

As they were driving and talking about Slim they were passing Sheep Mountain on their left, giving Bud the Tour Guide a chance to change the subject. "Off to the left is Sheep Mountain. I doubt we'll see any sheep today 'cause they've all gone to lower elevations for the winter, but in the summer it's not uncommon to see 'em up high."

"Sheep?"

"Yeah. Dall's Sheep. They look kinda like Rocky Mountain Big Horns, but they're not quite as big."

"Aha. Pretty cool bit o' real estate in these parts," Lew spoke, while his head was on a swivel. "I think I'm speechless."

"Uh, yup, that happens a lot in these parts."

"WELL, would you look at that," Word said to Frenchy as they were stacking wood to take inside.

"What?" Frenchy replied.

"The thermometer."

"Yeah. So? What about it?"

"Well, instead of getting colder overnight it warmed up."

"Hmm. How 'bout that. Only in Alaska. It does feel a bit warmer, now that you mention it." Frenchy hoisted the arm load of wood and headed for the door. He was more interested in getting it inside than talking about the weather. "What's it say?"

"It is a bone chilling, mind numbing, finger biting, nose nipping..." Word started to kid.

"Yeah, yeah, quit goofin' around. What's the temperature?"

"Ooh, we're a bit touchy this morning! Okay, Mister Gripe Gut, it's a whopping Minus Two Degrees, Fahrenheit. Did you roll out on the wrong side of your sleeping bag this morning?"

Frenchy shoved the door open with his shoulder and Word followed him inside to give him a hand. "You call two below mind numbing? Feels more like a heat wave to me. The Pineapple Express must have blown through overnight," he said, referring to the breeze. "No, I didn't get up on the wrong side of my sleeping bag. I'm just grumpy 'til I've had my morning coffee."

"Oh, well, if that's all there is to it, here," Word said, handing Frenchy a cup of steaming brew. "Here. Have a swig. I ground up some new beans last night."

After enough time for a swallow or two Word asked, "Whatchew think?"

After sniffing the cup before taking a mouthful he answered, "Um..." Frenchy made an agreeable sound as he slurped another mouth full, "that's really good stuff." Frenchy's grumps were evaporating as quickly as the steam from his cup. "What is it?"

"It's a new blend I got from Big John in Fox. He calls it Gitupengo."

"Well, it's got my vote for a super java. This is what I call a great cup of coffee! Man, this is tasty stuff," Frenchy said, draining his cup and pouring himself another. Then changing the subject he continued, "speaking of Big John, have you seen his Twin Towers?"

"Oh yeah. How cool are they? What a great idea to grow two ice towers in Remembrance of Nine Eleven," Word continued. "They're really gettin' up there, too."

"We oughta stop by on our way in."

"Now, that's a great idea. I'm glad I thought of it."

"So, now that you've had more time to peruse Dan's notes, what other nuggets have you managed to dig out of 'em? What's that question you were gonna ask?"

"That's it!", Lew burst out.

"What?"

"That's it. I've found it!" Lew went on, sounding like he'd just discovered gold.

"You found what?" Bud asked, trying to figure out what Lew was talking about. For the past several miles they had not done much talking. Bud had been busy on his side of the truck and Lew had been absorbing Dan's notes. They had made a pit stop in the last bit of civilization in the Yukon Territory. Beaver Creek. With a winter time population of about 150 hardy souls and just a few miles from Alaska.

"I figured out why Dan was killed," Lew answered

"Really? Just like that you figured it out?"

"Well, um, not just like that, but I have figured it out."

"Really," Bud responded incredulously.

"Yeah," Lew reacted.

"That's good news, I think. Oh, by the way," he continued, "I checked on the trailer and it's nice and warm in there. We're still about 300 hundred miles from my place. So, if you wanna find a place to camp, here in this bustling metropolis, we could have a nice leisurely drive tomorrow. Or, we can head on out and get a little closer before calling it a day."

"Well, it's totally up to you. You're the one drivin'. I'm just along for the ride. By the by, how'd you get the trailer nice and warm?

"Oh, gettin' the trailer warm was a piece of cake. When I first got the rig I put in electric baseboard heaters and an additional alternator in the truck and the only thing it runs is the heaters in the trailer. So, now all's I have to do is turn on the heat in the trailer when I think it might be needed. I did that when we stopped a few miles back. You wanna camp here or go one aways? It's about five hours to Fairbanks and I don't wanna drive that far still today."

"Clever. I'm beginning to see how a real Alaskan thinks. Let's camp here in this, what did you call it, a bustling metropolis? It looks like we can find a good place for the rig. By the way, how far is it to Alaska from here?"

"Yup, Beaver Creek, the last bustling metropolis in the Yukon. In fact, it's the farthest west community in Canada. Alaska is about 20 miles straight ahead of us, more or less, and I know just the place to camp," Bud said, starting the engine and heading North to Alaska.

"You like S'mors?" Bud asked.

Sitting around the campfire munching S'mors and talking about nothing in particular and everything in general, Bud asked Lew, "So, you gonna tell me what you figured out, or are ya just gonna keep it to yourself?"

"satan did it," Lew stated.

"Yeah. I thought we had already decided that. But, you said you had figured out the why. So, why did satan kill him?"

"Okay, think with me here. Dan had been studying what "the church" has called the rapture, and in his notes he wrote about finding new, or different, things concerning that teaching. He has documented everything he's found."

"Yeah? What's he found?" Bud asked, thoughtfully.

"Well," Lew began, "for one thing, he's found that the book of Revelation wasn't written when we've been taught it was."

"Oh? How so?"

"Now, I don't know about you, but I've been taught, and have heard for years, that it was written around the year 90 AD However, according to Dan's notes, he's found it was written about thirty years earlier, or around 60 to 65 AD

"Okay... so how's that important?" Bud asked.

"It's important," Lew responded, "because John said he wrote the book while he was on Patmos Island, and Dan has found that John was there until shortly after Nero's suicide, which occurred in 67 AD. After Nero was gone the fifth caesar after Nero commuted his sentence and he went back to Jerusalem."

"The fifth caesar? Why did it take so long for Rome to commute his sentence?"

"Because all of the next four were either killed or committed suicide, and that happened within a year of Nero's death."

"You mean there were four caesar's in one year?"

"Yup. Four of'em in one year."

"Interesting. Where did Dan dig up all this information?"

"From historical writings of the time, primarily a guy named Josephus."

"Joe who?"

"No, Joe wasn't his first name. Flavius was his first name and Josephus was his last name."

"Well, if my parents had named me Flavius I'd gone by something else, too."

"Cute. But I think Flavius was probably a pretty common name of the day."

"I suppose. Now, about that question."

"Oh, uh, yeah. What was the question?"

"Me? You're asking me what your question was? C'mon... I haven't a clue. You had a question for me."

"Yeah, well," Lew began, "um, uh..." he thought out loud.

"Noah," prompted Rapha, Lew's angel.

"Uh... oh yeah!! I got it. Thanks, Lord. It was about Noah. Here's the question... who was left on the earth after the flood?"

"Well," Bud thought, "it was Noah and his family."

"Right. Where was everybody else?"

"Uh, well, they drowned in the flood."

"Right again. So, who was taken and who was left?"

"Well," Bud thought out loud, "Noah and Company were left, so I guess that means all the others were taken."

"How about at the battle of Jericho?"

"What?"

"You know, where the walls came tumblin' down."

"Oh, yeah," Bud answered, more than a little confused. "What about it?"

"Well, who was taken and who was left?"

"Um," Bud began, "you sure you're still on the same subject?"

"Trust me," Lew answered.

"Right. Well, all the people in Jericho except the spies and that Rahab girl."

"Exactly.

"Why was she and her family spared?"

"Because she did what she was told to do to be safe from the... there it is," Bud practically shouted. "She did what she was told to be safe."

"Bingo," Lew answered. "Just like it's gonna be when Christ comes to get us. He's only goin' to get the ones who have done what they've been told in order to be safe."

"So, all this talk about the Christians being "raptured" off the earth is not how it's going to happen. We've been looking at it with a skewed perspective."

"Yeah," Lew agreed, "and that's why Dan was killed."

"What? That's a bit of a stretch, isn't it?"

"No, not really. You see what Dan found is this. The rapture thingy is a hoax told by satan and he doesn't want the church to know it's fake."

"Well, that's an interesting way of looking at. A skewed perspective." Bud agreed.

Lew went on, "Paul does teach that we Christians are going to meet the Lord in the air. It has just been the assumption that we're going to heaven when that happens. As Dan points out in his notes, if Jesus comes back, then takes us away, and then returns yet another time to set up His Rule and Reign, wouldn't that be His third coming?"

"Yeah... it would." Bud spoke in agreement. "He is only returning one more time, His Second Coming. Now this makes sense."

# THE INN

Dᴵᴄᴷ, Jack, Xan, and Scott having been holed up a couple of days in the Alpenlite Hotel, were getting a little antsy waiting for the weather to clear. Fortunately for the small band of worn down travelers it had gotten warmer. The eighteen degrees below zero had been replaced with cloudy, snowy weather and the temperature on the Freddy's sign said minus two degrees. They were laboriously making their way across the parking lot to what they had come to call 'their' restaurant, but with the additional foot, or so, of snow on the ground it was a rather daunting task. They were also realizing there really is a difference between eighteen degrees below zero and two degrees below zero. They could not believe it, but they were actually working up a sweat inside their winter clothes.

Since arriving in Fairbanks almost two whole days ago they had found their dining/eating choices were pretty slim. Especially since their only transportation was what had been provided on their birthdays. There was the deli at the grocery store, and the "Mexican phone company", as they referred to Taco Bell. Then there was the food bar at Freddy's, and The Lord's Inn. They were headed to the latter for dinner and were chatting along the way.

"Now, this is not bad at all," Jack was saying. "It's not near as cold as it was when we got in."

"Oh yeah?" Xan picked up. "That's easy for you to say. I'm freezin' my whatever off."

"Wimp," kidded Dick. "You sound like one of those cheerios, or whatever they call'em."

"Cheerios?" Scott chimed in. "You mean cheechakos?"

"Cheechako! Yeah, that's the word! Thanks, Scott. Yeah, Xan," Dick continued, "you sound just like a cheechako."

"Yeah, well, call me a cheechako or cheerio or whatever," Xan mumbled through the scarf she had wrapped around her head. Even through all of her new winter wear she was still feeling sorry for herself. "I really don't give a rip. It's cold and I'm freezing, and I don't think I'm ever gonna be warm again!"

"Okay, Cheerio," Jack kidded, "it's not much farther and when we get there you can have the seat closest to the fire and warm your coldness."

The building was made in the English Tudor style and upon walking through the heavy wooden doors with leaded glass windows, a person was seemingly transported back a hundred years or so to a time in England when knights and ladies gathered together to enjoy the grub, the grog, and the company of friends. The night Word and Frenchy had chosen to have dinner at The Lord's Inn was no different.

The tables were made of thick dark wood and four high back chairs were placed around each. There were only two unoccupied tables when the two friends walked in. They chose the table on the left side of the fireplace. The other was directly in front of the fireplace. There was a fire, and while not 'roaring' it was warm, inviting and was creating a cozy glow all around the room. At the other end of the room was a small stage and four musicians were playing gospel music with a country swing and flavor to it and Frenchy began the conversation, "They're pretty good, those guys over there."

"Oh yeah," Word agreed. "I guess they're here every Friday and Saturday night. I don't get to town very often, but when I do I try to make it on the weekend just so's I can come in and listen. I guess the leader, I suppose you'd call him the leader, he's the guy that does most of the singing anyway, well, I guess he's a pastor in Tok, and from what I understand the drummer is his son. I don't know the bass player or the other guitarist, but they sure seem to love the Lord and love their music.

"Whoever they are, they're pretty good." Frenchy added, "it looks like we got here just in time."

"Yeah," Word replied, looking around, "it looks like this one and the one right there are the only tables left," he concluded with a motion toward the adjacent table.

The two were talking while removing their parkas and Word happened to glance toward the door and was pleasantly surprised to see his brother walk in. There seemed to be a stranger with him. He had never seen the guy before, but they had definitely come in together.

Word raised his hand, "Bud. Bud! Over here," he semi-hollered, "Over here, Bud."

Bud finally saw his brother, and he and Lew began making their way over to the table.

Word was on his feet as Bud got to the table and the two brothers were immediately giving each other the kind of bear hugs only brothers can give.

Bud said, "Hey Bro, sure is good to see ya!"

"You got that right," Word said. "I wondered if we were going to ham it up tonight, seein's how it's Friday. Who's your buddy?" he asked as he motioned to Lew.

"This is the guy that I met in Colorado. Word, meet Lew. Lew, Word. Sure am glad you remembered me this week, but I don't think we'll need the radios," Bud kidded.

"Nope. Don't think so," Word laughed. Grabbing Lew's hand, Word said, "Hey Lew! Welcome to Alaska! I guess you traveled all the way from Colorado with this guy?"

"Yup, sure did. It was quite the trip, too, let me tell you."

"Boy, I heard that. I've traveled with him before. You must be one tough old bird." Then motioning to Frenchy, Word continued. "Lew, Bud, this is my buddy from Nowhere, Frenchy. Frenchy, Lew and my brother Bud. He really is my brother, but most of the time I try not to claim him, if you know what I mean," Word kidded.

Getting to his feet Frenchy went around the table and began shaking hands with the two men, "Hi Bud. Hi Lew. Nice meetin' both of ya. We talked the other night on the radio, if you remember."

Bud picked up the conversation, "That's right and we've talked about it quite a bit over the past several days. Course, that's not all we talked about, but we definitely remember that conversation. Right Lew?"

As the four men sat down around the table, Lew went on. "Oh yeah. That was somethin'. You know what, Frenchy?" Lew said, looking intently at Frenchy, "I think we've met somewhere before. What do you think?"

"Um, well, um... now that you mention it," Frenchy answered, trying hard to control his feelings of excitement and wonder and amazement that were brought to the surface by seeing the guy who had thrown a twenty foot hunk of spruce tree all by himself, "I think we have met before." Wanting to sound interested but not skeptical he asked, "Have you ever been to Alaska?"

"Well," *'Oh dear,'* Lew thought, *'Lord! I could sure use some help here,'* he prayed, "um yeah," Lew said, "I made a short trip up here. Not too long ago, as a matter of fact."

*'No! That's just too weird!'* Xan thought to herself as she, Jack, Dick, and Scott were wading through the snow in the parking lot. *'It can't be! I must be losing it!'* Seeing a pick-up that looked just like the one she had seen in Colorado, Xan continued her thought process. *'There's just no way. It's gotta be a different truck. C'mon! That truck's not the only one like that. That's gotta be what it is. That one just happens to look like that other one. Why would it be here anyway?'* Xan went on arguing with herself, but somehow felt she was losing the argument. *'No! I'm losing it. That's what it is. I'm losing it. No, that's not it. It's the cold. It's gotta be the cold. This blasted cold has finally frozen my last brain cell and I'm just seein' things. It's all a cruel, cold coincidence and my frozen brain has short circuited.'*

Nissi, Jireh, Rapha and Tsidkenu, the Guardian Angels, or the HAFs, of the four men were in the rafters over the guys and were really enjoying themselves. Nissi, Word's HAF, said, "Oh, this is gonna be good!"

"Oh yes," Tsidkenu, Bud's HAF responded, "this is gonna be better than good!" Meanwhile Rapha and Jireh found convenient perches in the exposed beams overhead. The naastis, on the other hand, were not having such a good time. They were bound, gagged and otherwise incapacitated. The Angels had wrapped their tails around their necks, hung them from some of the rafters, and were forcing them to watch the proceedings. Just about that time the four Angels were joined by four more Angels. Olam, Scott's HAF; Elyon, Xan's HAF; Shammah, Jack Marshall's HAF; and Kadosh, Dick Phelps's HAF just came in, along with the bound, gagged and completely dumbfounded naastis that tried to control the newcomers. It was going to be quite a party.

Just as the four of them were walking through the front door the song the group had been playing ended, and there were a couple seconds of semi-silence. Just enough silence to allow the four guys to hear the outdoor noises for a second, and they all turned toward the door to see who had come in.

When they saw the foursome coming through the door they all thought, *'Just a bunch of cheechakos.'* All of them except for one. Keeping an eye on her, and hoping he wasn't obvious and that he was staring, he averted his eyes as the four began walking toward what the HAFs had conveniently arranged to be the only table for four left in the entire restaurant. The table right next to theirs.

As the four new arrivals were making their way toward the empty table a pair of eyes happened to fall on a familiar figure. *'It can't be!'* was the thought that ran quickly through the brain cells. *'It can't be, but I think it is.'*

"Lew?"

*'Oh man,'* Lew thought. *'Of all the people. Of all times. Of all the places. Oh man, oh man, oh man. I could use some help here, Lord,'* Lew prayed inside.

"See?" It was Tsidkenu who spoke up. "I told you this was going to be better than good."

Lew looked up, and the eyes were unmistakable. He heard himself say, "Xan?"

"Is that really you, Lew?"

"Xan? What are you doing here?"

Bud, Word, Frenchy, Jack, Scott and Dick. All six of them stopped. Stopped completely. In mid-motion of whatever they were doing, in mid-sentence of whatever they were saying, in mid-thought of whatever they were thinking, they stopped in their tracks. When they heard the conversation begin, they were more startled than a frog in a hail storm. Here, in Fairbanks, Alaska, in the middle of the largest state in the union, two apparently total strangers were looking at, and talking to, each other as though they had not seen each other for years.

Dick broke the silence, "Xan," he began, "you know this guy?"

Xan was dumb-struck.

"Xan?" Dick went on.

"Uh... um... what? What did you say?"

"I asked if you know this guy." Dick answered.

"Uh, yeah," she heard herself stammer, "um... we know each other. At least we used to."

Sixteen knees started to buckle as eight people began grabbing chairs, tables, the wall, anything solid and unmoving to steady themselves as they sat down, mouths agape. During that awkward moment Lew and Xan caught each other's eyes and did not, could not, deflect their eyes away. Both thought they were seeing a ghost, and because of the events of the last few weeks they figured anything was possible. They even began wondering if there was something more going on here than was meeting eight pairs of very large eyes.

Olam and Elyon saw diablo and stench coming in like a flash and using their shields they stopped the two demons in mid-flight before they could reach Xan and Scott.

"That's far enough," Olam said.

stench and diablo screeched to a halt, almost bumping into each other not realizing the two angels were any where near, as Olam and Elyon had used their ability to be hidden.

"You can't do..." diablo began but was stopped short by a gargantuan hand around his throat.

"Know this," Olam commanded. "We can! Furthermore we will! Now, shut your foul mouths, both of you, and get over there with your cohorts where you belong," he continued his command, pointing to the others in the rafters.

The two demons looked at Olam and Elyon and knew it would be useless, not to mention very painful, to resist, and turned to join the other demons.

As they were moving Elyon pointed toward the sky.

"NO!" diablo yelled. "It can't be!"

At the sound of diablo's scream of terror the other demons also looked toward the east. Then all of them turned and looked toward Elyon and saw the other angels had joined him. They all smiled a knowing, threatening, smile.

It was Jack's turn to break the silence. "Would somebody please tell me what's going on here?"

"We used to be married," Xan said.

"Married! You and this guy were married?" It was Scott who spoke.

"Yeah," Xan said. "We were married."

"A long time ago..." Lew paused, "... long, long ago and far from here."

"And you never said anything," Scott said.

"Like Lew said," Xan continued. "It was a long time ago. Besides, you never asked."

"Yeah," Lew agreed. "It was a very long time ago."

"Wow!" Bud said. "That must have been in one of the previous chapters in your life."

"Chapter nothin'..." Word began, but his words were cut short by a flash of brilliant white White light.

V ERNA found herself flying. Again. She was not in a jet-liner, but she was flying... on her owne... barely feet above the tree-tops. One second she was leaving her house in Minturn, Colorado and the next she found herself just out-side Jerusalem and instinctively knew she was over the place where Advocate had been taken off the earth.

Looking around she realized she was not alone. Pastor Mac and Sharon were there. Also Dan and Donna, and she noticed Dan was showing no ill-effects of having been shot in the head. Lew and Bud were also in the group. She had never met Bud but somehow knew his name.

Looking to her right she pleasantly saw Xan and grinned at the amazed look on Xan's face.

Millions of other people were there and she knew their names as well.

"This," she said to no one in particular, "is different. Didn't think it would be like this."

THE entire earth experienced the bright light at precisely the same instant and all people who were completely sold-out disciples of Advocate were changed. They found themselves in the air over a mountain near Jerusalem. The majority of them had never been to Jerusalem but they somehow naturally knew where they were. They also realized they had been left, but that realization only heightened their awareness of where they were, and, more importantly, why they were where they were.

Meanwhile, back in Fairbanks, and all over the earth, from the smallest hamlet to the largest city, the people who had not made a decision to follow Advocate were gone. They simply vanished and were found no more. They had been taken. Away.

The naastis from all over existence were instantly transported to the skies over a vast plain called Megiddo, a few miles north of Jerusalem. Having no idea how they got there, they could tell from their point of view that their outlook was not good.


"HELLO family", UNICINC messaged to the entire body amassed before Him. Using the Direct Thought Link He was downloading instructions and information to each one individually. But not with words as we know them. It was more like an instantaneous transfer of knowledge on a mental level.

"Hallelujah's", "Thank You's", and "Praise You's", were just some of the simultaneous responses echoing across all of creation.

Lew, Bud and all the others in the massive group recognized one another, even though their bodies had been changed. They still looked human enough to know each other but there was a shine, a glow, a light of some kind emanating from in or around them.

"If you look around you," UNICINC continued, "you will see the enemy thinks he is ready for us, but we have more than a little surprise waiting for him and his minions. You all have your co-ordinates and assignments so let's go kick some demon butt!!" The entire universe rocked and rolled with thunderous approval.

"Nice time for a battle," Nadia said.

"Now always is," Obed agreed.

"See you around," Bud said to Lew, heading for his assigned position. Lew was waving to Bud as he saw Verna go flashing by. Tsidkenu had joined Bud and Deum had joined Verna. He watched as Deum, with a sword in his hand, slashed and sliced a demon in two. It was completely cut in half and both halves went sailing toward a massive hole that had opened up in the earth. Verna was watching in amazement. Tsidkenu and Bud then headed for sacre, Bud's naasti, while Frenchy and Jireh headed for thordan.

As Lew was heading toward zoltan, his target, his angel, Rapha, joined him and together they headed toward their encounter with zoltan. Their attack path taking them over the gaping hole. Looking into the hole below him. Lew saw the boiling raging fire in the very center of the earth. There were so many demons and pieces of demons falling into the inferno the sides of the hole appeared to be covered with demons and demon parts.

Word, and his angel, Nissi were reaching their objective just as UNICINC and Advocate were engaging diablo himself. After dispatching kije, Nissi and Word were watching diablo approach UNICINC and Advocate. diablo whipped a long burning chain toward the pair, but it was a feeble attempt. As the end of the flaming weapon was about to wrap it's blazing end around Advocate's neck UNICINC reached out His hand and grabbed the weapon with a hard jerk, pulling diablo out of control, sending him sailing backward toward UNICINC. As Advocate saw diablo flying toward His Father he loosed the belt from around His waist and whipped the end of it around diablo's feet. diablo's feet were bound together. UNICINC then whipped His belt around diablo's neck. As a team, UNICINC and Advocate pulled, stretching diablo like a rubber band. The timing was perfect. Advocate let go while UNICINC continued to whip him like a sling shot, and diablo went sailing head over heels, screaming in agony, to the hole in the earth and the tortures it contained. Even though the truth was not in him, diablo was aware of his fate and went screaming and wailing down, down, down, into the fiery lake.

As diablo splashed into the combusting pit Lew, Bud, Xan, Verna, Frenchy, Word and all the others cheered and praised UNICINC and Advocate for this, the ultimate victory. Somebody on the far side of the battle scene yelled out, "They tried to kill us!" and somebody else chimed in, "yeah-but we won!" To which Advocate replied, "Let's eat!" The atmosphere of the entire universe vibrated with the exuberant shouts of the victors.

While sitting around the miles-long table that had the appearance of pure gold UNICINC downloaded more information. "Each of you were absolutely amazing out there just now. Take your time enjoying the feast which we've set before you. When everyone is completely satisfied we'll go to the wedding."

# CONCLUSION

W HAT you have just read contains significant truths which should not be ignored; truths that can be Scripturally and historically verified. I trust that your own life's journey has been enhanced by reading this book.

T HE following is a list of references which may assist in follow-up reading.

Simmons, Kurt. *The Consummation of The Ages*. Carlsbad, NM: Bimillennial Preterist Association, 2003

Eberle, Harold R., and Trench, Martin. *Victorious Eschatology*. Yakima, WA: Worldcast Publishing, 2008

Whiston, William. *The Works of Flavius Josephus*. Grand Rapids, MI: Baker Book House, 1974

Eberle, Harold R. *Living and Dying with the King James Bible*. Yakima, WA: Worldcast Publishing, 2010

# GLOSSARY OF TERMS

ADW = Air Defense Wing

AirOps = Air Operations

CHP = Colorado Highway Patrol

CIC = Combat Information Center

COMHAF = Commander of Hemispheric Angelic Forces

COMNORHAF = Commanding Officer of the Northern Hemisphere Angelic Forces

COMSOUHAF = Commanding Officer of the Southern Hemisphere Angelic Forces

DSI = Department of Strategic Intelligence

EFTO = Encrypted For Transmission Only

EHF = Extremely High Frequency

ELF = Extremely Low Frequency

END = Extended Nerve Desensitizer

GPS = Global Positioning System

HAF = Hemispheric Angelic Forces

HQ = Headquarters

IAF = Initial Approach Fix

INTSIG = Intelligence Signal

NAASTI = Network of Atmospheric Agents of Sub-Terrestrial Impieties

NASQUAD = NAASTI Squadron

NORHAF = Northern Hemisphere Angelic Forces

RFR = Rear-Facing Radar

SEMIVISAK = Semi-Visible Sector over Alaska

SEMIVISROKMONT = Semi-Visible Rocky Mountain Sector

SID = Specialized Instruction Division

Tac One = Tactical Channel One

TP = Thought Processors

UHF = Ultra High Frequency

UNICINC = Universal Commander In Chief

VHF = Very High Frequency

VLF = Very Low Frequency

WATCOM = Watch Commander

WORSPADCO = World Space Defense Command

# AUTHOR'S BIOGRAPHY

Bob Ledbetter is a man of many talents and past professions. Both his dad and granddad worked for the railroads and he took his first steps while riding one of Union Pacific's streamliners. Understated, he is enthralled with the big "iron beasts," the smells, and the noises. Bob was a music major in college, a radio announcer and broadcasting instructor, as well as a professional photographer. His dream of a lifetime arrived when he found himself living in Alaska, the Last Frontier. There he became a tour guide in the summers while doing other jobs during the winter. One of the things you do to survive in Alaska, if not working for the government, is to work two or more jobs. He is now semi-retired and resides with Meg, the love of his life, on the Oregon coast, a close second to The Last Frontier. He still maintains his hobbies of trains—riding, collecting, and photographing them.